BATTLING BROKEN SHADOWS

THE ERASEHER SERIES BOOK ONE

SARA NICHOL QUINCY

First published by Milcann Hunnee 2022

ISBN: 978-1-957719–00-9 (Epub)

ISBN: 978-1-957719–01-6 (Paperback)

ISBN: 978-1-957719-10-8 (Hardcover)

SaraNicholQuincy.com

For Phoenix

The scared little girl that I locked up in a dark place in my mind for so many years because I thought I hated you and that you would never be good enough. I was wrong; you've achieved more than I could have ever imagined and I'm sorry. You are enough; you have always been. This is for you beautiful, be free. I'm proud of you!

CONTENTS

I

THE GREAT COLLAPSE

"Open your eyes, Kaleah," a soft yet stern masculine voice whispered. "Kaleah, come on… please open your eyes. Tell me you're still in there somewhere… You gotta be… I need you to remember me…" He spoke again hesitantly like he knew what he was asking wasn't realistic.

All I could see was a dull hue of black, with bits of brownish-gray shadows floating around. I tried to open my eyes, but I couldn't. I tried to move my body, but I couldn't.

"Kaleah… please open your eyes…" With every plea, he breathed closer and closer against my cheek, filling my senses with his warm, heavy breath. "Kaleah?" He continued, his voice growing more frantic the longer I unintentionally denied his request. "Dammit, woman… please, Kaleah… please open your eyes." His voice started strong, then morphed into begging.

I couldn't feel my legs or my arms, nothing except warmth against my face. Frustration started to overwhelm me when suddenly I was hit by an onslaught of thoughts.

Why can't I remember anything?

I have no movement, no feeling, no nothing… Where am I?

Wait… Who is this man and what does he want with me…?

. . .

Roughly 2 months earlier…

The Sicari were coming. Even if I changed my mind it was too late. They knew where I was now. "Deal with it Kaleah. Stop being a wussy." I tried to console myself but my dueling thoughts never let me rest. I was tired of hiding, tired of being alone, and tired of doing nothing but surviving. More than that, I was bored… completely and utterly bored out of my mind. Some days it was minds, plural. I'm sure I had more than one of them.

The sun was beginning to rise. The sky was hazy but elegant as the sun slowly grew larger and larger with brilliant rays of pale yellow and burnt orange. I was sure it was the last one I would see as a free person so I figured I should savor it. It looked more beautiful than normal but I knew that was probably a product of my active imagination. It liked to play tricks on me. Sometimes I thought I saw people I knew weren't there too. I tried not to talk to them but I wasn't always successful. My favorite I named Fred. I liked to talk to Fred.

I had been alone for almost three years. It'd been seven since the last of civilization had fallen apart, though. There was a war, but not one like the other wars we had seen in history. It was really just the collapse of our society and all the aftermath that went along with it.

The war started innocently enough, as do most I would assume, but unlike in the past where they used bullets or arrows, in this war the principal weapon was information. Whether it was the truth or not didn't matter. It's what they used, and they wielded it as any great army would. The date the war actually started was unclear because the symptoms of the collapse started slow. The growth was gradual enough no one tried to fight until it was too late and fighting was all that was left.

There were two sides, like in any war, both fighting over money and power. The lust for power may be what sparked it, but hate for the opposition was the fuel. Each side had no problem supplying ample fuel to their followers to keep them motivated, either. It was the same as the mob's lust for death at a witch hunt or the blood of a gladiator in the Roman coliseum. They poisoned people to believe their side was the right side, anyone else was the enemy, and the enemy must be eradicated. However, in time, both sides became poisoned, and there was no right side anymore. But that didn't matter. Each person had to pick one, and if you didn't, you were an outcast. I didn't. So for this grievous sin, I was labeled a Gypsyin, a traitor to both camps. The truth is, I'm just a survivor. I will do what I need to, pretend to be who I need to be, whenever I need to, for the sake of myself… and Fred.

Once a unified nation, the country, now torn by a second civil war, consisted of two distinct sides. First there are the Coldiers. Named by their enemies for their reputation of being 'cold soldiers,' probably referring to their souls since they are an evil, merciless people—in my mind, anyway. Then there are the Sicari, though I don't know what gave them that name. I have yet to see them act as heartless and malicious toward me as the Coldiers have, but either way, neither were people I agreed with or wanted to be a part of. The Coldiers were the side that considered themselves politically advanced while the Sicari held more traditional values. After years of slipping behind each side's defenses, I couldn't really tell much difference between either of them, though, honestly.

It might have been easier if one side took the left half of the nation and the other took the right, but I guess as with any divorce, things don't always end with such clean lines. After the reunification rallies in the first years of the war, the Coldiers took the larger cities to live in and govern, leaving the Sicari to take the smaller towns and countryside. Initially, even though they were outnumbered, strengthened by their resources, the Sicari connected all the smaller cities and towns to become a network, preventing the Coldier cities from merging and becoming too powerful. Now, just like with a draw during a chess game, no one can move for an ultimate win, thus neither side can take full control and overcome the other… yet…

I sat silently on a small cliff overlooking the valley I had called home for the last 4 months. The sun had been up for a good hour now, so the beams of light were no longer as wispy and innocent as before. Now they had turned to full-on rays of light that were bright and warm against the fair skin of my chest and face.

Although I wasn't sure, I assumed the Sicari would arrive by horse, not by vehicle, for two reasons. One—Coldiers had a monopoly on gasoline so a Sicari with a car was one special son of a bitch. Two—I had yet to see it, a Sicari with a car. Not to say it didn't exist but, well... not in my world. Fred said he hadn't yet either.

I sat there for what felt like hours in deep thought. The cool wind of fall had settled nicely into a smooth, peaceful breeze. It gently blew my long, wavy hair back and forth. Now and then a dark brown strand would fall into my face and I would have to tuck it back behind my ear again. It was peaceful here, but lonely. Fred wasn't very good at holding a conversation.

The idea of changing my mind criss-crossed its way through my thoughts. If I didn't want to still go with them, I could just hide. I mean, they'd probably still find me but, hey, a good game of hide and seek might be fun. I knew I was likely to die either way. That was the point. I didn't want to be on my own any longer. I was tired of being alone. *Why not go out with a bang? Right, Fred?*

The Sicari executed their prisoners by lethal injection. Coldiers, on the other hand, preferred to use death by hanging. Why they chose that method was unbeknownst to me; I just knew that wasn't the way I wanted to go. I didn't really want to die either way, but I knew the risk of seeking settlement after being an outcast. It was the price for temporary companionship, a price I was now willing to pay. To believe I wasn't a spy of the enemy and let me live had dire consequences if they were wrong, so it was rare to find someone that decided to side-swap. Either you belonged, you were alone, or you died.

I hugged my knees as the crisp fall breeze brought a sharp chill through the holes in my jacket. By my calculations, from the position the sun now took in the sky, it was close to noon. I figured they would soon find me. Hollows Edge at Cave's Creek was where I was supposed to be, now I just had to hope whoever came knew where this landmark was located. The rock cliff where I had been perching was set into a large hill overlooking a deep valley. Near the edge of the valley, ran a narrow band of road. The road set against the hill to one side and followed a small creek running along the other. I assumed the creek was named for the many caves that were scattered along the hillside, but I didn't know why they called the cliff Hollows Edge.

Suddenly, I noticed that the birds, who had been quite noisy for most of the morning, had stopped chirping. In the silence they left, the sound of footsteps grew louder behind me, crushing the fall leaves underfoot as they approached.

"Quiet, Fred, they're here... You gotta stop talking to me now or they'll think I'm crazy... We can't have that." I murmured.

There was only one set of footsteps. I thought that was odd. *Did they only send one man?* I didn't know what to expect. I knew it wouldn't be a parade, a horse-drawn carriage, or anything special. Still, I was surprised and very underwhelmed at the Sicari's one-man response to my letter. In it, I was very clear that I not only had valuable and specific information about their enemies but also that I was a well-trained Coldier Agent and would only come willingly if they provided food and a proper escort for protection.

Was this the best the Sicari station could send? Either this guy was well worth his salt or they didn't take my letter as seriously as I had hoped. Granted, none of what I had written about myself was true. I didn't have any combat skills and was pretty pathetic as a fighter, but still... I felt slightly offended.

Winter was coming, and I knew I couldn't survive as an outsider again for another one, no matter how far south I tried to move. The real reason behind my letter was to trick them into sending an escort to get me and take me to the Sicari's central station, known as the Praetorium, way quicker than I could get there on my own. I was fairly far south at this point and quite a ways from the Praetorium, the only receiving station for prisoners. If they only sent one man and with no horse at that, then it could be two to three months before we could make it to the Praetorium. Traveling north in the winter on foot was crazy, even for me. I wasn't sure about him but the way I planned to die wasn't by freezing or starving. Ideally, something that sounded more painless, like lethal injection would be better.

A semi-husky male voice suddenly yelled, "Don't move!" interrupting me mid-thought. I couldn't help but crack a quiet smile. It was a real voice, a real man talking to me this time. I could only imagine the ways I was going to enjoy his company.

"*You* don't move," I yelled back, trying not to let the smirk slathered across my face reverberate in my tone.

"DON'T... MOVE!" He shouted again at the back of my head. "And slowly put your hands where I can see them."

His voice was quite stern and serious. I paused to think about whether I wanted to obey his commands. Perhaps it was from all my alone time, or maybe something more, but I felt impish and thought I would play with him a little. I realized the end of this escapade had a high likelihood of ending in death either way, especially considering my whole pretense in getting him here, so I might as well enjoy myself and have a little fun in the process. After all, it had been an awfully long time since I had talked to a real person.

"Why can't I move?" I countered. "I need to see you before I turn myself in."

"Stop... If you move, I'll shoot." He barked. Even though I suspected he was exaggerating, I didn't really want to be shot, so I didn't test him.

"You can't shoot me. I'm too valuable." I yelled, then giggled to myself, amused.

He huffed in irritation with the volleying conversation and began to walk toward me. "Do as I say or you're going to get hurt." He said, his voice drawing closer.

"I don't think you can hurt me. I'm pretty sure I'm invincible at this point. Believe me, Fred has already seen—" I stopped suddenly. *Dammit, I forgot I wasn't going to mention Fred.* "Uh... I mean, I don't… uh… don't shoot me. I'll bleed…" *Shoot, now I sound like an idiot too!*

"What the…" he mumbled from behind me. "Just stop talking and don't move." He yelled out before more leaves rustled, then more mumbling. "Invincible, my ass!"

I too, growing tired of our exchange and now less amused, decided to give in. "Fine… I'll comply, just chill out." I said, letting my smirk relax as the amusement faded. I was expecting a response, but there was nothing but silence for a few seconds longer than I wanted to wait. Before I could turn to see who exactly I was talking to and why he was not responding, a quick flash of black passed my peripheral vision as something hit my back, right about the middle, shoving me forward. Now, pressing my face against the cold, damp rock I had been sitting on.

"Ow, get off of me!" I screamed out as best as I could with what breath I had left. He was quick. With his left knee pressed firmly into my spine and his right knee on the ground, I could feel him staring down at me. Before long, he let up about half his force from my back, then removed his knee altogether. At the release, I rolled over and away to look up at what appeared to be a man with profuse confusion.

"You're not dangerous." He relaxed, slowly rocking back to sit on his heels. He had a lean muscular build but was not small by any means. His face was lean, with a strong jaw resting beneath a short stubbly beard. His traveling must not have taken long because his clothes weren't weathered or tattered like my own. "Are you armed?" He asked, motioning toward me as if he expected me to tell him.

"I bite!" I said, trying to not laugh. His surprised look quickly changed into an irritated one. Seeing how he moved, I figured he probably knew what he was doing after all. He acted like he meant business, and what he stumbled upon wasn't everything he was promised. I felt bad for him upon this conclusion. Poor guy wanted to capture a spy and here he was with a crazy lady.

I sat up for a second, trying to formulate my thoughts. I didn't want to be body-slammed again, nor did I want to create any higher level of irritation between us, seeing how he appeared to possess enough skills to beat me into submission if necessary.

Without officially agreeing to my thought, my mouth decided to go the pity-me route and blurt out a response of its own accord. "I'm sorry I'm not the prisoner you were promised. No… I don't have any weapons on me."

Irritated with myself and my traitorous mouth, I immediately sat forward and put my head on my knees. "Stupid mouth… Fred, why didn't you stop me?" I spoke again involuntarily. *Oh my gosh, control yourself before you make this man think you're psychotic. Wait… what if you are?* Straining to clear my head, I squinted deeply only to be interrupted when he spoke again.

"What's wrong with you?"

I looked up to now see extreme confusion covering his face. His eyes were shaped like two heavily hooded almonds, mysterious looking with a piercing stare. I had no idea at this rate what odd behavior I was putting off but he was incredibly attractive so I hoped for the duration of our time together I could control myself.

"I'm psychotic." My mouth blurted out again. I rolled my eyes and looked down to try to stop myself. I took a deep breath, then released it slowly. "I'm sorry. I've just been by myself now for—" I paused. I knew, but I didn't want to tell him. "It's just been a long time since I've talked to a real person," I said as I fiddled with the tongue of my shoe.

"So you're alone?" I suspect I heard a small touch of sympathy leak through his voice. Until I looked up and his face appeared just as irritated as it had been. I wasn't sure if he was asking out of concern or trying to gauge his position. Still gazing toward me, he brought a hand up to scratch the side of his face. His skin was tan but ruddy like he had gotten more sun than usual recently.

"Yes, for a few years now," I said, hoping my honesty might ring through.

There was a moment of silence as I looked him in the eyes, watching him formulate an opinion. "Bullshit!" He said with a snappy tone and definite assurance I was lying. "You're a woman, and what maybe 120 pounds soaking wet? No woman can survive that long out here all by herself."

Any tension I was holding in hoping he believed me, slowly released and dissipated. *Dammit...* I didn't have a plan, but deep down I still hoped whoever captured me saw how pathetic I was and petitioned for me not to die after we got to the Praetorium. At this rate, however, it appeared he was not likely to come across that conclusion on his own.

"Believe what you want," I said with disappointment. "It doesn't matter. I know what you people plan to do with me when we get to the Praetorium." I lowered my head still looking at him from the corner of my eye now, waiting for his response.

He didn't say anything. Apparently, whatever I said went right over his head. He stood up and reached behind him into a pouch on his belt, searching for something. Then he stopped and pulled out a long, slender dark green cord.

I knew what it was and what he was planning on doing with it. Although I wanted to fight him and tell him I wasn't dangerous and that it wasn't needed, my train of thought could only focus on the other questions I had been pondering before his arrival.

"Where's your horse... ah, horses... you know, whatever brought you here? What are you planning on using to take us back?" I asked with absolute hope that I didn't really know the answer and I was wrong about my miscalculation of him.

"Stand up," he said firmly, with the authority of a military man. He looked down at my hands as he gestured for me to turn around. "You know as well as I that agents don't travel through the grotto lands, and I wasn't about to go all the way around with a horse, either. I don't have time for that," he said it with a twinge of disgust as he took each of my hands one at a time and wrapped the cordage around them in a way I was sure I would not be able to break free from. I, however, really had no idea what he was talking about and didn't know what he meant by grotto lands.

I didn't reply, hoping that he would feel the need to fill in the silence with more information. But nothing… He was completely silent as he continued to fiddle with the cord and my hands. At one point, he stopped and pulled up the sleeve of my left forearm, I assume checking for my identification tag. Not seeing anything since I didn't have one, he slid it back down and continued with restraining me.

Since he didn't, I continued talking for both of us, hoping I didn't annoy him so much that he'd want to gag me. I didn't know how much longer I might live, but I didn't want to spend my last few months with a filthy old rag shoved down my throat.

"You seem pretty good at this. You're not very talkative, though. Can I ask you something else?" I said softly in an apologetic tone as he finished wrapping my hands and took hold of my arm to turn me around to face him. He raised his head, now connecting his eyes with mine. He was tall for a man, and I wasn't short for a woman. He looked to be about a head taller than me.

"What?" His voice was softer now, but I could still hear the impatience in his tone.

"I like to talk," I said, then immediately regretted it. "I mean, I want to talk to you but I don't want to annoy you by talking too much." Seeing I didn't have the capability to control what I was saying, I realized the next few months weren't likely to go how I planned them in my head. My lack of companionship over the last few years had crippled my ability to keep anything I was now thinking to myself. I suddenly felt completely impulsive and afraid of what I might say and how I might say it. "Ugh… sorry it's just nice to talk to someone other than myself and uh… Fred." I let the words roll out of my mouth then completed it with a tiny apologetic smile.

He just stood there and stared at me, almost expressionless. I'm sure at this point he was pretty confused why he had traveled all this way for someone that appeared to be of no importance whatsoever.

"Either you're a brilliant Gypsyin or an idiotic one." He murmured as he checked his pockets, searching for something else.

I sighed in disapproval of him calling me names, but said nothing to combat his observation of me.

"There it is." He pulled out a darkened piece of paper from his left chest pocket. The corner of his mouth turned up in a self-satisfied half-smile. Now, giving me his full attention, I could see his face better. For his profession, he didn't have as many age lines as I thought he should have. He couldn't have been much older than me I would imagine. "Do you know what this says about you?" He held the folded letter between two fingers as he used it to point at me, replacing his half-smile with a smug grin.

"Of course I do, I wrote it," I said innocently like that was normal behavior.

His brows furrowed over both eyes, this time with a very strong look of frustration. He didn't say anything but looked at me for a second with his face frozen like that. His eyes flickered back and forth, then back again to my face. He stepped back, then looked down and then back up to get a better understanding of who he was working with. I could imagine the wheels in his mind like cogs as they spun to try to figure out what in the world he was doing here.

"It says you're dangerous, which you're not. It also says you are a Coldier Agent, which I can see by the lack of tag on your arm, you are not. So... I don't know what else you're lying about but that's not my problem ya see, that's gonna be yours when I turn your little lyin' ass in." He said, then grabbed me at the top of my arm and proceeded to push me in front of him back in the direction he had come from.

"Okay... you caught me," I replied over my shoulder, trying to look back at him as I moved forward. I didn't fight, but walked along with the pace at which he was pushing me up the hill.

"You're not a Coldier, you're a Gypsyin. If you're a Gypsyin, you've got no people of your own. You're free to roam about as you wish, travel where you want. Why the hell would you turn yourself in and say you're dangerous when you obviously aren't... say you've got inside information, when you probably don't... all so I can take you in just for them to hang you?" His voice rather full of irritation sped up a bit as he heaved me forward.

"Hang me? What?" I huffed and slowed my pace a little in defiance. "I thought you guys used lethal injection. What happened to the lethal injection?"

He stopped pushing me as his hand slid from my arm down my waist and away. I turned to see him just standing there, staring at me in amazement. After a moment, a large grin grew on his face. "You're insane!" He said emphatically, with eyebrows slightly raised as he leaned toward me and took my arm to push me again. "I don't know what to do with you." He busted out with a loud chuckle. "You're crazy... You're a crazy Gypsyin... What the hell have I got myself into?"

I didn't say anything, but kept walking the way he was pushing. I guess deep down I had wondered myself just how crazy I was or if anything I was doing made any sense. I didn't argue with the idea, but I was a little put off by what he kept calling me. I knew what he meant by Gypsyin, but I didn't like that he hadn't asked me my name yet.

"I know I might be your prisoner, but you could at least stop calling me that and call me by my real name. If we're going to spend the next few months traveling north together, we can at least be civil to one another."

His hand tightened around my arm. "All right, what is your name then, Gypsyin?" He asked with thick sarcasm.

"Kaleah," I said softly.

He was silent. Still just pushing me along in front of him. His hand loosened slightly. "Well then, Gypsyin," he said with little emotion in the tone, "it won't take no *few months* to get you there. Maybe when we do, I can talk them into giving you that injection you'd like rather than hangin' ya."

What an asshole... I didn't reply, I just kept walking. We crossed over another hill when finally I saw what he'd traveled there in. Sitting like he'd parked it in a hurry was a small two-door car. I almost missed it due to its faded red color blending in so nicely with the fall foliage. It wasn't a horse, that was nice but I wasn't sure if I felt happy or sad about this new development. Why wasn't it a horse? That was odd, I thought, but I quickly dismissed it with the assumption that he must have just been that one special son of a bitch.

2

A STRAY CODDY

We'd now been on the road for a few hours, however the speed we were traveling at was slower than I would have expected. I assumed he had his reasons, but hoped the main one was our safety, especially considering my side of his pathetic little vehicle had no seat-belt.

He didn't speak much unless I spoke to him first and even then he didn't always care to respond. He acted somewhat callous in most of our exchanges with one another. When he did respond, he was frigid in tone, but deliberate and guarded in speech. His looks, however, weren't guarded at all. He was quick to make direct piercing glances whenever I said anything he didn't feel like responding to.

I had no idea exactly what lifestyle he had come from or what agent experience he had, but I got the idea by many of his mannerisms that he went by the book. Hell, I'm sure he lived by the book, bowed and prayed to it even.

Despite sitting across from him, I still felt completely alone. Even Fred seemed to disappear. The car was starting to grow stuffy as well. The warm dry heat radiating from the vents blew almost at full blast. The silence between us felt like it grew louder in the white noise of the blowing heat and the low hum of the engine. The tension between us also seemed to grow thicker the longer we drove.

I hadn't been in a moving vehicle in so long; I tried to gather what joy I could out of the experience without appearing giddy. My hands were still bound but thankfully he released them and retied them at my front before we left.

"What's your name?" I asked softly while looking out of my window, trying to break the tension between us with light conversation.

"Why do you care?" A snappy voice spat back at me.

I turned to look at him, curious why he'd have a bad attitude. I realized I could respond in many ways, and many shot through my mind in rapid succession as if quickly sifting through a paper filing system trying to find the right one. I could counter his moodiness with my own, though I wasn't sure that would lead to my original intent. Or I could try to soften his hardness with kindness, but I knew that was risky as well and might come across manipulative, which I didn't want to do. I chose the latter and hoped he would see my true nature.

I looked back toward my window, intentionally leaving a long pause before I decided to reply. I could see the mist in the air starting to formulate droplets against the window seal. The sky wasn't necessarily dark, but rather a muddy gray. It looked quite chilly out. At that moment, I was happy to be somewhere that produced manufactured heat, even if it did threaten to suffocate my senses.

"I do care," I said, keeping my eyes out my window. "I know you probably don't care for me and I guess I don't blame you. I assume that's your job. Be a bad-ass, get the bad guys, you know kill those Coldier bastards…" I paused, then turned back to look at him again.

He didn't turn to look at me, he just kept his eyes straight to the road ahead. His facial expression had changed, but I couldn't discern exactly how, or what it meant. He was a hard read if I had ever seen one. Almost always, with a stony expression, he seemed rather emotionless most of the time. He lifted a hand from the wheel and brought it up to his hair as if to comb it to one side. Apparently, he had forgotten he was wearing a hat, though, and inadvertently knocked it off into his lap instead. His hair was a light sandy brown, smooth and glossy like it'd been freshly washed. Had it not been for his usual sour look, I would have thought he was quite handsome.

Finally, he broke the silence, relaxing back into his seat and releasing his hard grip a little from the wheel, while lowering his left arm to rest on the door. "What do you know about the Coldiers?" He asked, his voice still deep and stern, with a twinge of gravel in the lowest inflections.

Seeing as how he intended to unofficially interrogate me, I thought it was a clever time for a bit of quid pro quo.

"Ha…" I unintentionally released a small chuckle at the thought of my cleverness. "Sure… I'll tell you everything I know, since I don't have any reason to hide anything. But first, you have to tell me your name." The words departed slowly, leaving a half-grin in their wake.

He took a deep breath inward, releasing it with a small sigh. His right hand raised to flip the windshield wipers, clearing the mist that had started to cloud his view. Again, his face was emotionless like I had been talking to a brick wall. "Jake," he relented as he glanced over to connect with my eyes, probably seeing if I believed him. Then he quickly looked back to the road, returning his right hand to the wheel again.

"Jake… Hey, like that commercial? What are you wearing, Jake?" I asked. Amused and unable to help myself, I followed it with a slight chuckle, though stopping abruptly with his quick reply.

"Do you think this is a joke? You're about to die for no good fu —" he stopped himself to lower his voice before continuing. "You're about to die for no reason, no reason!" The inflection at the end made his voice half crack like he was holding back some sort of emotion.

I paused to genuinely think about the question, looking straight ahead then down at my fingers while I continued to fiddle with the cordage between them, as I had been doing for the last 3 hours. "No," I said. Tightness started to develop in my throat, as my eyes began to cloud over. I blinked a couple of times rapidly to delay what I expected to be happening. "It's not a joke," I said softly under my breath as my voice started to break up. "But I don't care if I die. I'm tired of being alone," I murmured, then swiftly lifted my gaze back toward my window to make sure he couldn't look at my eyes. I waited a few seconds, then leaned my face over to my shoulder to wipe away a stray tear that had formed and fallen to my cheek.

Without missing a beat, he continued with his questioning, now his voice a little less stern but still void of any compassion. "All right, now what do you know about the Coldiers?"

"They're all assholes! That's it... That's all I know..."

Immediately, he swung his head around to look at me, apparently surprised by my remark. He stepped on the brake as if he were about to stop the car, pull over, and verbally whip me, but he quickly released it and continued with the gas. His face looked a bit more irritated than usual now with a small splash of suspicion added to it. At this rate, I was amazed by his self-control and started to admire the way he used it in the face of an understandably unusual captive.

"Fine then, be that way. You're entitled to your secrets. But they won't save you, whether you tell me or not. So I guess—" he hesitated, looking straight ahead while adjusting himself to sit a bit higher and closer to the steering wheel. His eyes squinted then he leaned in farther as if trying to see something in the road ahead. "What the..." he said as his hands clutched the wheel tighter.

Before I could fully turn my head away from him to see what we had come upon, my whole body jerked forward as if a large force were pulling every inch of me toward it and away from my seat. In the same split second, my eyes caught a glimpse of his hand as it reached out in front of me and pressed against my chest, I assume, as a buffer from the blow that I was surely about to endure.

For a moment I was weightless, a warm rush of heat seemed to engulf me, then suddenly everything turned black and silent. For that moment alone, my thoughts as well were silenced. Slowly, though, one-by-one feelings of warmth and tingling began to grow and spread back through me. I could feel my pulse in my throat.

Realizing I must still be alive, I relaxed a little and began mentally checking my body for pain while all my senses returned slowly at their own pace.

"Gypsyin?" A voice spoke as if calling out loudly, but to me it sounded like no more than a whisper. "Are you all right?" It spoke again with sincere concern in the tone.

"Yes," I mumbled, trying to get my lips to work and respond in a manner I was used to. I opened my eyes only to see the bottom side of the dark dusty dashboard a good inch in front of my face. "I'm dizzy, that's all... and... well... I'm pretty sure my seat has me wedged into the floorboard."

A few moments later, light from outside flooded into the tiny space as well as a brisk chill that came in with it. He stood there for a moment, surveying my situation.

"Yeah, you look stuck." He said matter-of-factly. He reached down and took a hold of my left leg to pull it up and out. Next, in one quick shift, there was a release of tension on my right foot as he pulled it out to meet my other leg. With my legs now dangling from the car, I could see Jake standing there, peering down at me. With his eyes darting left to right, he looked at me with determination on his face. The usual sour scowl melted momentarily while he tried to figure out how to get the seat pulled back away from me. His eyes briefly moved up to meet mine and for a moment, I could see concern and compassion.

He lowered himself to a knee, leaning in over me, reaching for something past my head. He smelled like the woods after a thunderstorm—clean and earthy with a hint of citrus. For a moment, his jacket fell into my face before I turned my head to let it slide away from my cheek. He mumbled and grunted quietly to himself, pushing with his left arm on the seat as he pulled on something behind my shoulder. Then, with a sharp jolt, the seat slid backward and away, releasing me. He leaned back and braced himself against the car to stand. Looking at me again, he gave the smallest smile I had ever seen. Then he reached out a hand toward me, motioning for me to use it to pull myself up.

"I can't," I said, looking down at my wrists, seeing the cordage taut between them and the chassis below the seat. "It's caught."

"Oh ok, hang on…" He said then reached down to untangle the wad of confusion and pull me free. When it wouldn't come, he reached around to his magical treasure trove in the back seat and pulled out a large black knife from one of his black duffle bags. He gently dug it in between the cordage strands and with short quick strokes sawed until suddenly my wrists were loose and free again.

"What happened? What did we run into?" I asked as I wiggled myself free of the floorboard and pulled myself to my feet, using the car door as leverage. The road was nothing like it had been pre-war. Now, the asphalt was heavily aged, with large tracks of grass and weeds. Littered between them were random abandoned vehicles sprinkled here and there, left behind as their owners ran out of gasoline. We must have swerved to miss something, causing us to hit one sharply in the left rear.

He didn't reply, he just stood there looking me over, checking to see if I was hurt.

"What made you swerve?" I asked again, confused, as I peered toward the road. "What did you see?"

"A man," he said finally with a low monotone voice before he turned to walk over toward the front of the car. "I think he'll be all right, though." He said as he looked down almost straight in front of the tires.

"What?" I shouted, unable to contain my excitement. Not that I wanted to see a dead body, but just to come across another man so soon was exciting to me, at any rate. I walked over to stand next to Jake, then looked down to see what he was looking at.

There *was* a man! His body rested against the car in an awkward position, but there didn't appear to be a scratch on him otherwise. He was knocked out cold. Unlike Jake, he was smaller and scrawny-looking, with dirty scraped-up skin. He had long, matted, straggly hair not so graciously flowing into his unmanaged mane of a beard. His clothes were weathered like mine, too.

Jake towered over him for a second, then squatted down onto the balls of his feet. He leaned forward to grab the man's left wrist and twist it around toward him checking for his tag. There it was, a small blue disc shape inset into the upper meaty portion of his forearm.

"He's a Coldier!" I said, inhaling sharply as I took a step backward.

Jake turned to glance up at me, squinting his eyes a bit, but with no other expression on his face. "So he is," he said, gently laying the arm back against the body and returning to his feet.

"Aren't you going to kill him, then?" I asked, assuming that was the way this whole enemy thing worked.

"No," he said sharply, staring down at the man. "I'll take him to the station with you, they'll deal with him there." He leaned down again toward the man's face and reached out to give it a few swift pats against his cheek. "Wake up, Coddy," he said loudly.

The man began to stir, then slowly opened his eyes followed by a quick jerk and a gasp as he looked up at Jake. "What the hell, man?" He murmured with a cough as he held his stomach. His voice was scratchy and weak. "Dude, you hit me with your car!" He sputtered again. This time, I recognized his accent. He sounded like he was from the East coast.

He spoke quickly, churning every word out as fast as possible. Like darts, they pierced the air. He sat up slowly, surveyed himself briefly, then glanced up at me. His eyes tarried for a moment before looking back over at Jake. I could see the thoughts of confusion start to accumulate in his mind.

"Barely," Jake said, defending himself while looking down at the man before he looked back up and across the hood at me. I had backed myself away slowly a few steps every time neither man was looking. "You better not run." Jake yelled, lifting his arm to point at me like it would strengthen his implied threat. "Gypsyin!" he said again with an urgent controlling tone, apparently already anticipating my next move.

My body knew what it wanted to do long before my mind knew it was going to do it. Without even thinking, I turned, picked a direction, and began to run, all while arguing with myself not understanding this primitive gesture of escape.

I didn't make it far and quickly lost my heading as my body was forced to collapse under what had to be a solid mound of muscle. After squirming my face free to breathe again, I resigned to lay there in defeat. Trying fully to collect my breath, I let out a long sigh, expressing my irritation. Not irritation from my failure to escape, but rather, I knew it would take a long time to get rid of the taste of the soil that had now been ground into my teeth.

Without much effort, Jake pushed himself to his feet and looked down at me, still laying flat where he pancaked me. "Why?" He said pointedly. This time, his face actually showed quite a bit of expression. His eyebrows were closer together with his mouth still half ajar from the question.

Painful as it was, I heaved myself from my elbows up into a sitting position as I looked up at him with my own disbelief. "I don't know," I said, shrugging. "He scares me." There it was again, my mouth blissfully unaware of the fact that I would like to keep some secrets.

Jake's face showed his usual confused scowl, this time a bit bigger than before, as if he was more confused by me than normal. His stare was harsher as well. With his eyes staring down at me, his body language froze to indicate further confusion. "Him?" He said with a bit more liveliness than normal in his voice. "Him?" he asked again in an even higher pitch as he pointed toward the front of the car. "What the hell do you think he's going to do to you that I won't?" He said with his voice raised as he stood there looking down at me.

"He's a Coldier. We can't trust him!" I said, raising my voice back. "And now look, we can't even use the car anymore. Believe me, you don't want him with us when we're walking by foot through the byway lines." I paused briefly. "Besides, I doubt you got enough food in your little fanny pack back there to feed him too," I said smugly while trying to stand up and brush my pants off.

"You said you didn't know anything about Coldiers..." He

replied, eyeing me as he angled his body towards me in case I needed to be tackled again.

"No, I told you they're all assholes, remember? Twice…" I said emphatically as I held up two fingers at him. "Twice, I wandered on the wrong side of their line at Nashville and twice…" I paused as I broke eye contact. "Let's just say they are shitty people and I would rather die in the hands of a Sicari than allow what they did to me to be done again."

His brows creased like he was trying to understand. "What did —" He stopped when he was interrupted by a sharp, whiny voice coming from the ground in front of the car.

"Guys, are you planning on doing this all day? I think you broke my leg, man. You're not going to leave me here, right? You can't—"

"Shut up!" Jake interrupted, hollering back. Then he walked over to me to grab a hold of my arm. "Look," he lowered his tone as he started to walk me back around toward the front of the car, "he's coming with us whether you like it or not. Don't run again. I won't let him hurt you." He finished as we rounded the hood. "Now what do I do with you?" He said as we both peered down at the man in the road.

3

A GOOD PRISONER, I AM

We stopped to camp for the night beside the car. Jake seemed uneasy about the idea that I might run again, now that he didn't have any other way to tie me up, so he suggested I sleep in the trunk. I didn't think it was a great idea until I realized I didn't really have a choice. He cleared out his travel bags and the extra gas cans and gently manhandled me to get inside, as I may or may not have thrown a few knees and elbows his way in rebellion. Thankfully, Fred made his way in so I didn't have to spend the night alone again.

The morning came earlier than I would have liked. Jake opened the trunk to release me well before the sun had started to rise. "Come on, get up, let's go." A rough, deep voice greeted me as a cool brisk gush of air flooded into the trunk. "I got the bags ready, I'm gonna need you to carry one." He said, being way more chatty than I had seen him thus far. He also didn't appear to be perturbed in any way that we were now going to have to walk instead of drive, substantially lengthening our travel time.

"Where's the Coldier?" I inquired, looking around.

He motioned toward the right side of the car, where there was a small embankment. "Down there. He's waiting." He said as he took me by the arm to help lift me out of the trunk. He started to release his grip once I was out and on my feet then stopped and looked down at me. "Are you planning on running again?" He asked, his voice oddly not sounding as stern as it had any other time in the past.

"No," I sighed, wondering why he thought he could trust me when I knew better than to trust myself. He loosened up his grip on my arm as he walked me around to the side of the car. I couldn't believe it was that easy. *Maybe he enjoys tackling me and wants another opportunity?*

"Good," he said, looking smug, "because guess what will happen if you try it again?"

I hesitated. I didn't want to know. I thought maybe if I didn't answer he wouldn't tell me.

"I'll chase you down again, and as soon as we get back, I'll let ole Coddy here have his way with ya." He pointed down at the man now sitting patiently next to the fire.

I swallowed hard, but didn't say anything. I knew I didn't want to hear it. I looked at him with my best mean face, trying to scowl as deeply as possible, then I yanked my arm away from him.

He took the hand that was holding my arm and rested it on my shoulder against my neck. "Good, I'm glad we have an agreement." He said with a half-smile as he lightly squeezed my shoulder with his hand.

"You're supposed to get me there safely, remember? That's what I demanded in the letter." I said, snapping at him.

"Yeah well, you also said you were something that you're not, *remember*?" He snapped back, face flushed with the brisk air then looked over at the Coldier. "Don't run again and we won't have any issues. As long as you're with me, I won't let him touch ya. Deal?" He said then glanced back at me.

"Fine," I muttered, now thoroughly irritated then looked down at the man as he began to lean against one of Jake's large black bags.

Something's not right. I paused to observe him, trying to think about what I felt was off about the situation. Jake continued to talk to me as he opened the car door to get something, but I tuned him out, trying not to deflect my thoughts away from the Coldier. I didn't know exactly what I thought was wrong, but I continued to stare at him while waiting for Jake to be done. Good thing the man wasn't looking back at me. I'm sure the suspicion that started to build up inside my head had now begun to translate into my face.

Something's not right, Fred... Something seems fishy about that man. One thing I couldn't get past was if this man was a Coldier, why was he not under just as much guard from Jake as I had been up to this point. After all, it was obvious that I was harmless, and this man could be anybody, but Jake didn't make him sleep in a trunk.

This time I held complete control over my mouth and was able to restrain it from saying anything. I didn't know what they talked about while I was in the trunk, but I resolved to wait and watch their behavior before I concluded what the real motives were of either man. After that I would decide what to do with myself depending on the outcome. Either way, I was sure I couldn't trust Jake anymore than he could trust me.

Jake, now finished in the car, shut the door and turned back toward me. I broke my stare and turned toward him to gesture for him to go ahead. Though not believing I would follow, once again he took me by the arm and pushed me forward in front of him towards the makeshift campfire.

The man looked up at us coming toward him. A quiet smile inched up his face as if he was trying to look friendly and approachable.

"Howdy, Gypsyin," he said in a mellow tone. "Did ya get a good night's sleep?" He spoke quickly with a speech that was indistinct, cramming the words together as if in a hurry to get them out of his mouth.

I looked down at him, waiting for my brain to decide how to proceed before replying.

Before I could, though, Jake moved me to the side. "You both can get better acquainted while we walk." He said, bending down to pick up the largest of three black bags—two duffle, and one backpack. He then picked up the backpack and handed it to me. "You carry this one." Then he picked up the second duffle and handed it to the Coddy to carry before we began to walk.

***

We were walking for hours. I tried to not say much, but just watch both of them and their mannerisms as we went along. The Coddy told us his name was Seth. He appeared to be rather witty and enjoyed talking, though most things coming from his mouth at that point were merely just pleasantries about the countryside and whatnot. He walked with a tiny limp; I assumed from the car, but couldn't be sure it wasn't from before that. He came across friendly, though I surmised it was forced and not organic to his true nature. I still couldn't tell exactly what he was up to or figure out his real motives for following along with us. I could only assume for his sake, Jake was pretending to be a fellow Coldier. If not, I was unsure of why else he wouldn't have already tried to cut and run or fight with Jake over something.

For being a man that didn't live out in the wild, I observed Jake had no trouble traversing this unknown terrain. He moved swiftly with precision and stealth, even when unnecessary. He didn't talk much. He let Seth do all of that. He also let Seth travel in front of him and me behind, but frequently would turn to make sure I was keeping up the pace and not planning any other attempts at escaping.

As the day drew on, the sun was now high above us and had already burned off the chill from the cool air of the morning. Warming up from that and the exertion of hiking, Jake stopped briefly to remove his jacket. His shoulders were broad, with smooth muscular lines curving down his back, ending at a trim waist. The clean lines of his muscular arms were also now visible through his long sleeve black shirt. I had to admit there were worse things to look at during a long hike.

Seeing the way he cared for himself brought my own condition into sharp contrast as I started to feel self-conscious about my tattered appearance. My hair only being brushed with my fingers was surely wild looking, at best. My over-sized jacket was a good deal past its prime, and my shoes were on their last leg, literally and metaphorically. Both of them were in dire need of new shoestrings and the tongues would constantly slide forward, irritating my feet, making it difficult to walk. I had hoped the next time we ran across an abandoned house maybe I could find some replacements.

"Stop for a minute, Seth," Jake yelled out ahead of him as he turned to walk back a few steps toward me. "Turn around," he said, looking at me. His eyes squinted more than usual from the direct sun shining into them. His lashes were naturally long and dark, an effect I had only been able to pull off myself in my pre-war days with loads of mascara. To say I was jealous was an understatement.

I turned, following his orders, assuming he wanted something out of the bag I was carrying, and he did. There was a gentle pull, then tug when I heard a zipper followed by some rustling of paper for a split second. In the brief pause from the noise, I tried to turn back around to see what he had wanted when he tugged again. "Hold still," he said curtly.

I complied. After all, I wanted to be a good prisoner. I knew it might work better for me in the end if I wasn't a pain in his ass the entire trip—when I could help myself, anyway. I didn't always understand the things I did or why I did them. Many times there was another voice feeding my thoughts, one I didn't always recognize. Confusing as it was, I figured it was just my subconscious's way of keeping me safe. Though, it had an odd similarity to the way Fred sounded at times as well.

I heard the rustling noise again, followed by the zipper. "All right, we need to turn and head east now," he said as he pointed toward the direction the sun was now vacating.

I had a rough idea of where the Sicari's central station was, but without looking at the map myself I had no idea if that was the direction we were walking or exactly what route Jake was intending to take to get us there. I turned around to see he had started to walk in that direction when he turned back toward me, noticing I hadn't continued to follow.

"What are you doing? Let's go!" He said in a strong commanding tone as he motioned again toward that direction.

"It doesn't feel right," my mouth blurted out. Though consciously I had no idea why I felt this way, still I hesitated, continuing to stand my ground along with it.

"Look, I've done this over a hundred times," he said, reassuring me. "I know where I'm going, and how to get there. And I know exactly what I'm doing out here, too. You don't have any say in the matter. Now let's go." He walked a few steps back toward me and took a hold of my arm to move me forward, positioning me to walk between him and Seth.

I glanced up to look at Seth, who had apparently obeyed without any hesitation and was now a few yards ahead. "Just trust him," he yelled over his shoulder as he turned to grin at me. "Besides, how d'you think you have any idea where you're going? You're just a Gypsyin."

There was an anger boiling up inside me hearing the way he called me that. I was annoyed with that label and what he meant by it. "You can go to hell, Coddy," I mumbled under my breath as I began to walk again behind him. "I'm sure that's to the East as well."

We walked for about another hour until we stopped to eat some of the food Jake still had left in the bag that Seth was carrying. Although I had been pretty hungry from all the walking we were doing, usually I didn't need a lot of food to keep me going.

While alone, I learned how to scavenge from whatever area I was living in at the time. Winter was the worst. In the spring, things were still a bit scarce. Summer generally was where I had the best luck finding things like herbs, small tree rats, a random animal carcass here and there, but mostly fish, I about lived on fish. Now and then I would venture off a bit to find another abandoned house that I hadn't explored yet. Sometimes I would find something good, maybe a can of food here or there. But most of the time it'd been so picked over by other free men that there was seldom anything of value food-wise to be had. Winter was hard. I hated winter. Even going south where it wasn't as cold and harder to freeze to death, any easy food source was still pretty scarce.

I could tell Jake liked to eat. And by the looks of him, he didn't seem to have any recent bouts of starvation that he had been forced to endure, like Seth and I. I observed them both as we sat to eat a lunch of dried fruit, jerky, nuts, and a bit of hard aged cheese. I didn't know how a man could keep that much muscle tone and not have plenty to eat. That was the benefit of being part of a station, they rarely had the same issues with food as free men.

Seth, however, looked like he hadn't had a decent meal in a while and was probably living off of the same number of calories I had been, just enough for a small female. His face looked a bit more hollowed out, with heavy shadow lines under his cheekbones. His body was quite gaunt, though he still appeared to have some muscle left from what I could tell looking at his exposed forearms.

I hadn't exactly formulated my full opinion of him yet. I wasn't quite sure how he was a Coldier but was out on his own living like a Gypsyin or why he would even want to live like that. I didn't know the rules they all went by; what exactly a deserter looked like if that is what he was or if that was even a thing. All I knew was he was confusing as hell and things didn't add up. He didn't look dangerous. He didn't have to look dangerous to actually be dangerous, though. Either way, he did look weaselly. When he wasn't talking, which wasn't all that frequent, his eyes looked as if he was mischievously concocting some plan of misfortune.

After lunch, we walked in the same direction, going toward the East until we found a water source. It wasn't much, a tiny stream that almost seemed to have appeared out of nowhere, probably a natural spring. Its taste was crisp and clean like it hadn't been defiled yet by an onslaught of random animals running through it. I had thought it would probably be a good place to make camp for the night, considering it wasn't guaranteed when we would find another freshwater source that nice. I figured why not make the most of it. Jake disagreed with me, though. He thought we should make as much distance as possible and overruled any input I put forth. After a few minutes sipping, freshening ourselves up, and collecting what we could carry of it with our single thermos, we trudged on.

After covering many miles, I was exhausted, but knew it wouldn't do any good to complain. I was also completely over listening to anything that came out of Seth's mouth. It didn't take long for me to conclude that maybe his unit kicked him out because he wouldn't ever shut up. Quite frequently, as we went on, I found myself daydreaming about picking up a random rock and throwing it at him. I even considered asking Jake if I could borrow his gun so I could just put myself out of my misery already. I didn't though, assuming he wouldn't appreciate my kind of humor.

I honestly didn't see how letting the Coddy tag along with us was of any benefit. Not only the shortened supply of food he now created concerned me; but also what we might do if we ran across another Coldier. Jake was definitely a pretty formidable force, but I wasn't sure how well he would do if he had to deal with multiple enemies at once. Especially since I wasn't in any position to help defend him.

The sun had started to sink lower in the sky, though with the time of year it was, that didn't indicate it was actually that late. I figured it would probably start to get more chilly as we went on. Not only was I getting more and more tired, but my shoes were really showing their wear at that point. They were old when I found them, but now they had traveled several miles past their expiration. The insole on my left shoe was about worn through and the rubber at the heel was pretty thin itself. My right shoe didn't fare much better, the seams weren't nearly as tight as they used to be and I was afraid it wouldn't be long until the adhesive holding the suede to the outer sole would finally give up the fight.

It didn't take long for Jake to also notice the growing lack of sun and warmth. Only a few minutes later, he decided to announce his decision to stop for the night and find a suitable place for camp. Where we stopped wasn't much to look at in the way of scenic value, but it seemed to be a decent spot for good coverage from the brisk air that we'd be sure to encounter during the night.

We'd been walking beside a decently dense pine grove for a good way when Jake finally took us up into it. He looked around for a few minutes, and then settled on making camp under one of the larger trees he'd found. It didn't take him long to get the area ready and make a fire. I could tell Jake had been serious when he told me earlier how proficient he was outdoors. It wasn't more than five minutes or so after we collected a bit of dry wood and a few pine cones that he had a good fire going. Though, he probably would have been a great deal faster if not for the constant verbal interruptions from Seth. The more Seth would talk, the more annoyance I saw on Jake's face. I was secretly hoping he was just as over his non-stop chatter as much as I was.

"So how 'bouts are we sleepin'?" Seth rapid-fired, while he stood holding his hands close to the fire.

I admit I wondered the same earlier in the day as my mind thoroughly processed all the aspects of what this journey was going to entail. I wasn't sure how Jake was going to manage two prisoners at the same time, all while he needed to sleep himself. I wasn't sure Jake knew yet what he was going to do, either.

No sooner had I thought it, I saw I was wrong. He must have already considered his options because it didn't take long after Seth's inquiry before Jake shared his predetermined plans with both of us. "You're going to lie over there," Jake, talking to Seth, motioned toward the right side of the fire, "and she's going to sleep next to me over here." This time Jake motioning toward where he was sitting on the other side of the fire closer to the trunk of the tree.

Seth looked over at me as if waiting for me to make some sort of disapproving gesture. And to be honest, yes, normally I would very much object to the idea of having to lie next to a man that I barely knew. However, in this instance, the idea of sleeping beside Jake was actually rather comforting. Thus far, he had done nothing to make me fearful of him or any of his intentions when it came to me. Also, being closer to him put me farther from Seth, of whom I was still very much fearful of.

"Ah, well that's a shame man, I's hoping you'd have her sleep here by me." Seth continued as he got down and started to lean over onto one elbow. "I'd sure like all that extra warmth right up next to me. I'd say it looks like it's been an awfully long time since she's had a man's—"

"Enough!" Jake huffed, interrupting him. "You seriously talk too much, man."

Finally, I thought to myself, hoping Jake's rebuke might shut him up a little, if nothing more than long enough for me to get to sleep. Being as tired as I was, I didn't intend to wait any longer to get myself positioned and ready to sleep. I crawled over toward Jake until I was between him and the tree away from the fire and Seth.

"Is this where you want me?" I asked. I just wanted to lie down, so I didn't mind much what position Jake intended for me to lie in.

"That's fine right there," Jake said while eyeballing the distance between himself, the fire, and the tree. "Go to sleep and I'll lie down next to you when I'm ready to."

I didn't argue one bit. I was so completely exhausted and would have been ready to collapse almost anywhere at that point. I slowly lay down behind him, pushing some of the pine needles up under the hood of my jacket to use as a small makeshift pillow. I was a bit more chilly than before now, having Jake sit between the fire and me, but that didn't seem to affect me much as I quickly drifted off.

Before long, I was awakened by Jake gently curling himself up behind me. He nestled in tight to my back then placed his hand on my shoulder, resting his forearm alongside my upper arm. I assumed it was the best he could think of to prevent me from running again and perhaps to make sure Seth kept his distance. However, at that moment, I didn't care what his tactics were. I was overwhelmed by the pleasantness of the heat he was now radiating toward me, and it wasn't long before I gently drifted back to sleep.

4

RAINDROPS AND SHOESTRINGS

The next morning, I woke up from a crisp chill in the air and was greeted by incessant chatter from Seth. Jake had already gotten up and had the fire put out. I must have been exhausted, because I hadn't even noticed when he got up to leave my side.

"You hungry, Gypsyin? I'll share my portion with ya. You look like you haven't been eatin' a whole lot. You could use a bit more to eat, put some meat on 'em bones of yours." Seth sat glancing over the now non-existent fire at me. "You sure are pretty. Why you can't be much older than my sister. She woulda turned 25 this year, bless her heart. I sure do miss her. I loved that girl." The word love seemed foreign coming from his mouth. Although it appeared he was trying to be kind, I couldn't help but wonder if this little speech of his had ulterior motives.

"Eat, Kaleah. We need to get going soon." Jake interrupted Seth to interject.

I looked over at him, surprised that he finally used my name. I wondered if us having to sleep next to each other made him less irritable toward me. I wasn't sure, but didn't mind. I was growing tired of being called Gypsyin, so I very much welcomed the friendly gesture. I took a small portion of the food that sat between us and ate, ignoring any of what Seth had offered me. I didn't want to appear ungrateful, but I didn't intend to give in to any of his acts of generosity. Not without knowing yet if they were genuine or manipulative.

Not much time passed before we set out again, this time with the same positions we had been in earlier the previous day. Seth was leading, with Jake behind, and me trailing them both. I felt better having rested, but my feet were still troubling me quite a lot. If I was going to be walking so much, which I imagined would be a lot, I needed better shoes.

The terrain we were currently on wasn't too rough. It consisted of relatively flat ground with only a random small hill here and there. Jake didn't want to walk anywhere near the roads that were nearby. I overheard him telling Seth the day before that he wanted to stay in the country more and avoid any roads. I didn't hear him say why, so I could only assume it was to prevent coming across the wrong set of people. At the rate we were going, I knew I could decently manage with the shoes I was wearing, but figured they would soon turn into a hindrance if we came to any bigger hills.

"Jake," I yelled shyly toward his direction, "can I talk to you for a minute?"

He paused for a moment and turned around to look at me with mild curiosity. The sky was overcast, making the air a bit more brisk, so he was wearing the same hat as the first time I saw him.

"What do ya need?" He asked in a pleasant tone. Before I could answer, he hollered up to Seth to hang on for a minute, then turned and backtracked toward me a few steps.

"I don't think I can keep up at this pace with these shoes," I said as I looked down at my feet.

He looked down briefly at them, then back up to my face. "Yeah, I noticed them myself last night. I don't know how you've made it this far in those things." He said with a gentle smile. "Give me a second, let me look at the map." He then motioned for me to turn away from him.

"What do you want with the map?" I asked as I turned around.

"To look for the nearest road," he said. "Where there are roads, there are houses, and where there are houses, generally there are shoes. Besides, it wouldn't hurt to find one, or maybe two, to look through. There are a few things we could use. I didn't pack planning on taking this trip by foot. We would have been there already if we hadn't… if I hadn't wrecked the car." He mumbled, looking down at the map, eyeballing where he planned on taking us next.

"All right, let's head north for another mile or so. Then we'll turn east and should run into something before long." He folded up the map and put it back in the lower zipper pocket of my bag. "Here, you need to drink," he said, holding up the thermos that he'd been carrying.

I nodded, then took a couple of gulps before handing it back. "Thanks," I said with a smile.

We walked another half an hour or so when I noticed the sky was starting to get darker. It wasn't even close to midday, so I knew it was probably a storm rolling in. My instincts wanted me to find a place to hide until it passed, but I ignored everything my mind was telling me to do. I figured Jake had it under control. I would await his orders, hoping they consisted of getting out of any rain that was sure to come. With how cool the air was, I could only imagine how miserable we would be if we were wet at the same time.

No sooner had I thought that, then Jake spoke up, having also noticed the weather. "Seth, ya see that big red tree ahead?" He asked, pointing toward a large maple in the direction we had been walking. The leaves on its branches that hadn't already fallen were a brilliant red with hints of orange at the tips. It had a few larger-looking limbs, but mostly it consisted of a lot of smaller ones that would be an excellent cover from the rain. "Run toward it, we'll meet you there," Jake yelled up to Seth.

Seth started to run as Jake turned toward me and stuck out his hand in my direction. I stopped and eyed it with a bit of confusion. It had started to rain, and the wind was picking up a bit, but wasn't very substantial yet.

"Your bag," he clarified, motioning for me to hand it to him.

"Oh," I nodded, then pulled it off my shoulder and slung it in his direction, where he caught it without much effort.

"Ok, let's go." His voice picked up to counter the noise of the wind.

I trotted toward him. He put his hand on my back and pushed as to help me move more quickly toward the tree. We made it not even a third of the way when suddenly the lace of my left shoe decided to finally break under all the strain of running. This set off a cascading effect. Once the lace broke, the shoe slipped off my foot, causing me to stumble and fall. Jake, still pushing me forward at a run, lost his footing and in trying not to bulldoze me found himself landing elbows first on the damp ground.

I didn't tarry. Knowing the rain would probably get heavier any second, I pushed myself up slightly and looked over at him. He had already returned to his feet and was now bent over collecting the bags. I leaned back to adjust myself to stand when suddenly Jake's arm wrapped around my waist and hoisted me to my feet. The rain was now coming down pretty substantially.

"Don't worry about your shoe, just run to the tree." He was shouting over the sound of the heavy rain spattering against the ground.

And that I did. I ran, with one shoe, soaking wet, muddy and now quite cold, over to the tree where Seth had been waiting and in no hurry to help. Once I made it, I reached out to lean against the trunk with one arm and down toward my knee with my other to rest and try to catch my breath.

"Take off your jacket, now." I looked up to see Jake in a haste to remove his own jacket. "Now!" His tone grew emphatic.

I stood up, a bit exhausted by the exchange as well as the chill that had started to set in, and took off my jacket. No sooner than I had, he took his and wrapped it around my shoulders and pulled it tight to crisscross itself at my front. It wasn't wet at all. The material was slick but sturdy. It was definitely much warmer than my own, although it didn't seem to do much to combat the shivering that had started to take over my body.

I looked up at Jake, now just in his long sleeve shirt and hat. "How are you going to stay warm?" I asked, noticing my teeth had begun to chatter.

"Don't worry about me," he said, trying unsuccessfully to not look concerned. "I won't be able to start a fire here and if you get too cold, your body will go into hypothermia." He said as he bent down and started to rummage through one of the bags. He pulled out another long sleeve shirt and pulled in on over his other one, then looked back up at Seth. "You warm enough?" He asked, gesturing toward him.

"Yeah man, I'm good. I didn't get in the rain like y'all did. This tree is pretty nice. It's been keeping the rain off pretty well, I'd say. What do you plan on doin' with her? I can warm her up if you think it'd help. You know my body heat would probably help her out quite a bit right now. I mean I'd hate to see her get sick from this, the pretty little—"

"I'll warm her up, she'll be fine." Jake interrupted, standing back up. Then he looked down at me, trying to assess my current condition and what to do about it. "Come here," he said firmly, motioning me toward him. I moved closer at the same time he took a step in my direction. He pulled the front of his jacket open and slid his arms in between it and me, wrapping them around my back and pulling me tight against his chest. "I hope this works," he said, "'Cause I doubt you'll like the alternative."

With my teeth still chattering, I was too worn out to pay any attention to his innocent threats or to respond. The wind wasn't helping my condition either, as it had now begun to pick up and be a bit more blustery.

Seth began again. "Are we gonna stay here for long? It doesn't look like it's gonna end anytime soon. Maybe we should—"

Jake interrupted to finish Seth's sentence for him, "Sit down and shut up? Yeah, that's a great idea, Seth, just sit down and shut up." I could hear the frustration in his voice as it reverberated through his chest and into my ear.

"Okay… Yes sir, buddy," Seth said sarcastically, as he reluctantly obeyed.

After standing there another minute shivering against him, Jake started to slide both his hands vigorously up and down my back, trying to create heat from friction. He didn't say much and was pretty quiet the whole time, likely because of the unsettled tension that had been between us up to this point.

His arms, like his hands, were large and brawny, clutching me firmly between them. I held my forearms parallel to each other tight against his chest, just below where my head was resting against him. Seth was right; it had been a long time since I had a man's body wrapped around my own, and I didn't want it to end. The warmth I was receiving from him was slowly overtaking the chatter of my teeth. However, even though the experience was quite satisfying, I figured I shouldn't try to manufacture phony shivers to lengthen it once my real ones dissipated.

He relaxed slightly and pulled back just enough to create a small gap between us, moving his hands to lie flat on my back just above my waist. "Are you feeling better now?" He asked, like he genuinely cared.

I wanted to say no. I wanted to step forward and bury my head back into his warm chest and nestle the rest of myself into his burly torso, but I didn't. I realized not only was it out of character, but he probably wouldn't want to continue with it either once he figured I was fine.

"Yea, I th… think I'm probably all right now," I said, still with a bit of shiver in my voice.

He pulled me back in against him, a little less tight this time, and continued to rub my back. "Liar," he said, sounding like he was grinning a little.

We stood there a couple more minutes until Seth broke into the silence yet again. "I got some food out of the bag for ya. Here, why don't ya come eat some of it, Jake? I can take over now man, she's probably sucked most of the heat outta ya. It wouldn't be nothing. I didn't get wet, so I'm still pretty toasty up under this coat I got on. It may look a bit raggedy but it's done good for me so far."

Before I got a chance to oppose, I could feel Jake tense up a little, I assume in irritation. He didn't say anything, but Seth stopped talking for a moment, so I figured Jake must have sent a disapproving glance his way to insinuate that he needed to shut up again.

"I'm fine now," I said as I started to slowly pull away from the soothing heat emanating off of him. "Thank you." I gave a small smile while looking up at his face. His eyes looked peaceful. Maybe he'd also been enjoying the opportunity for us to stop and rest. For a second he lifted a corner of his mouth and nodded, then finished pulling his arms back out from underneath the jacket. He reached down and took a hold of the zipper at the bottom and zipped it up. "Wear it for a little bit. I'm warm enough without it. We'll look for you another one when we look for you some shoes," he said as he backed up a couple of tiny steps, then sharply turned to head over toward Seth as if breaking free from a trance.

The rain was still coming down at a decent rate, but the sky wasn't as heavy-looking as it had been, indicating that it might let up soon. I leaned back against the tree while wrapping my arms around to hug myself. My foot was now freezing. I looked down at it and tried to wiggle each toe one by one, reassuring myself that they would thaw out eventually and I would be fine. I wondered if going back to get my shoe from wherever it had landed in the field once the rain had stopped would be of any benefit. I could try to put it back on and maybe it would help me manage the distance of the next mile or so, but it would no doubt be soaking wet at that point. I wasn't sure whether walking in a wet shoe or just walking with only a sock would be better for my ailing foot.

Jake came back around to hand me some food. "Here," he said, placing a couple of chunks of cheese and a pile of nuts in my hand, "you need to eat something if you're going to have enough energy to keep going. Who knows how many extra calories you burned with all that shivering." He smiled, then leaned his head back and dropped a few nuts into his mouth.

"How long is the food we have left going to last?" The question flowed out of my mouth with no forethought.

Jake paused, looking at me, his brows turned inward a little. "Not long enough," he said, being vague. "I'll hunt when I need to."

"With what?" I asked, looking down at the gun he had holstered along his left thigh. "I doubt you brought enough bullets to hunt *and* protect us."

"I don't need many," he said, breaking eye contact to bend over and rearrange things in his bag. "That's not something you need to worry about. That's my job, not yours. You're just the prisoner. I'm the Capture Agent, remember?" He glanced back up at me. His eyes now looked at me the same way they did when we first met, guarded and distant. With this look, I quickly gathered he didn't like his prisoner management questioned. I could see with this exchange his attitude quickly returned to his previously icy demeanor as well. I thought to apologize for myself but felt it best to just leave it alone. I didn't expect he'd believe me if I told him it was Fred's idea, either.

"Looks like the rain is easing up. I think it's a good time to move on now, don't ya think?" Seth asked smugly while readjusting himself against the tree and glancing over at Jake. It was obvious he was catching on to Jake's irritability from being questioned by me, and trying to use this opportunity to further irritate him. I didn't know if he intended to make Jake less happy with me or if he was trying to test Jake's authoritative boundaries. Either way, I just hoped that Jake could see through his manipulative strategy as much as I had.

"We'll move on when I say we will." Jake's tone was firm again as he continued to rearrange things in his pack.

Seth looked up at me, winked with a sly grin, then back down toward Jake. "Yes, Sir," he said.

It wasn't more than another twenty minutes or so when the rain had pretty well died down and Jake decided it was time to move on. Forgotten in all the shuffle, my shoe was still out in the field where we both tripped and fell. I intentionally didn't remind either man that I was now traveling with no shoe on one foot. I figured it wasn't all that obvious when I pulled the pant leg of my jeans down over my dark sock, since it kind of resembled a shoe. Looking down, it was easy to trick myself into thinking that I still had both shoes and I might have if my foot wasn't already cold and stiff. I knew it was a risk, but it was one I was willing to take. I thought if nothing else it would hopefully guarantee we wouldn't keep traveling too far without finding a house first.

5

FUZZY PEEKER

e walked for another half an hour or so until Seth, observant as he was, decided to mention my single foot shoe-less-ness to Jake.

"Too bad your Gypsyin only has one shoe," he said, looking back at Jake briefly. "She probably can't walk too much further without us stopping soon. Man, I bet her foot is pretty cold. If my shoes weren't so big I might think to let her borrow one, but you know we can't keep letting her borrow everything or we won't have enough to keep ourselves warm." He managed to slip it in before Jake sent a glare in his direction to cut him off. We were all walking relatively close together but in the same pattern as normal, so it wasn't difficult for me to hear what things Seth decided to ramble on about.

Jake looked back at me, then down at my shoe-less foot. "Why didn't you say something?" He asked rather pointedly.

"I thought you were mad at me," I replied, looking at his eyes, then down at the ground.

"So you decided that was a good reason to lose a foot?" He ended with a high inflection.

"I wasn't really thinking about that, I just—" I paused not wanting to tell him the actual reason behind my behavior. "I didn't see how mentioning it to you would have changed anything." I shrugged.

"Well, he would have probably given you one of his shoes like he gave you his jacket." Seth piped up. I could hear a touch of sarcasm in his voice, but it wasn't glaringly obvious.

"Seth, I swear man, if you don't shut your mouth, I'll cut out your tongue while you sleep!" Jake shouted forward at him while pointing toward the way we were walking. "Keep moving!"

Seth turned back forward with his head a little lower and his posture now less erect and continued to walk as Jake ordered.

Jake turned back toward me. "I can't get you to the station before winter if you only have one foot to walk on," he said, acting like that was the reason for his concern.

"I'm sorry! Is that what you wanted to hear?" I raised my voice to match his apparent level of irritation. "I'm sorry I didn't tell you about my foot. I'm sorry I asked you about the food. I'm sorry I asked you about your gun. I'm sorry I made you trip and get wet… I'm sorry I ever even wrote that damn letter asking you to come get me." Upon releasing the words, I relaxed feeling relieved to have let it all out. "I'm sorry," I said this time in a softened voice with sincerity.

Jake's face relaxed. His mouth started to open, about to say something, then he was cut off by Seth. "Ah hey, guys, I think I see what we're looking for. It's not much to look at, but I bet it'd do. It looks like it probably has a shoe or two in it. Hell, maybe we can find ourselves some more food. You know I could use a different coat. This one is getting a bit raggedy."

Jake now walking beside me turned to look at me again. "I've had prisoners worse than you," he said in a lower tone as Seth a couple of yards ahead of us continued to talk, thinking we were listening. "I know why you didn't remind me about your shoe. I'm tired of walking too. Believe me, this isn't what I had in mind either when I traveled down to get you. I know it's a pain in the ass. He's a pain in the ass." Jake motioned to Seth who was still chatting away. "But we'll get through it. And maybe when we get to the station I can convince them you're not who you said you were." He looked back over at me and smiled a little. "Now, let's see if we can find you some new shoes."

The sky was still quite hazy but now with small ribbons of light shining through the clouds. The house we came across was small, and fair to Seth's point, not much to look at. It set about a quarter of the way into a small hill on one side. The paint on the wooden exterior was still pretty well intact without much fading or flaking, not as I had expected for a place with no upkeep. The landscaping in front of the house, however, was another story. Vines now covered a good deal of the houses' south-facing wall. The porch which set next to that was partly covered with the same thick vine growth. There was a large shrub on either side of what looked like it had been the entrance to the porch, but was now no longer accessible. Also, to my surprise, the house still had most of its windows intact. Only a couple looked to be broken.

Jake took his position in front of both Seth and me and walked slowly toward the house, setting the pace at which he intended for us to advance. He had handed Seth his bag to carry before drawing his gun. He gripped it with both hands and carried it low out in front of his chest. His steps were cautious and methodical as we started to go around looking for the best way in. We passed the porch and started to head toward the back of the house, looking for a secondary entrance. Halfway down the side, there was another exterior entry. The screen door on the outside was slightly ajar, with the top section of the screen badly torn.

Jake reminded Seth to be quiet by moving his finger to his lips and mouthing "shh" while looking at him, then he motioned for Seth to set the bags down and continue to follow him. He passed the door and started to go on around the house, the entire time keeping his gun up and looking around thoroughly for anything that might make it dangerous for us to enter. The entire process seemed lengthy, but understandably so. After a few minutes of sneaking around, he slowly straightened up to his full height and re-holstered his gun.

"Okay," he said quietly as we started to walk back to where he instructed Seth to leave the bags, "Seth, you look like you're a strong guy. Why don't you see if you can get that door open?"

I don't know if it was obvious to Seth, but it was obvious to me that he couldn't have really meant it. He was just using Seth in case there was actually any danger in opening the door and he didn't want to get himself hurt. Though I figured that's what his intentions were, I didn't say anything. I just followed them both back toward that side of the house.

Seth hesitated for a second but then just went on ahead. If he knew what Jake was up to, he didn't act like he much cared. He walked over and pulled on the wooden screen door. At first, it seemed like it was a bit stuck and wanted to rub on the scuffed up cement slab below it. But with another hearty pull, it loosened up and swung out past the halfway point and out of his hands, making a hard thud sound as it hit the side of the house.

"Oops," he said as he turned toward Jake, looking for permission to talk again. Jake shook his head slightly, declining the request. I assumed because he didn't want to hear any more out of his mouth rather than due to it causing us to be in any more danger. Seth huffed a little in this apparent rejection as he turned back toward the inner door to open it next. He reached to turn the knob and, without much effort, the door swung open and in. He then turned toward me and gave a gesture for me to enter in front of him. "Ladies first," he said, looking at me from the corners of his eyes while he did some sort of half-bow thing with his body.

I gave him a look that wasn't probably what he was expecting, but before I could say anything Jake stuck his hand out in front of me, I guess, assuming I was about to step forward. "No, you can go first." Jake said, looking at Seth, "She'll follow me in."

Seth shrugged his shoulders like 'ah well I tried' and then turned to enter first. As Jake went next, he turned to make sure I wasn't far behind and following after him.

Once we entered, Seth turned to the left where there was a small living room and Jake turned to motion for me to follow him to the right into what had been an eat-in kitchen. The space was small, probably the only reason he didn't make Seth take the same route as what we did. As I looked around, I could tell we had not been the only ones to explore the place. The kitchen counters were pretty bare, with the random non-kitchen object strewn here and there. I could hear from the other room Seth was comfortable enough to talk again. He narrated almost every move he was making to us as he made it and listed out everything he found as he found it.

"I'm going to look for you some shoes, Gypsyin." He yelled from the other room. "Who knows, maybe I can find ya a nice li'l dress you can put on for us. Ah, I bet Jake would like that. Oh, you know what would be nice? I'll look for a blanket. It's getting pretty cold. We could use a blanket to sleep under. Who knows what we might find. I love looking through houses. You never know what you're gonna come across. Oh look, another DVD. These people really liked their movies. Too bad you can't do nothin' with DVDs these days…" His speech started to get garbled as he rummaged through the debris in the coat closet.

I bent down a bit and started to open and explore the cabinets in the kitchen. Jake walked around a little island that separated the kitchen from the living room, bent down and began to search for stuff in the cabinets below it. I had no trouble finding lots of things that were useless, but nothing we needed. I think Jake was having the same luck when he decided it was time for us all to move along and explore the back of the house where the bedrooms were.

"Come on, Seth, we're going to look back here. If we're going to find some shoes or clothes, they're more likely to be in the bedrooms, anyway." Jake spoke loud enough that Seth would hear him over his own jabbering. After a couple of seconds, Seth came around to the hall. He was carrying a large pitcher I assumed he thought we could use to carry more water. Also, wrapped around his neck was a small pale blue baby blanket he had turned into a makeshift scarf for himself.

"Don't be jealous, Gypsyin," he said as he looked at me, "it wouldn't have looked good on you anyway, being blue and all. You know, my neck has been a bit cold here recently. I've been needing one of these." He was cut off by Jake, taking him by the arm and pushing him ahead in front of us down the hall.

Jake then turned toward me and pushed me in front of him as well. He obviously didn't trust me and probably wasn't sure if I still wanted to escape. I figured he'd know better with me only having one shoe and all, but I could understand his reasoning.

I followed Seth a little further down the hall until he cut off and went into a small bathroom that was to our right. I figured if there was anything of value in there he would get to it first. Plus, I didn't want to share such a tiny space with him, so I went further down and to the left where I entered a small bedroom. As I walked in, there was what was left of a bed to the right with the headboard against the wall and a pair of box springs sitting below it, with the mattress completely gone.

The room, like the rest of the house, was tiny. I started to look on the floor to the left between the bed and the wall. I didn't want to reach down and rummage through all the crap lying around, not knowing what I would come across, so I used the foot that still had a shoe on it to kick things around a bit, trying to uncover anything of use. I found a few small children's toys and some rope. I started to reach down for the rope then realized it wasn't something I wanted Jake to see or have, so I took it and threw it under the bed and pushed a bit of other random junk in front of it.

"Gypsyin..." Seth's voice spoke quietly behind me. I turned to look toward him while standing back up. I hadn't been paying much attention to who was behind me as I was looking around, trying to find things. I just assumed Jake was in the hall between Seth and me.

Seth was standing inside the doorway of the room, staring at me, his eyes appearing darker than normal. He had a smirk on his face that sent chills down my spine. "I have something you're really going to want." He singsonged, clearly enunciated his words for one of the first times since I'd heard him talk. His eyes stayed locked on mine while he held something behind his back. Feeling uneasy, I backed up toward the corner of the room. I wondered where Jake was, but didn't want to seem skittish and overreact to Seth by calling out for Jake if there was no need to. Until... Seth suddenly took a few steps closer to me hastily.

"Jake!" I called out now terrified, changing my mind on the previous notion. Then I brought my arms up in front of me to block Seth in case he got too close.

"What?" Jake yelled back from down the hall as he came quickly into the room. I looked past my hands and over at him. He looked at Seth, then back at me, as if trying to determine what was going on and how Seth got between us. "What are you doing, Seth?" His tone was sharp and agitated.

Seth turned toward him and put his hands out in front, displaying what he had. "I found our little Gypsyin a shoe." He said as he motioned for Jake to take it.

He really had found a shoe. It was a man's shoe, but I didn't mind. Better to be too big than too small. It was for the side that I was missing, too. From what I could tell, Seth was also wearing new pants as well. Jake took a few steps toward him as he glanced over at me. "Are you okay?" He asked.

"She's fine," Seth said as he looked back at me and smirked with squinted eyes, looking sly. "I didn't have time to touch her. You're too quick for me, I guess." He said, looking back at Jake.

A scowl quickly appeared on Jake's face as he stared at Seth. "Touch her and you won't make it to the station," he said quietly but with a serious, stern tone, the only tone where I can hear the huskiness in his voice. The intensity of his stare left no doubt that he meant it.

Seth threw up his arms in surrender. "You got it, man. She's all yours. I hear ya loud and clear. You don't want to share her, fine. I mean, I think you're being a li'l bit selfish with her, but I guess I understand. You do know, though, she is just a Gypsyin," he continued. "I don't know why we can't both—"

Before I realized what he was planning, Jake stepped forward and threw a fist into Seth's gut. Seth let out a loud cry as he hunched over Jake's arm that was still steady against his stomach. Then Jake bent over to whisper something into his ear. Seth nodded his head a couple of times as he let out a bit of air and some small whining noises. I couldn't hear what Jake was saying, but I could hear Seth agree to whatever it was. "Yeah, dude eh, fine… ok…" he said, wanting Jake to let him go and probably forget about the whole thing.

Jake stood up, gave him a strong pat on the back, half like sealing an agreement and half like he meant to cause him more pain. At that, Seth let out a loud coughing sound then slowly stood up and started to gingerly walk past him to wait at the doorway outside of the room. Jake looked over at me. At the moment, I probably had a decently shocked look on my face. He didn't say anything for a second, just looked at me, then away for a split second as he sighed to himself before speaking "I found some stuff for you in the other bedroom," he said, then motioned for me to follow him.

I started to walk toward him when out of the corner of my eye I saw something fuzzy peeking out from behind the mirrored sliding door of the closet. "Wait, is that something?" I asked, reaching past Jake to grab for it. He spun around to see what I was looking at. I pulled it toward me with a gentle tug, then held it up and looked at it. It was a sweater—purple, soft, and fuzzy. I was pretty pleased with myself for finally finding something. I held it up against me and looked in the mirror on the closet's sliding door to see if it would be big enough to fit. But all I noticed as I caught my reflection was how awful I looked. My hair was wild and disheveled-looking and my face was filthy, not to mention the mud that was all over my pants. On top of that, I only had one shoe.

Jake noticed my brief hesitation as I looked at myself like I hadn't seen this person in what might have been years. "It'll fit, and you can clean yourself up if you'd like before we leave. But for right now, follow me. I want to show you the other stuff I found," he said.

I followed him out and to the left further down the hall, passing Seth who was now sitting down near the doorway of the second bedroom. As we entered the room, I noticed there were a lot more clothes in this one than in the one I had been in. Jake reached down toward a swivel stool that was sitting near the door that had a few articles of clothes draped over it. He picked up what looked like a large coat. It was dark blue with a hood that had a fur trim. "Here," he said as he held it out toward me. "It's not the prettiest thing, but it'll keep you warm."

"Okay," I said, enthusiastically. I started to take it from him, but then motioned instead for him to hold on. I unzipped his jacket and handed it back to him first, then reached out to take the new one.

He hesitated to grab it as he looked down at my chest. Wondering what he was looking at, I looked down at myself when I noticed my shirt was still wet and dirty. "Oh yeah, I might need to change this too," I said, then realized suddenly how exposed I was since it was thin and I wasn't wearing a bra.

As I looked back up at Jake, I could see him looking past me now, toward the doorway. I turned to see Seth had gotten up and was standing there waiting for us to finish. He must have still been experiencing aftereffects from Jake's disciplinary action, though, because he was quiet, not saying a word, just standing there watching.

Jake showed me a few more things he found before he was satisfied that I had enough to continue traveling with no more serious wardrobe complications. He took Seth and went outside, letting me have a minute to myself to change and tidy up.

I came out to them standing there, holding the bags waiting for me. Seth was talking again and Jake was pretending to not be ignoring him. Seth looked up from the ground toward me as I stepped out. "Well… looky, looky, Jakey." He paused and looked over to make sure Jake was looking at me as well. "Don't you sure have yourself a fine looking little bit of woman you get to curl up to tonight?"

Jake *had* been looking at me. His face was a bit more open than usual, but with the same piercing eyes intently surveying what I had changed into. When he heard Seth's verbal garbage, though, he turned from me to glare at him. At this, Seth slightly turned away and pulled his hands briefly up to his stomach. I looked over at Seth and scowled. "Dude, don't you ever learn your lesson?" I asked as I walked past them to pick up my bag.

6

PILLOW TALK

We kept walking. One day turned into the next. The routine was pretty well always the same. As soon as the sun even started to look like it was about to go down, Jake would scout out a place to make camp for the night and make a fire. Seth always slept on his side of the fire begrudgingly while Jake slept curled up against my back, with us on our side of the fire. Jake's morning routine always started early, generally before the sunrise, with him up preparing breakfast and reorganizing the bags before I was even aware of the lack of heat against me.

It'd been about 3 weeks since we ran out of the food that Jake originally brought. But true to his word, he had no trouble finding more for us to eat. Just like he said, he didn't need many bullets. When it was time, he reached down into his ostensibly bottomless duffle bag and pulled out a decent sized spool of wire. With this he had Seth and me help construct snares galore, of which he was able to catch for us more than enough rabbits, tree rats, even the random groundhog or two, to keep us going.

Seth, having already exceeded my patience not far into our first few days together was now obviously stretching the length of Jake's humanitarianism as well. After days of non-stop chatter we now knew all about his entire family, where he came from (the East coast, as I previously suspected because of his accent), his ex-girlfriend, the reason he joined the Coldiers shortly after the war started, and numerous other meaningless facts about his life.

Of all this newfound knowledge about the man, one thing he never cared to divulge however was why exactly he was no longer at his base and how he came about being in the middle of the highway. I suspected Jake, for the same reason as me, wasn't in any hurry to inquire on the matter, though. Probably somewhere deep down, we both figured that if we didn't talk to him, he would stop talking to us. It wasn't working yet, though, unfortunately.

Jake, every so often would make small chat with one or both of us. He rarely went into any great detail about himself, nor did I, but I did get a decent idea about how he was raised and where he was originally from. He was about three years older than me and enjoyed sports in high school. I wasn't able to get much out of him at a time, probably because there wasn't a lot of room between Seth's endless gabfest for Jake to get much of a word in edge-wise.

He, too, like Seth had a younger sister. Although I assumed, unlike Seth's, Jake's was still alive. He didn't say anything about being a Sicari or which station he came from. I didn't know what Seth thought about him or what he knew, but I figured he wasn't mentioning it due to whatever tension it might cause between them being on opposing sides and whatnot.

Over the last few weeks, Fred and I continued to watch the behavior of both men. Though I couldn't say I wasn't still slightly confused. I developed enough of a conclusion to each of their motives, what I could perceive them to be, anyway. It was obvious Jake hadn't been treating Seth as I would think he should, as another prisoner like me. He didn't watch over him or stay as close to him as he did me, although I will admit I hadn't seen Seth try to run. I figured maybe that was why Jake wasn't as overbearing with him as he seemed to be with me. Maybe, he thought, if the prisoner doesn't feel like a prisoner he would be less likely to act like one.

It was easy to see why Seth wouldn't run. Looking at him

compared to Jake, it was clear Seth was probably having more difficulty finding enough food for himself, and obviously Jake didn't. I think Seth was nothing more than an opportunist at best. Why flee from the hand that is willing to feed you? Maybe his reasons for being willing to walk with us to the Praetorium were simply the same as mine. Maybe he was tired of being alone and starving and for whatever reason the Coldiers wouldn't take him back.

My mind had days to ponder so many questions that I wanted to be answered, but wasn't about to ask. It seemed clear enough why Seth stayed with us, and why Jake didn't treat him like a prisoner as much as he did me. However, I couldn't help but return to the same question. *Why Jake would put up with Seth if he didn't have to?*

If it were me and I was a Sicari, I would have already found some way to discard him. I couldn't see what value he brought to Jake for Jake to keep him around. I could only come up with one conclusion. He must have been holding on to him because with Seth he actually had a real Coldier prisoner. Whether he was a high-ranking agent spy like my letter said probably didn't matter. His mission was to pick up a dangerous Coldier Agent. What would it look like if he came back with just me, nothing more than a supposedly pathetic, ignorant little Gypsyin?

What if his plan this whole time was just to use Seth to fulfill his duty and I would appear to be nothing more than a straggler he picked up along the way? In that case, they might be less likely to interrogate me, and less likely to kill me when I didn't have any of the answers they were looking for—answers my letter promised to deliver. Or maybe because I wanted that to be Jake's plan this whole time, I just made it up in my head to make all my suspicions fit my narrative. Deep down I hoped my conclusion was correct even if it was an assumption.

Jake, who was generally well mannered and extremely patient, though sometimes cold, possessive, and prideful, had been easier for me to figure out than Seth. On the outside, there were times that Seth came across as well-meaning, but there was something about him that was ugly deeper down under the surface. I could see it when he would make his off-hand comments toward one of us, mostly toward Jake, but about me.

I wasn't concerned that he didn't like me. To the contrary, I was afraid he liked me too much. The way he would look at me when Jake wasn't paying attention led me to this conclusion. His eyes were pleasant enough to look at, but then sometimes he would stare at me and let his eyes linger longer than a man should.

I couldn't piece it all together in my mind. I didn't like him but I didn't know all-together why. I wanted to come up with more reasons than just his obvious lustful advances toward me, but I settled on the thought that maybe it was just because he was a Coldier. And whether I wanted to or not, I couldn't... *wouldn't* like a Coldier.

We were mainly walking into the same dense countryside as we had been since we started. Jake wasn't a fan of getting close to any of the roads unless we had to, or unless he was in a car, apparently. Now and then, we would randomly come across a house nestled out in the woods we were traveling through. Generally, they would have long graveled drives and be pretty hidden from view to anyone traveling along the main road.

Coming across these was like finding an extra present on Christmas. Jake's eyes would light up and he would get all excited in the most subtle way that he does. I could tell even though it would probably be barely visible to most. Whenever this would happen, we would all take our assigned positions and go through the established routine. He would slowly walk around, holding his gun, ready to pounce on whatever might be dangerous to us.

Both Seth and I rearranged our wardrobe every time we came across something better or more suited for traveling. I was actually able to find a pair of women's shoes, a tad bit small but in general way more comfortable than anything I had been wearing to that point. Seth exchanged his accessories numerous times. Now instead of the small blue baby's blanket adorned around his neck, he was wearing a muted red, almost pinkish flannel shirt tucked in around his coat's collar. He briefly changed his loafers out for a pair of boots he found, but before leaving decided it was a bad trade and went back to swap them back out again.

Jake didn't take much, if anything, from any of the places we went into. He was completely satisfied with his clothes and didn't feel the need to upgrade anything. After wearing that jacket of his for an afternoon, I completely understood why. It must have been military-grade or something because for as thin and light as it appeared, it was still quite hardy and held its heat in substantially well.

The last house we stumbled upon had been pretty deep out in the woods. It didn't appear to have been visited by many people if any, after it was originally abandoned. It was a treasure trove for Seth, who frequently found way more than he could carry. Before we would depart almost every house, he had to sit and sift through his new collection and decide what things he had to part with and what things Jake would allow him to bring along. Considering Jake was quite possessive of his bags, Seth wasn't allowed to use any of their space to store his treasures. Because of this, he looked like a legitimate hobo walking around with random items hanging off of him this way and that.

Of all the houses we had been in so far, this one was my favorite. Upon walking in, I was taken back to the pre-war era. Everything was still sitting in the place where it looked like it belonged, exactly where the previous occupants would have left it. It was hard to tell why whoever had been living in it would have vacated, but when they did, they didn't seem to take much with them. As I walked slowly around observing the area, Seth was the first to comment, of course, on the fact that there was still a bed with a mattress in both of the two bedrooms. Part of me felt elated at this finding. At the same time, I was torn with feelings of sadness; I suppose from all the pre-war reminiscing the house was stirring up inside me.

"Can we sleep here for the night?" Seth asked Jake, like a small child giddy with excitement, similar to myself. "We can each get our own bed. I mean I'm sure you're gonna make her sleep with you…

but hey, if you've had enough of her—" he stopped himself for once. "Whatever… you know what I mean." He finished as he started to rummage through some papers still sitting on the kitchen counter.

I could see Jake's wheels turning as he thought of the condition of the place and the consequences if we were to stay here. He looked up at me, connecting with my eyes, trying to gauge my position on the matter. I half smiled as I tilted my head slowly to the side with a very slight shrug. I knew what I wanted to do, but ultimately I wanted to be safe, so I didn't want to do anything that would steer him one way or the other.

"Fine." He said finally with a small huff. I think inside he really wanted to as well, but he didn't want to let us in on that fact.

Supper didn't take nearly as much work to make, but it could have just felt easier because we were all in an elevated mood, plus we had a wood stove and pans to work with. Even as drafty as it was, the house had been quite a bit warmer than we were used to at that time of the evening. After eating, while Seth and Jake continued to talk and rummage around more, I sat down in the only recliner in the tiny living room and stared out the window. I didn't always get to watch the sunset, but this time I was enjoying the view as well as having real furniture to sit on again.

As the sun had started to go down, I could tell Jake was ready to go to bed. He was not a night owl. Even though that's what I would have considered myself, I didn't buck at it. When he was ready, I knew I needed to be, too. He wasn't a super heavy sleeper either. Seeing how frequently I woke up and hadn't even noticed that he left, I figured I probably was.

Even though it had been a good three weeks since I had tried to run last, he still insisted that we sleep the same way every night, with me tucked in neatly under his arm and my back nestled up against his chest. I figured it was the easiest for him to keep track of me that way, maybe along with other benefits like warmth.

"Kaleah," Jake said my name, trying to call me away from the dreamy state I had fallen into staring out the window. I glanced over to see him standing at the entrance to the hall, waiting for me to follow him to the bedroom. I stood up and started to walk toward him. Seth wasn't in the room any longer, so I assumed he had already taken an early trip to his private escape where he had a real bed probably for the first time in ages.

I walked into the room behind Jake, then passed him to go over and crawl onto the large bed that set nicely centered against the wall. It didn't have any sheets, but there was a decent-looking quilt that was laying over the bottom corner, half on the bed, half on the floor. I turned around to see Jake shutting the door behind us. I hesitated to lie down as I watched him, but wasn't sure if he could see me all that well now that the room was pretty dark. I didn't figure that he had any bad intentions, but I was a little dismayed in either case. He must have sensed a bit of trepidation on my part, because it didn't take him long to speak up.

"Don't be scared," he said gently with a sweet demeanor as he sat on the edge of his side of the bed. "I need it shut to make sure Seth doesn't come in while we sleep."

I relaxed, "Oh… ok. That makes sense." I responded as I started to remove the thick outer sweatshirt I had been wearing. "I know you wouldn't do anything." At least, I hoped that was the case.

"You're still scared of him, though." He said as he lay down on his back.

I hesitated, but then decided to open up, hoping that I could trust him with the knowledge. "Yeah," I said, lying down next to him on my back. "I just don't trust him being a Coldier. You know? I mean…" I hesitated.

"What happened?" He asked softly.

"What, when I was at the Coldier base?" I knew what he meant, but was prolonging it to think about how I wanted to answer him.

"Yeah… did they hurt you?" His voice was now low and delicate.

"No," I said with a brief pause. "I mean, I don't remember much. I was trying to escape and they—" I paused again. He lowered his arm from his chest down to where my arm was between us. He felt around for a second, then grabbed a hold of my hand. "I think they shot the guy I was with." I finished, then took a deep breath.

He didn't say anything for a few seconds, but continued to hold my hand. "I'm sorry." He said finally like he was the one who pulled the trigger.

I swallowed hard, trying not to sniff or make any noise showing that I had started to tear up.

"What happened the second time?" He remembered I said I'd been there twice. "Unless you don't want to talk about it. I understand." His voice was tender.

"I was hungry," I said slowly while thinking, trying to bring up the story to myself first. "I didn't want to be there again, but I hadn't taught myself yet how to find food out on my own... I went into a room with the wrong guy. I didn't realize the way you're supposed to barter there, ya know?" I asked, seeing if he was still listening.

He squeezed my hand a little, as if lending me the courage to continue. "He said he'd give me some food. I followed him to get it... I didn't know he'd look for a tag. When he didn't see it, he called me a Gypsyin and said the only way Gypsyins got any food was to pay with—" I paused again to swallow. "I didn't know what a Gypsyin was... He did things to me that I've... I've... I didn't want the food anymore. I didn't want to be there anymore. I didn't even take the food, I just left as fast as I could after he—" I let go of his hand to bring both of mine to my face to wipe it off. "They're evil. They're all evil... Please don't let Seth hurt me." I said, as I looked over at Jake. Though the room was too dark to see his face well, I could still see a good portion of the white of his eyes looking back at me.

He turned from his back onto his side, keeping his face turned toward me, then reached up and took a hold of my hand again with his. "It won't happen again." He said gently.

I couldn't keep holding it back, the emotions were too much for me. I started to cry as quietly as possible, thankful at least he couldn't see my face. Hoping he couldn't really hear me either.

"It won't happen again." He said again this time with a little more strength behind the tone. He must have known I was crying. He released my hand and brought his up to my face, resting his palm against my cheek as he wiped the tears under my eyes away with his thumb.

After a few swipes, he tightened his grip slightly against my face and pushed himself closer to me with his other arm. His face was now closer to mine with the white of his eyes bigger than before. "I won't let it happen again." He said once more with a sweet yet stern voice.

"Okay," I sighed, relaxing into the bed, hoping I could trust him, begging myself to just give in and trust him.

He moved his hand from my face to my back, pulling me toward him to hug me. I let the top of my forehand rest against his chest. "Try to trust me." He said softly as though he could read my thoughts.

I moved closer toward him, letting my cheek sink into his chest. "I'll try," I said.

He slowly rubbed his hand along my shoulder, then moved it to the center of my back and pulled me in tighter.

This was new—his sincerity, his openness, his tenderness… This wasn't the same man that captured me on the hill. I wasn't sure what changed him or why but I hoped it stayed this way. I needed him to stay this way. Though it seemed crazy, I wanted him to want me. That was the only way I suspected maybe I'd be allowed to live, if I was more to someone that just a Gypsyin, a wanderer, a nobody.

I snugged in closer, appreciating his warmth and the comfort of no longer being alone, even if it was temporary. It wasn't long before I fell asleep.

7

DANGEROUS COMPANY

The next morning I woke up alone in the bed covered with the quilt that had been laying along our feet. The sun was actually up to my surprise. Jake normally never waited that late before getting me up.

"Gypsyin…" I could hear Seth calling for me. "You're going to miss breakfast if you don't get up, sleepyhead. You sure do like to sleep. Aren't you supposed to be the one who gets up before us men and makes us something to eat. Why do you get to sleep in? I want to sleep in…" His voice got louder then stopped as he neared my door.

"Kaleah, it's late. We need to get going soon." I heard Jake that time. He didn't sound hasty, more like he didn't want me to linger unnecessarily.

I pulled my sweatshirt back on and went out to see them. Jake had made a small breakfast for us before we set out to leave again. He wasn't exactly more lively, but I could tell he wasn't as hard in his responses when we would talk to him, either.

"I found this," he said as he reached over to hand me what looked like an antique hairpin. It was a darkened silver color. One end of it came down to a point almost like a pen would but without the ink while the other end displayed a small bouquet formed in metal. Each flower was set with a small turquoise stone. I stared at it in observation for what had to be a solid minute. "I thought you might like something to hold your hair out of your face." He said with a tiny smile.

"Oh my gosh, thank you," I said softly still looking at it, mesmerized by its beauty.

"Oh my gosh, thank you," Seth muttered out in a high whiny pitch, trying to mock me. "Is that the best you can do?" He asked now looking over at Jake. "I got something for her, I'll give it to her tonight." He turned back to look at me his face now displaying a pompous grin as he winked.

I didn't say anything. I just turned back around and continued to eat while still examining the hairpin, fiddling with it between my fingers. Suspicious of how quiet everyone was after a moment, though, I peeked back up at Jake, looking out from the top of my eyes without lifting my head. He was leaning against the kitchen counter with his arms crossed in front of him, glaring at Seth. His face was red and tense.

"Get the bags. Let's go." He said still looking at him, then stood fully up, pulling himself away from the counter, and started to walk around me toward the door. I felt like a kid in school. When one idiotic student irritates the teacher, now everyone has to pay for it. I rolled my eyes to myself, then reached down to collect the remaining bit of my food and quickly shoved it into my mouth as I stood up.

We all grabbed our assigned bag and walked out onto the porch. Jake looked back at the door then turned around to shut and secure it. I think he was trying to keep the intact condition of the house for future visitors. That was admirable of him.

We hadn't taken our usual walking positions yet as we started through the yard and over toward a small outbuilding that was next to the drive. This time I was walking on Jake's left with Seth to his right. It was nearing the end of fall now, so the trees were pretty bare, leaving the ground covered with all the dead leaves that they had shed over the past few weeks. This made it relatively difficult to walk through them with any grace or stealth. Every step we took sent out a loud crackly crunch.

Before I had sat down to eat, Jake told us his plan for the first half of the day. We were going to head east towards the sun, then he would look at the map and reevaluate which way he wanted to take from there. As we started to walk farther from the house, I set the sun as my heading and began to walk toward it. I hadn't taken all that many steps, though, when I heard a loud whoosh of leaves to my side where both men had been walking.

I looked over suddenly. To my mind, it looked like Jake had just vanished into thin air. At first, I was stunned. Like a deer caught mesmerized in a car's headlights, I was caught, staring at where he once had been, in a moment of confusion. I glanced around, trying to figure out what had happened. *Where did he go?* In all my staring, my gaze settled on Seth who appearing to be stunned like myself, was just standing there, his face contorted with confusion.

Only seconds lapsed when I started to hear a rustling sound that would soon help resolve my confusion. I looked down to see Jake below us in a large hole, now shuffling around, trying to bring himself to his feet and knock off the leaves that had collapsed onto him from above. He was deep. My first thought was how were we going to help him get out, but my second thought quickly barged its way through to take precedence.

We...

I looked up again, locking eyes with Seth, who was now staring intently at me. His face was turned down, looking at me from the top of his dark, mischievous eyes. His body positioning suggested that he had come to the same thought quicker than I had. Each of his arms were raised up and away from his sides as he bent over slightly, posturing like he was about to catch a loose chicken that had flown the coop.

I froze for a moment. My mind was like a truck trying to shift itself into gear, jerking, trying to make me pick an action—fight or flight?

There was no more hesitation. Without even thinking about my next move, my body completely took over and decided. Run! I needed to run. At that moment, everything became a complete blur. I didn't have time to analyze what was the best way to proceed. My instinct to survive propelled me. Throwing my weight from one foot to the other, I quickly spun around. My eyes locked onto something far into the distance, and I began to run.

Within seconds, I knew he was behind me. I could hear him. The sound of deep panting escaping his throat mixed with the pounding of his feet against the leaves. He was gaining on me. I wanted to turn and see how close he was, how much faster I needed to be, but my body wouldn't allow it. I was locked on a target and I was dead set to make it there.

I wasn't fast enough, though. He caught me. The sounds of the leaves under his feet were now nearly indistinct from the sound my own feet were making. No sooner than I realized this, I could hear his voice directly behind me as well. His breathing was heavy. "Come here!" He belted out. "Stop running, Gypsyin!" He screamed again as a solid force slammed against the center of my back, thrusting me toward the ground, forcing me to plow my face into the leaves.

"Dammit, woman, you're not going to run from me." He huffed, lowering his tone to a sinister growl.

I pushed up to my knees and tried to crawl away just far enough to get back up to my feet. Then a hand grasped my ankle and pulled me back toward it until my stomach was back flat against the ground. "I'm tired of watching Jake get you all to himself every night," he said, his voice now seething. "Did he think I wasn't gonna make him share you? He'll believe it now!"

I pushed the top of my body up onto my elbows, trying to pull my knee forward again to crawl away, but he still had a hold of my foot. He pulled it back and twisted, turning me over, with my back now in the leaves. "You're gonna stay down and stop trying to get away. It isn't gonna do ya any good fightin' me. Jake isn't here to stop me now is he?" His face was bright red from the exertion, though his tone lightened like he'd caught his breath.

I looked straight at him, staring at his face. Thinking maybe if I show him less fear he might stop, all while trying to still figure out a way I could turn around to get myself back on my feet to run again. He hovered over me, glaring down, watching as I tried to slowly crawl backward. "You think you like what Jake does with you every night," he said, starting to bend over to grab a hold of my foot again. "Wait until I show you what I'll do to ya." I pulled my foot away as he reached for it.

Suddenly, I heard a loud rustling in the leaves back toward where we left Jake. I glanced away from Seth toward it, desperately hoping that there was some way Jake had managed to get free from the hole on his own. "He isn't gonna save you, Gypsyin." As Seth reached down again toward my foot, I brought my other foot up and kicked him hard, square in the jaw. He stumbled back and away just long enough for me to turn around and get my feet under me again to run.

It took me a second to find and reset my eyes on my original goal, but without much effort, one leg quickly followed the other as the sounds of the leaves returned to my feet. Kicking him must have only granted me a few seconds though, because it wasn't long before I started to hear him behind me again. Each leg swooshed through the leaves followed by a distinct crushing sound with each step. "You're not gonna like what I'm gonna do to ya when I catch ya!" Seth, furious, shouted forward at me, while now running again.

Before long, the singular sound of the shuffling of leaves turned into two distinct sounds when suddenly I heard Jake calling out as well. Still running as fast as I could, the strong sound of the leaves directly behind me began to dissipate and trail off.

I continued toward my mark, an outbuilding in the far distance. I intended to run as fast as I could, giving it everything I had, and that is what I did. I didn't look back. Once there, with one quick motion, I pulled the door open, threw myself inside, and shut the door behind me hastily as to not be seen. It was dark, damp, and cold. I lowered myself to the ground and curled up against the side as far back in a corner as I could crawl to. I closed my eyes to drown out any light that was still visible, just as a child would cover theirs during a scary movie.

Somewhere inside, I felt like if I couldn't see him, he couldn't hurt me. My heartbeat pounded deep inside my ears as every other sound dissipated and faded away. It sounded fast and hard and felt like it was thumping itself against my brain, trying to penetrate my thoughts. I tightened my eyes, telling myself to breathe... *Just breathe, slow down and breathe.* I curled up tighter, wrapping my arms around my legs, pressing my face into my knees as hard as I was able. I wanted to cry. I wanted to shout out for help. I wanted to pass out. I wanted to give up so that maybe it would all be over faster. "Breathe," I told myself again, trying to stop myself from having a full blown panic attack.

The light started to increase intensity through my eyelids even though they were as tight as I could possibly have shut them. I knew he found me. I knew hiding in the shed wasn't the best plan, but I didn't know what else to do. Upon this revelation, my body sent out deep intense shivers that I wasn't able to control. Realizing that running and hiding hadn't worked I opted for begging. "Please don't hurt me." I cried out. "P... Please," the shivering started to deepen. "Don't h... hurt me. P... Please," I cried out again, straining to get a full breath as my breathing quickened, my ears rang and my head began to feel heavy, soon to black out.

Two hands gently gripped my arms, then they shook me slightly to rock me back a little. "P... Please don't h... hurt me." I begged.

Slowly, as if my hearing had started to fade back into my thoughts I could hear a small voice every time the hands shook me. "Kal..." the volume of the voice slowly increased. "Kale..." Then as if all at once "Kaleah," said a soft, gentle voice.

I slowly opened my eyes, still hesitating to lift my head. "Kaleah, it's me. Kaleah..." The hands moved down and around to my back as a large warm body pulled himself closer to mine.

"Kaleah... you're okay. It's me, Jake. You're okay now. I've got you. You're okay now." The voice repeated itself over and over. But nothing stood out to my mind until after it echoed itself multiple times.

Then, as if everything broke away, instantly my mind recognized his name… Jake.

I finally looked up. His eyes stared soothingly into mine. He continued to repeat the same words. "I got you. You're okay now. It's just me…. It's Jake."

With the tension of my mind and body at its absolute peak, the moment the realization set in that I was safe, I broke… "Jake!" I cried out, then released my knees and leaned into him.

At the same time, with his hands against my back, he pulled me tight into his chest. "Shhh… You're okay now. I've got you. You don't need to be scared anymore. You're okay now."

Still sobbing, I relaxed against him, letting my mind completely go and surrendering to the idea that I really was okay now.

We sat like that for what, I'm sure, was only minutes but felt like hours. I didn't want to let go. I was still in shock.

"He's gone now," Jake said, finally breaking the silence.

8
UNDONE

"Are you okay?" Jake finally pulled back and looked down at me but it was still dark so I'm sure he couldn't see me well.

I nodded hesitantly; I wasn't sure if I was yet or not. I still felt pretty shaken up.

He reached up and pushed the hair back from my eyes. "You look okay… Here let's go back outside where we can see better." He said softly, then reached down to take my hand. "I'm not sure because of all the leaves but I think the hole I fell in was a hand-dug well the owners probably didn't care to fill in before they moved on." He said, pulling me to follow him back outside. "When I finally realized where I was, I tried to find a way out. It was deep, though. Then every time I tried to move, all those freakin' leaves would re-collapse on me again."

He sounded frustrated with himself but I expected it wasn't the leaves that were the real culprit. "When I heard you scream and didn't see Seth, I figured he was after you. I tried to get out as quick as I could." He continued, sounding exasperated, as he leaned against the outside of the shed then slid down to rest as he motioned for me to sit next to him. "You're not hurt, right? He didn't get a chance to hurt you, did he?"

"No," I said softly. It was still hard for me to speak so I just shook my head as I leaned up against the shed to sit beside him. I wanted to ask him how he finally made it out of the hole but I couldn't get myself to speak more than a word at a time so I just assumed it was either his agility, his athleticism, or maybe just his sheer will to get to me. "Wait… Where's Seth?" I asked suddenly. Apparently that question was important enough I was able to speak it.

"When I got out of the hole, I could see him chasing you, so I yelled, hoping he'd stop. When he saw I was free, he veered off toward the woods. By the time I caught up though, I couldn't see where he went." Jake said, leaning forward, then turned to look at me to see how I took the news.

"What?" I wasn't all that keen on him not knowing where Seth went.

"Well, I could have tried to follow him, but at that point I realized he could be anywhere. I didn't know if you were hurt but I saw where you went so I figured it'd come find you first to make sure you were okay."

"Oh…"

"Believe me, Kaleah, I didn't intend for any of this to happen. If it wasn't for that freakin' hole… Ugh…" He stopped then stared off into the woods, frustrated. I could tell he was agitated, obviously not only with Seth, but I think a little with himself.

"It's not your fault… I don't blame you for anythi—"

"No, it is…" He interrupted, still acting irritated with himself. "I should have seen the hole. I'm sure if I was looking where I was going better than I was, it would have been obvious."

I didn't say anything. I just nodded, then reached over and rubbed his back. I realized even though he may be brave, capable, and fearless, sometimes he also came across as a bit prideful. The idea that he couldn't stop a man, a pathetic excuse of a man at that, was likely eating at him.

After we both sat for a minute gathering our composure, his usual assertive behavior kicked in and we didn't tarry any longer. He said with not knowing exactly where Seth went and what he would be planning, he wanted to get me out of there so we could make as much ground as possible as quickly as possible. In no way was I opposed to this determination of his and followed along tight to his every move. We cautiously walked back toward the house to gather the bags that had been flung about in all the commotion. Jake took both duffles and handed me my backpack, then looked toward the East, the original way we had started to walk.

"We're going north now, not east." He said firmly, with no explanation, low almost under his breath, but loud enough for me to hear him.

We walked for another 12 days. Each consecutive morning, the frost would bite more bitterly than the previous. I also now noticed when Jake woke up each morning. Once I felt him pulling his heat away, I would fully wake up myself without him having to say anything to me. The pace we had been going was quite a bit faster than before when we had Seth tagging along. I wasn't sure if it was easier to go faster because it was just the two of us now, if Jake was intentionally trying to make better time because of the worsening temperatures, or if he was trying to set more of a distance between us and wherever Seth might be.

Just knowing Seth was still out there was constantly on my mind. Jake half wrote him off, saying he would probably either die from starvation, freeze to death or live in the last house we left, seeing it still had so many treasures he'd likely not want to leave behind. I didn't know if Jake really believed himself and didn't think Seth was any longer a threat or if he was just trying to play it down, knowing the truth would cause me significant mental anguish. The thought that he might trail us weighed heavily on me. I knew it could just be paranoia. It didn't help that's all Fred talked about. I knew I didn't have the best history of mental stability, but even with no evidence of it, I couldn't shake the feeling.

I'm sure Jake noticed I often looked back in the direction we had come from. I didn't like to talk loudly anymore either. I wanted to be able to listen for any sounds that might indicate approaching danger. It wasn't just me, either. Jake was more vigilant as well. I didn't know if it was because he also thought we might be in danger or if it was just for my sake, but while walking the first day after the incident he shared with me his decision to change a few of our previous protocols.

Although I'm sure he didn't mind the way we had previously slept, since it was nice and warm, he said he didn't feel it was still the best for our safety. Now, when it was time to stop and make camp, he did a more thorough job of scouting out a place that was hidden better than before. He started making the fires smaller than he used to as well. It sucked not having as much warmth, but ultimately I thought he felt better knowing we were less visible.

Each time it was time to make camp, he now found a nice large tree and instead of both of us laying down between it and the fire, he'd sit leaning up against it with his back to the trunk and I either sat leaning against him or would lie down against his side. He still found some way to place his hand on me. I didn't think it was because he suspected I would still run anymore, but probably just to make sure he'd wake up if I moved away from him for whatever reason.

Jake was more engaging now that Seth wasn't with us, too. Even though I could tell he still wasn't completely open about everything, I was able to have more meaningful conversations with him. His overall demeanor was less domineering as well. I figured this could be because he was now the only male and he didn't have to be quite as assertive toward the group, or maybe because he started to trust me; I didn't know which.

Frequently, while walking he would help pass the time by telling me stories about his childhood, his parents, and what he was like before the war. From everything he was saying, he didn't seem anything like what I had observed about him originally. I got the idea from his stories he used to be rather kind, attentive, and even intriguing. I could see a bit of it coming out in him the more we talked.

He would smile more, even if it was only the corners of his mouth most of the time. When he did, it was nice. He was letting me in a little, not to mention he had a pretty handsome smile. As his comfort with me grew, he also became the slightest bit playful. It was still very subtle, but I could see it. Now and then, when he realized he didn't need to be so serious he might make a joke. He was quite witty, something I grew to enjoy very much. In either case, I appreciated him no longer being as cold and short during our exchanges.

I knew from earlier conversations that he was originally from the North-East, but this time he was more comfortable giving me additional details. He was raised in New York, strongly emphasizing to me it was the state, not the city. Apparently, he wasn't much of a city guy most of his life until the last few years before the war. He said he had wanted to be in the military since he was a boy and was going to join up after he spent a few years working for the family business. But before long, he could tell things were starting to get out of hand and the collapse was inevitable. He said when he saw that; he changed his mind altogether and opted for civilian life, not wanting to obligate himself to only God knows what would be ordered of him. I thought it might be a good opportunity to ask him about being a Sicari, and why he chose that side, but the conversation quickly ended and I got the idea that it was a bit of a sore subject and he didn't want to talk about it.

After a brief period of walking in complete silence, he decided to restart the conversation by asking me about myself. I told him as much as I could remember about my childhood. I was from Tennessee and my parents were both lawyers. I was decently used to cold winters, though probably not as accustomed to such low temperatures as he was. I tried to share what I could with him, but I knew there was a problem. I couldn't remember a lot of my past. I'd had that problem for quite some time and wasn't sure when it began. A lot of things just didn't make sense, and a lot of my memories were pretty hazy if not completely gone altogether. I didn't share that with him though; I wasn't sure if it would make him think less of me.

It was nearing late afternoon when Jake decided to slow the pace to pull out a few of his snares from his bag and set them. We'd had a decent amount to eat the previous few days, but our supply had started to dwindle. Jake never let it get too low before figuring out a way to find more. We walked along a small path. He was quiet, just looking around, observing game trails, scat, and such until he stopped. He squatted down, resting his weight against his legs, and began fashioning a snare. He twisted the wire, creating a loop then glanced around, looking for the perfect place to position it. After a couple of minutes of fiddling with it and a couple of small twigs close to the ground, he slowly turned and started to stand back up.

"All right, let's set a couple more, then we'll go rest and wait until we catch something." He said softly, trying to not alert the wildlife. I stood behind him, waiting beside the bags, and watched as he did the same thing a couple more times in different spots.

"Thank you," I whispered as he knelt over his bag, fiddling with more wire.

"For what?" He asked softly, with his back still turned, his hands now taking the wire to create a loop.

"Not treating me like everyone else does… just a stupid little Gypsyin they can take advantage of," I said, trying to keep my voice low.

He paused for a second, his fingers still holding the wire tight. "I do the best I can… but you know I still gotta do my job, right?" He let out a small sigh, lowering his hands to his thighs as to stop and think. "I know what you really are, but that's not what they think you are… I still gotta take you in."

"I'm not asking you not to," I said slightly lifting my voice. "That's not what I was saying." I trailed off, thinking about what I *was* trying to say. "Look, I know you got a job to do… I know I'm… just… the job." I paused again to take in a large breath.

"Do you know what my superior would do to me if I don't have you when I get back?" He asked still turned away, his voice like mine no longer whispering.

"You're right," I let my voice level out. "I'd hate for anyone to do to you what I know they plan on doing to me. No reason we both have to die." I said with slight sarcasm.

"Do you think I want that?" He asked, his voice taut and tense as he lifted his head and turned toward me. "Do you think I want them to hurt you?" His face slowly turned flush. He set the wire down and pushed himself back up to stand facing me. "Do you not think I've already thought about it… what I should do with you?"

"Sure I have, you're gonna turn me in because I'm your prisoner." I scowled. "I'm nothing else to you… I know that. I didn't expect anything else." I said dejectedly.

"Well, you should have!" he snapped back, now with pain in his eyes. "You should have expected something else… I don't wanna turn you in. I don't want you hurt… If I didn't care about you I wouldn't have stopped Seth. I wouldn't have kept you warm this whole time. I wouldn't keep feeding you…" His face was now fully flushed but not quite angry.

"You're only doing that because I'm your prisoner," I raised my voice again, taking a step toward him. "It wouldn't do them any good for you to bring in a cold dead body now would it?"

The tension was thick as he paused, locking eyes with me. He let his shoulders relax slightly as his eyes stared into mine with piercing ferocity.

"You're wrong." He said, lowering his voice back down to a near whisper. "You're more than my prisoner… Despite how hard I try, I can't change it. I wish I could just turn you in and not care. But instead, every ounce of me wants to save you. Save you from them and from yourself."

I didn't say anything back. I just kept looking at him, lost in his eyes. He raised his hand toward my face and gently brushed the hair away from my left eye. Then he lowered it to rest on top of my shoulder briefly before moving it to cradle the back of my neck.

Without saying anything else, he looked down toward my mouth, then back up into my eyes. With gentle pressure pulling me towards him, he leaned down and kissed me. I could feel every ounce of tension that had just risen between us melt away as our lips sank into each others. He kept the pressure against my neck, holding my face tight against his, not yet ready to release the kiss. When his other arm came up to wrap around my waist, I realized without effort mine were already both wrapped around his. His face was warm against mine. That alone made me want to continue longer than probably either of us expected we would. But every good thing must come to an end and after a lengthy moment, he relaxed the grip that had been pulling me toward him.

Without stepping back, he let go of my waist and I lowered myself, returning my heels to the ground. I looked down and slightly away, feeling a touch of embarrassment. "I'm sorry I did this to you," I said, raising both of my hands to his chest to lean my forehead against.

"You'd have done it to anyone." He said as he again wrapped his arms around my upper waist and held me tight against him. "I'm not easily smitten by any means but no matter how hard I've tried you've… you've undone me," he paused. "I've been trained by some of the most elite… They taught us to control our emotions, every single one of them. I was trained on how to be a stone wall, how to be interrogated, how to overcome every tactic an enemy might fight me with. But you… they didn't train me for you."

I smiled to myself, happy to hear how he felt about me along with realizing I apparently had a superpower I didn't know about. It was peaceful resting against him. I didn't want to move. I didn't know where this would take us. I wished I could have read his thoughts, but settled on the idea that we still had time to figure it all out.

9
PROWLER

We walked for another two days. I could tell he was conflicted. Most of the time, we would only have small talk and nothing deep. I didn't bring up the kiss or how he felt again. I knew the whole situation was difficult for him; my existence was difficult for him. I knew he was probably trying to process to himself what he wanted to do, and he didn't need me trying to muddy it up in his mind. I don't even think I had resolved within myself what I wanted him to do.

Deep down, I knew I cared for him as he did for me. Knowing this and knowing what trouble he would be in if he didn't turn me in, I wasn't sure that we shouldn't just go along with the original plan. He was perfectly fine and alive before he caught me. If he released me over to them, he could then go back to being both perfectly fine and alive again without me. I didn't want him to be punished or have his life threatened on my account.

The next day, we didn't make as much distance as we normally had each of the previous days. Possibly because it was the first day it had snowed since we started walking. I wasn't super fond of snow to start with. Pre-war I think it was just one of those things I resolved to be content with until it melted away. I never really liked to go out and play with it either, as far as I could remember, probably because I have never enjoyed being cold.

Jake, on the other hand, seemed to like the snow quite a bit. I could tell he was doing everything in his power to not play with it. At one point while we were talking, he bent over to pick a handful of it up. He acted like he was creating a snowball but then before throwing it, as I had expected him to, he just slowly squished it between his fingers, acting as if he had only been observing its integrity. He also commented about how he liked that it would make it easier when he looked for game trails. I, however, didn't see much benefit unless it snowed enough for us to use it as a shelter. In my mind, it was useless at best, but more likely hazardous.

Sundown would be soon so we had been walking around the same area for a few minutes, trying to find a good spot to stay for the night. Ideally, I would have loved to find a cave. I had found caves to be my preferred places to camp, but they were generally hard to come by. We muddled around for a bit until we finally found a place that seemed relatively decent. It wasn't great, but Jake didn't want to spend more time than necessary looking; especially knowing if we didn't have a spot before the sun finished setting, we would be in a lot more trouble.

The place we settled on was under a large spruce tree he found. It had modest enough branches, but underneath was still bare without much snow cover. There were a lot of bushes, small trees, and undergrowth all around it, so I figured it would work well for what we needed. It also looked like a great spot to make a fire and not worry too much about it going out on its own while we slept. When we got there, Jake asked me to go around without getting too far from the tree and pick up any small twigs or sticks that I could find. The dryer the better. Meanwhile, he would start to clear a small spot for the fire and see what he could do about dinner.

I tried to stay close to the tree, but I wasn't having a ton of luck finding a lot of loose dry things, so I inched my way a little farther than he probably wanted. I think we both knew at this point that I didn't intend to run again, so he wasn't nearly as cautious about keeping me in his sight as he had been the first few weeks.

The sun was now close to setting, but the moon was up and almost as bright as the sun had been. I figured it was probably close to being a full moon. The snow, now about an inch or so, was doing an amazing job of reflecting the light and created a lovely evening glow.

As I walked around, not only did I try to find twigs and sticks like I was instructed, but I thought I would also keep an eye out for a game trail. I figured if I found one then I could show Jake and he could set up a couple of snares before we went to sleep. That way, hopefully we could catch something by morning before we set out again. I walked slowly and methodically looking close to the ground. Until I was stopped, frozen by what I ran into that was obviously not what I had been looking for and not what I wanted to see.

There in the snow, with its gleaming crystallized compression was the print of a shoe. It was distinctive. I squatted and stared at it for a second. Confused who might have made it, I quickly looked down at my own shoe. *Had I already walked around this area? Had I unknowingly walked in circles?* However, without even picking my foot up to look and try to match the tread, I could tell it wasn't mine. It was much too large to be a print from my shoes. It couldn't be Jake's either. Jake wore large boots with super heavy tread. This print had tread like that of a… I paused. Instantly I felt faint. My brain was trying to cycle what to do next. It was the print of a man's loafer. It had to be Seth's.

I couldn't decide what to do. I didn't want to make the wrong move. I didn't want to run, even though that was what I felt like doing instinctively. If I was wrong, what would Jake think? I decided I had to go back and tell him. I didn't know what he would do. How would he find Seth? Where was Seth even at? Was he hiding behind some tree ready to pounce on me as I walked by? How did Seth find us? Was it even safe for me to run back to Jake? Would Jake hear me if I screamed for him, and then if he did hear me, would he be able to find me again?

I softly dropped all the twigs I had collected to the ground and slowly rose back up, making sure to look around and stay vigilant of my surroundings. I couldn't have wandered that far away from Jake. I looked down at the trail I had made in the snow up to that point and tried to follow it back while still staying aware of everything else going on around me. I shouldn't have gotten too awfully far, I didn't think. Before long, looking through the underbrush, I saw part of Jake's figure standing in front of the tree, looking toward the side. I almost called out for him, but then realized wherever Seth was, I didn't want to alert him that I knew he was close. I walked softly as fast as I could, trying not to scream or run or show in any way that deep down I was terrified. I just wanted to make it back to Jake. That's all I had to do, I told myself. *You'll be okay. Just make it to Jake.*

As I got closer, I could tell there was something wrong. He wasn't standing right; he was tense and stiff. There were so many small trees and shrubs between us I wasn't able to see much more than that. Maybe he had already caught on that Seth was here but didn't know where I was, so he was upset and trying to figure out how to come and find me; I thought to myself, trying to make sense of how he appeared to be acting. As I got closer, I could see he was turned where he wouldn't have been able to see me coming. He was already tense, so I didn't want to sneak up on him. I didn't want him to pull his gun on me, not knowing if it was me or Seth that was coming near him.

I wrangled myself through a couple of shrubs that were to the far right of the tree, blocking him from seeing me. Then, after I did, I saw why he was tense. I was too late, and now exposed, Seth found him first. He was standing there facing Jake, holding a gun aimed at him. Both men saw me return almost exactly as I saw why they were frozen, glaring at each other.

"Well, well, welcome to the party, Gypsyin. I thought you might return if I was quiet enough." Seth grinned at me while still holding the gun toward Jake.

Jake looked in my direction but kept his body straight toward Seth. I could see he still had his gun on his thigh.

"How did you get a gun?" I asked Seth. The words slipped out before I could decide if bantering with him was even a good idea.

"Oh, wouldn't you like to know," he said smugly, "I know a lot of things that you don't." he continued, taunting me. He sounded different from what he used to. His speech was slower and more poignant than it had been. "You know there are even things I know about Jakey here that you probably don't." He used the gun to motion toward Jake.

I looked over. Jake was still frozen, though his face looked as if he were thinking hard about how to resolve the situation.

"Seth, you're full of shit," I said. Again, I couldn't help myself, wondering when I missed the class on how not to antagonize a man who's pointing a gun at you.

"Please woman, I'm not the one full of shit... he is. I've been honest with you this whole time. You knew I wanted you. I begged him to share but no, he wouldn't, and now look... Consequences..." He said, sounding like a lunatic.

"How did you get the gun?" I asked him again, thinking maybe I could use bantering to give Jake more time to decide how to get us out of this.

"I found it, stupid. You know when he locked you in that room with him all night? Yeah, I went around and thought I'd actually do a thorough job looking for stuff, seeing as it was pretty well untouched. I figured I'd be able to find something nice, and I did." He pointed to the gun in his hand.

"Seth, let her go and we can settle this like men. If you win, then you can track her down and have her, seem fair?" Jake finally decided to join the conversation.

I started to give him a befuddled glance, but didn't when I realized that probably was the best he could come up with. Seeing the both of them; it was more likely he would win the fight, anyway.

"Yeah right, do you think I'm really that dumb? Besides, you haven't asked me how I found y'all yet." Seth stopped briefly to think. "You know Jake, I'd think you'd be smarter than you act. Why, with me a Coldier and all, you really underestimated me, man. I mean, if anyone knows what I know and how to do the things I do, it'd be you." After eyeing Jake, he turned to look at me then back to Jake. "Besides, you should have known, not only would it be nice to have her to myself, but obviously if I was to take her in with that little letter of yours, I'd be reinstated." He smiled again insidiously.

"You said you lost your unit!" Jake quickly snapped back.

I started to think, trying to piece everything that I had thought I knew together. What each of them was saying wasn't making any sense. I didn't understand what or who they thought the other was. I looked over at Jake, who hadn't moved other than to look at me initially.

"Oh, you fool, do you believe everything everyone tells you? I know I'm on your side, but still… You should have at least wondered if I was lying." Seth relaxed a bit, enjoying his position of dominance over Jake for once.

"What's he talking about, Jake? What does he mean you're on his side?" I asked, still confused but hoping deep down there was a really good explanation Jake had hidden away, intending to eventually tell me.

"Ha, oh of course he didn't tell you. You're not very bright either, are you? Pity really with all that beauty. I guess it only makes sense. Brains… Beauty… you're not likely to have both…" Seth said, responding to me.

"Shut up, Seth!" I interrupted him, starting to quickly grow agitated with the level of confusion I was dealing with.

"He's a Coldier," Seth interjected. "Wow, I really do have to spell it out for you, don't I? With all that touchy-touchy going on I would have thought you would have seen his tag by now."

I must have frozen while staring at Seth. When he started to wave at me, my eyes blinked themselves free from their trance and looked down toward the ground. Though he seemed to clear some things up, I was still no less confused than before. All I could think was he must be lying. Jake couldn't be a Coldier. Then again, Jake wasn't saying anything to deny it, either. Seth was right. I hadn't ever seen Jake's tag. Seth also knew about the letter.

The more I stood there staring, thinking, the more things started to come into focus. I looked over toward Jake, my mouth ajar, hoping he would deny it. My eyes connected with his. Surely he was going to deny it, it couldn't be true. But that's not what I saw in his eyes. Now they were suddenly cold and dark. All I could see was what looked like remorse, not his usual soothing tenderness. Why would he have remorse? Remorse is only for when you've done something wrong…

"Deny it, Jake!" I pleaded. "Deny it!" My plea quickly switched to shouting.

"Oh yeah, Jake… deny it," Seth mocked me, looking at Jake. "Oh wait, you know what's better than that, why don't you just show her your arm. That's really the best way to show her that you've been lying to her this whole time." Seth's voice grew louder as he glared at Jake. Then he started to scream it as a demand. "Show it to her now, Jake! Then she'll see you for what you are, you lying bag of shit!"

I looked over at Jake. He didn't look back at me but straight on at Seth as he started to lower his arm very slightly to pull up his sleeve. There it was. His forearm had a little blue disc inset into it.

Instantly, it was hard for me to breathe. My lungs, no matter how fast or hard I tried, couldn't get enough air. I didn't know what to do. My mind was on the verge of collapse, and I wasn't sure I could control it. My body decided to take over. It must have thought it knew what to do. I surrendered to it. I took every thought or emotion and blocked them. They weren't useful at this moment, so I set them aside while giving my body total control. Seth must have seen it in my eyes because he started to shout at me. "Gypsyin, you better not run!"

Suddenly, everything was in slow motion, all my senses suppressed, channeling my strength into one motion: RUN! I turned, set one foot in front of the other, and began. At first, I couldn't hear anything but my breath, loud and rhythmic. Then, as I started to become more aware of my senses again, I could hear other things. It was almost like music. My ears added the crisp sound of my feet striking the ground, as if adding a beat to the rhythm of my breathing.

Soon I could hear other things behind me, those however weren't musical at all. I didn't turn to see, knowing I had to keep going and shouldn't look back. I heard a commotion, men's voices but only briefly. Then I heard a shot. At this I wanted to turn but realized I couldn't. I wouldn't let myself look back. Then I heard another shot shortly after the first. I didn't know what was happening, but I knew I needed to keep running, just far enough away until I could find a place to hide.

I ran until my legs started to hurt. Finally, feeling like I was alone and not being followed, I slowed down to walk. I knew since I'd gotten away, now was the time I needed to find a place to hide. I looked around, rummaging through the bushes, frantically trying to find a place.

Before long, I began to argue with my logic or maybe it was Fred; I couldn't tell the difference anymore. *If either of those men are still alive, they'll still find you. Hiding won't do you any good.* I knew my inner critic was right, but didn't know what else to do. For a second, a thought passed through my mind, hoping Jake was okay. Maybe Jake would come and find me. Then without hesitation, my body rejected the thought, reminding myself of what I now knew he was: a liar and a Coldier. He was a lying Coldier!

At that moment, I stopped where I was standing and sat down against the trunk of a large tree. It's like a switch flipped in my head. Why was I running? I was tired of running. The feelings of hopelessness were consuming me, and I no longer cared which man found me. The idea that Jake wasn't who he said he was started to sink in. It hurt. It felt like my chest was about to explode in grief. It wasn't just emotional pain; it was a real physical pain now too.

I brought my knees to my chest and wrapped my arms around them. I was starting to get a lot colder now that I wasn't running. I didn't know what I was going to do. I could go back and be taken prisoner again or I could stay by myself and freeze. I lowered my head to my knees and began to cry. With everything that had happened, I realized it wouldn't do me any good, but deep down I didn't care. The release from letting it all out was enough.

"Kaleah," a voice was calling my name, waking me. For a second, I thought I was in a dream. Maybe it had all been a dream. My mind began to argue with itself again. I opened my eyes, but it was still dark outside. *Maybe I just thought I heard my name, but no one was actually there.*

"Kaleah," it said again, bringing me further out of my sleepy state. I immediately realized where I was and it wasn't a dream. I lifted my head. The moon was dim now so I could barely see anything. There was a face straight above mine, though I couldn't tell who's.

Part of me wanted to hope it was Jake's and throw myself toward it. Though the other part of me would rather be taken prisoner and die by Seth's hand, before I would want to see Jake's traitorous face ever look at me again.

"Get away from me!" I yelled at him, realizing it would probably do no good.

"You've been out here for hours. You're going to freeze to death." I could tell now by his voice that it was Jake.

"Get away from me. I don't care if I freeze to death!" I yelled again toward the face.

He bent over and tried to grab a hold of me to pull me up. "No, get off of me. I won't go with you. You're a liar!" I yelled again as I batted his hands away.

"Yes, you are coming with me… whether you like it or not." He said firmly.

"No, I'm not!" I shouted.

He bent down again and wrapped his arms around the outside of my arms, not in a hug, but to keep me from flailing. Then he lifted me to my feet with one quick motion not yet letting go.

"I'm not going with you. I want to die. Leave me out here!" I shouted, wiggling and squirming, trying to get loose from his grip to run away from him again.

"Stop it, Gypsyin! Just stop, dammit!" He shouted back.

I stopped struggling and let my body go limp in defeat. I resigned from fighting him, "Just kill me then."

"Please, Kaleah. I'm sorry… Don't do this." He placed an arm around my back and bent to lift my legs with his other arm. "You're too cold. I'm taking you back. I'll explain everything there," he said as he started to carry me.

"I hate you," I mumbled like a small child that's mad at their parent.

He didn't say anything else, he just continued to carry me back to camp.

IO
BOTTOM FEEDERS

I had to have run far. He carried me for quite a while until finally I could recognize where we were. After laying me down beside the base of the tree, he quickly moved a few feet across from me to start working on a fire. I sat myself up and began to glare at him until he would look up at me, then I turned away and refused to let him look into my eyes.

"You can be mad at me if you want, but you're not gonna run again." He said gently, looking down at his hands. "I won't let you."

"I'm not just mad at you." I said weakly, "I'm scared of you."

He didn't say anything for a moment. I could see he was thinking about how to respond as he pulled a small black fire starting stick from his bag and started to scrape against it with the back of his knife, each stroke producing a tiny shower of sparks.

"I'm not going to hurt you. I don't want to hurt you…" he paused, looking down toward his hands. "I wouldn't have killed Seth if I didn't care about you. Just 'cause I'm a Coldier doesn't mean that… Ugh, I'm not the bad guy, dammit." He tightened his grip around the fire stick.

I didn't respond for a minute. I knew he was serious when he said I wouldn't get another chance to escape, and deep down I was terrified. I looked over toward where Seth had been standing. In all my fury toward Jake, I hadn't even thought again about Seth. "Where is he?" I asked, still looking in that direction.

Jake didn't respond at first. His efforts had lit a small bit of tender, so he leaned forward toward it and started to blow gently. "I've killed a lot of people. I'll be honest, I'm not a saint." He raised his head to look at me again. "But I don't think I ever wanted to kill someone as bad as I did him." He looked down for a second to collect a couple of small twigs that were around him, then lay them lightly on the small bits of flame he had created. "Don't worry about where he is," he said firmly, raising his head again. "He's dead, I made sure of it. He'll never bother you again."

"How do I know you're not lying about that too?" I asked, finally lifting my eyes toward his.

He stared at me for a second, his jaw tense with slight irritation, then his face relaxed to answer. "You don't have to believe me. Go look for yourself if you think it'll help you." He pointed with his knife over toward the ground under a small tree about 10 yards away. "I'd have moved him farther away, but I wanted to come find you first."

I sat staring at where he pointed, not wanting to get up and go look, though not sure how to resolve my plight if I didn't.

"Have you ever seen a dead body?" Jake asked gently, seeing my reluctance.

"I don't remember," I said, looking back over at him. "I mean I kind of remember my grandma's funeral and looking at her in the casket, but I... I don't know..."

The corner of his mouth slowly raised as he nodded, then he looked down as if thinking to himself. "Don't go look then. It's not pretty. You shouldn't have to see that." He said, reaching around for more twigs. The fire had started to take off nicely at this point.

"Why would you lie to me? This whole time you let me think you were a Sicari. How do I ever—"

"Trust me again?" He cut me off.

I closed my mouth slightly, looking down at my feet. "Yeah," I mumbled.

"I never intentionally lied to you. At first, I didn't care if you figured out what I was. I wasn't trying to hide it. But then…" He paused to lean back, now sitting with his feet close to the fire. "Then I saw how scared you were of him, how it made you run. So of course I hid it after that because I didn't want to deal with having to chase you down again. But after that night at the cabin—" He stopped to rub his forehead, pushing his toboggan slightly loose. "What was I supposed to do?" His volume gradually increased. "I didn't wanna lose you!"

"I don't know how to believe you. I want to believe you, Jake, I really do but…" I raised my voice gently, "You're just like him; you were both trained the same. Tonight, he acted like a totally different person. The whole time we were with him he was…" I paused, trying to collect my thoughts. "Couldn't you see… he had been acting, pretending to be something else? Just waiting for the right time to get what he wanted?"

"I'm not Seth!" Jake stopped me, his voice loud and firm. "What do you want from me? What do you want, for real? I don't know how else to show you that I care about you. Yeah, I lied. I didn't feel like I had a choice. This right here is why I didn't want you to know. I never wanted you to be scared of me." He stopped briefly to take a breath. "This is the last thing I wanted to happen. I never wanted you to look at me like you're looking at me right now." His voice slowly drifted into a murmur.

"You don't get it, that's the thing… You're gonna say exactly what you think I want to hear," I said, growing more animated. "That's what Seth did. He acted like—"

"Like he wanted to rape you!" He interrupted. His eyes were now focused on mine with his face tense. "He acted like he was going to attack you if I ever looked away." Jake was now becoming more animated as well with his voice getting louder. "And that's exactly what he tried to do. The first chance he got he tried to attack you. He didn't try to hide it."

"Okay, and what did you do to stop him?" I was upset but trying not to yell. "If you knew he wanted to attack me the first chance he got, why did you let him even come along with us? He was dangerous, and you knew it! I told you he was, and you still didn't listen." I took a second to breathe, but then answered the question before he had a chance to. "It's because he was on *your* side."

"I did stop him! I would have killed him before I let him hurt you, and that's exactly what I did!" He said, his voice heavy with intensity. "Do you even realize what will happen to me if they ever find out I killed one of my own? What they'll do to me if they knew I killed him in exchange for the protection of a Gypsyin?" His eyebrows drew closer together as his face started to scowl. "So, no to answer you, that's why I was trying not to kill him, not because he was on my side."

"No, but you didn't have to let him walk with us. He was right, you are naïve!" I said it, hoping it would sting. "You trusted him and because of that you almost got yourself killed. What do you think he would have done to me if he shot you? He wasn't worried about what they would do to him if he killed another Coldier. He was evil. They're all evil!" I was trying to stay calm, but was overwhelmed with anger. "That's why I can't trust you. I can't trust a Coldier. Every time, they lie, then they try to attack me."

"You can't say that!" I could tell he was trying not to shout as well. "If I intended to violate you, I would've already. I've had enough opportunities. If I wanted to do anything to you, I could have already." He briefly looked down at the fire, his face still distraught with agitation. "Hell, do you not see how much of a risk this is for me? For all I know, you really could be a spy just pretending not to be dangerous?"

I huffed slightly, trying not to laugh. "Are you freakin' serious? That wouldn't make any sense. Why would I do that?"

"That's what a spy would say." He looked up, seeing how I took his answer, keeping his own face stone cold.

I did everything I could, but couldn't stop myself from letting out a small chuckle. I hated that he was trying to break my intensity by making me laugh. I sat for a second, trying to forget it just happened and collect my composure. I figured he was trying to throw me off from asking more hard questions, but I didn't let that stop me. "How did you get the letter? I sent it to a Sicari station, not a Coldier base?" I asked smugly, trying to show him I was still upset.

"Oh," he huffed slightly now relaxing his arms against his knees, "nice try if you think I'm gonna tell a spy that kind of information," he said, doing his best not to grin.

I could see how he was trying to turn it around on me, whether jokingly or not I didn't appreciate it. "I'm not a freakin' spy!" I said, "Believe me, if I was, I would have already kicked your ass by now." Sensing the mood slightly change, I couldn't help myself from joking back a little.

He smiled and snorted, then brought his hand to his face quickly to act like it was just a cough. Then his expression immediately returned to what he was good at—being stern and cold.

"Where were you taking me then if not to the Sicari's central station?" Seeing he wasn't about to give me a genuine answer I figured I'd try another hard question.

"DC," he said matter-of-factly. "Originally anyway, but to be honest the last few weeks I haven't been exactly sticking to the course." His eyes returned to mine, trying to gauge how I was feeling before he went on. "I had orders... and they were pretty clear, really. They're always the same. I retrieve prisoners. It's what I do. And I'm the best at it, that's why they send me. What I don't do is wreck the car, kill a fellow Coldier, and fall in love with the Gypsyin prisoner." He finished with a rather stern tone like he just realized the weight of his actions and was irritated with himself.

Love? Is that how he feels? I don't remember ever being in love before but I've been feeling something new and different that I couldn't explain for a while now. *Am I in love?*

I didn't say anything. I didn't know what to say. I just looked at him, sheer shock radiating through me. His eyes were still intense but not as much with anger but rather defeat. I wanted to sit there and hate him. I wanted to hold on to my self-righteous fury... hold on to every ounce of rage I built inside myself when I realized he had deceived me, hurt me… broke me more than I was already broken. But without him even bringing it up or throwing it in my face, I remembered I lied first. My lie took a man, probably content where he was, and forced him to come to get me all because I was lonely and cold. Even though I wanted to hate him, I knew I couldn't, not unless I hated myself first.

"Fine," I said softly, "I'll believe you."

He looked at me puzzled. "That's it?" He asked. I only assumed this response was because he was used to fighting.

"I'm done fighting," I said, pushing my feet closer to the fire. "If I believe you maybe I won't die. If I fight you, I do." I softened my tone. "Besides, I have to believe you. You're all I have left." *And I want to be loved, so badly I want to be loved… needed, wanted, no longer alone.*

His face relaxed. "I'm sorry I lied to you. I never meant to hurt you, you must know that. All I can think about anymore is how to protect you. I've never met anyone like you. I mean sure, you can be a bit feisty and sometimes a pain in the ass, especially when you decide to run from me." He stopped to smile slightly then looked at the fire while poking it with a stick. "You're a hot mess if I've ever seen one." He smiled bigger now as he looked back at me. "But you can be my hot Gypsyin mess."

I smiled, trying to keep my word when I said I believed him. It was mostly true. I did, but part of me was still scared. I didn't know how to resolve it within myself, but I wanted to. "Am I still your prisoner? What about DC?" I tried my best to ask without indicating I was still afraid of him or afraid of his intentions.

His expression changed. He didn't answer right away, but took a second to think about what he was going to say. "You're not if you don't want to be," he said, but in a way like he hated to think of releasing me even if he didn't intend to still turn me in. "We're not going to DC anymore." His voice was assertive, having already made up his mind.

"Then what about your orders?" I asked. Both the complications and consequences popped into my mind suddenly. He'd be in danger. I didn't want him hurt, especially not because of me. "You have to turn me in. The things they'd do to you if you didn't, you even said yourself—"

"I've already decided!" He stopped me, now beginning to move closer to my side of the fire. "I couldn't live with myself if I turned you in."

"But what if they catch us?" I asked, becoming distressed by the thought. "I knew what I was getting myself into writing that letter. I don't want you to have to suffer along with me. If I die, I die, but I can't—"

"Stop acting like you don't care!" He interrupted again, gently pushing my legs to the side and positioning himself directly in front of me with his back to the fire. "Stop saying you don't care if you die. I know you care, or you wouldn't run every time you get scared. Let me worry about if we get caught, and making sure we don't."

I was conflicted. I wanted to believe everything he was telling me, but I was still so scared. He leaned forward, lifting his hand toward my face. I flinched slightly, then closed my eyes, trying to refrain from showing him my anxiety.

"Kaleah," he said softly, "I would never hurt you. Open your eyes."

I opened them to see him gazing at me. "I'm sorry," I said, trying to not look down and away.

He brought his hand back up toward my face again very slowly. "I promise I will never lie to you ever again. Please trust me." He tucked the hair from in front of my face in behind my ear, then rested his hand against the side of my head. "Trust me." He said again as he leaned his face in toward mine until our lips met in a kiss.

He was gentle, his lips were warm and soft. He slowly used them to brush upward against my own before firmly pressing them into mine. He held his hand tightly against my cheek as he brought his other arm up, between me and the tree, to my waist.

Every ounce of angst that I had been holding quickly dissipated with every kiss. Slowly, I resigned from all inhibition.

I let my hand slide down the side of his torso, feeling his tight muscles through his shirt. A strong shiver shot through my body as a warm heat crept up my neck. "Kaleah…" He whispered gently into my ear as he brought his hand up to intertwine his fingers into my hair.

I lifted my hands to the sides of his face to pull his lips back to mine. I wanted to trust him. I wanted to trust him so badly. *This feels so right.*

He brought his hand to my cheek and slowed his kisses until he stopped and pulled his face away just enough to look down and into my eyes. He stared into them for a moment, trying to read my soul, or maybe he was trying to show me his. I didn't know. Then he relaxed and moved to lower himself to rest against the ground, tugging my arm to relax against him. I lay my head against his chest, instantly feeling soothed by the rhythm of his heartbeat.

"See, some Coddy's have self-control," he smiled, looking down at me.

I relaxed, thinking to myself about the future and what it might look like for us now, all while trying to accept the fact that he was a Coldier whether I liked it or not.

"Why do you call yourselves Coddy's?" I asked curiously.

He let out a small sigh and slowly let his fingers caress my hair while answering. "Well, it was actually something the Sicari started calling us originally in a derogatory way, referring to a codfish 'cause it's a bottom feeder. But that didn't really bother us none. Seeing as what we knew about the Cod was pretty cool, we went ahead and adopted the name ourselves." He stopped to take a large breath. "They got a sharp bite and if you catch one they put up a hell of a fight," he said with a smile, knowing he sounded clever. "Don't get me started on the Ling Cod, those things…" He sighed, "Man, I sure wouldn't mind being referred to as one of them, they're ferocious."

I smiled. He *was* clever; I thought, trying to bring up other positive attributes I knew about him while suppressing any lingering feelings of fear. *Clever and kind... Gentle, sweet, caring, protective...*

"We need to rest now. We have a lot to do tomorrow and a lot of decisions to make," he said positioning himself between me and the tree, now giving me the position closest to the fire. He lay down behind me as he had every night before the first incident with Seth. Though instead of resting his arm along the top of mine like he usually had, this time he nestled it down against my waist. He gently tucked his hand under my side and pulled me in tight toward him. "Just in case you change your mind," he said softly into my ear, then kissed it. We lay there in silence until I fell asleep.

The next morning, I woke up much warmer than usual. As I opened my eyes, I could see Jake had already been up and got the fire going nice and strong. It took me a second to fully awaken and pull myself together before I tried to observe what was going on around me. As I sat up and started to look around, I noticed a large rabbit laying to the side waiting to be skinned and cleaned before cooking. It must have also snowed more while we slept; there was a thicker layer covering the ground now than had been there the night before. I didn't see Jake, but I saw a fresh pair of tracks his boots would have made sprinkled all around the area, so I figured he was close by.

It was quiet. All I could hear were the gentle sounds of the fire popping and cracking. Knowing there was no possibility of Seth lurking in the woods helped me feel more at peace at that moment as well. Now that it was starting to become light I looked toward the direction where Jake said he left Seth. Under the tree, surrounded by a thick blanket of fresh white powder was a dark oblong outline inset into the snow where his body had been.

Even if he was an evil madman, I was bothered and couldn't let go of the idea of how easy it was for his whole existence to be erased just that easily. I sat for a minute and stared at the emptiness. The thought of his absence hadn't quite sunken in yet, and though it didn't cause me to feel mournful, it did bring into focus the fragility of life. One minute he was there and the next he wasn't. I started to wonder about myself. Is that how simple it would have been if they turned me in? Would dying be as easy as just letting go of the fight I held inside... the sheer will to survive? Which way, I wondered, would hurt more, releasing the fight willingly or having it taken from you like it was from Seth?

I looked back toward the fire, realizing my train of thought was likely not taking me anywhere productive. I saw the rabbit again and figured I could help speed up the process if I cleaned it myself before Jake returned. I crawled over to the larger of Jake's duffles that was laying at the base of the tree and started to unzip the bottom pocket, looking for one of his spare knives. After rummaging around for a minute and not seeing any, I re-zipped it and looked into a larger pocket above it. Sliding my hand down into it I felt a handle and started to pull. Once I got it lifted out, I noticed from the corner of my eye something fall out and land on the ground below me. I looked down between my legs to see a large black woven bracelet made of cordage. I stopped for a second, looking at it laying there, then picked it back up and slid it back into the pocket. I started to zip it up when I noticed Jake walking toward me, carrying another rabbit.

"Mornin' beautiful," he said, walking closer. "The rabbits must like the snow." He bent over and gently tossed it down beside the other one, then looked back up toward me. "What are you looking for?" He asked like he wasn't hiding anything.

I hesitated, thinking about what I found and what it meant. "Nothing I was just... a knife... you know. I was going to help you by cleaning the rabbit before you got back."

"That's nice of you," he said, picking up a few small pieces of wood from beside the tree and placing them on the fire, "but what else did you find?" He asked, looking down at me.

"Your para-cord bracelet," I said, giving in.

"Hum," he huffed with a small smile, "right."

"I didn't know you had more cordage," I said as I watched him sit down near the fire and start to skin one of the rabbits. "Why didn't you use it to tie me up like you did the first day?"

He smiled, keeping his eye on the rabbit, "Why didn't you tell me you found a rope at that first house we went into?"

"What?" I asked shocked, "How d'you know about that?"

He looked away from the rabbit and toward me for a second, "You're not as sneaky as you think you are." He smiled then went back to what he was doing. "Believe it or not I didn't want you tied up. I needed an excuse to make you lay next to me every night." He smiled again and looked at me from the top of his eyes.

"I can't believe you," I said, cracking a smile.

"What?" He slightly chuckled, "I might not have bad intentions but I'm still a man and well... I couldn't let all that precious body heat just go to waste, now could I?" He grinned and looked back up toward me for a second before continuing with the rabbit.

I smiled, "No, I guess not... What did you do with Seth?" I asked, changing the subject and pointing to the now vacant space under the tree.

"I hid him real well. Hopefully, he doesn't have a tracker in his tag," he said as he started to pull the fur down and away from the rabbit's body. "If he did, and they were able to find him and see that he was shot—" He paused, "Well, that might cause some problems."

"How so?" I asked, intently watching him over the flames.

"'Cause I have a tracker in mine," he said, "if our trackers were together when he stopped suddenly... Well it doesn't take a genius to figure out there might have been some foul play going on."

"They're tracking you?" I couldn't hide the concern on my face.

"Yeah, but you don't need to worry about it," he said with a slight shrug, "I have a plan."

"Ah, ok?" I paused, with a look of confusion. "That's concerning. Did you intend to tell me about this plan of yours?"

He stopped what he was doing with the rabbit and looked up at me. "I took his tag. I'll keep it for a bit and then throw it into the next lake we come across. You really shouldn't worry about it, though. If he was a deserter, they're not likely to come looking for him, it's just a precaution." He looked back down and began to gut the rabbit.

"Yours, though, what about yours?" I asked, starting to feel restless.

"Right well... as far as Seth, mine shouldn't be a problem now. But as for us, yeah... I've been thinking about that. I can't keep it if I'm not gonna turn you in 'cause it'd put us both in too much danger. But not having my tag would also put us in danger if Coldier patrols ever caught us. Not to mention, it's kind of necessary if I ever intend to get supplies at a base again. So, I've decided I'm going to keep my tag but deactivate the tracker that's in it."

"Oh, well, if it's that easy why wouldn't everyone just deactivate themselves?" I asked, perplexed at this whole new problem I was just now learning about.

"Oh, 'cause it's not easy," he said matter-of-factly, then stopped and looked up at me to clarify. "I mean... it's not hard, I can do it. I just..." He for once stumbled over his words a little bit. "It's tricky is all." He smiled, trying to reassure me, but I could see through it. "I just gotta go to a base, find their tag lab, they all have them you know for the newborns, and deactivate it... simple," he finished, now refusing to look at me.

"That's not simple!" I said firmly, staring at him.

"Well, I doubt you have any better ideas," he said, finally looking up again.

"No, not if I didn't even know you guys were being tracked. I didn't even know you were a Coldier until last night," I said, defending my position.

"Okay, then we stick with my plan," he said with a small grin, probably feeling like he'd won.

I stopped arguing. I knew I couldn't change his mind; he was too stubborn. He finished dressing both rabbits and cooked them. We sat and ate the morning's portions in silence. I think he knew I wasn't very thrilled with the idea of where this was going to take us next, but at the same time, I wasn't about to complain about it either.

Less than two days before, I was knowingly walking toward my death, only hoping for a reprieve once we made it to our destination. Now I finally had someone to talk to that wasn't imaginary, and I was no longer alone or hungry. I knew whatever he intended to do was probably risky, but I figured at this point anything we did was risky. The only question was how much risk were we willing to take to produce the best outcome for what we both wanted.

"All right," I said, breaking the silence, "I know you weren't waiting for my permission. You're gonna do what you want, but I've thought about it and I'm willing to take that risk with you. I realize you know what you're doing and you've probably thoroughly thought about how you're gonna do it so… I guess I just wanted you to know I trust you and your decision."

He looked over and smiled. "Good! I'm happy you've come to that conclusion. There's just one problem," he paused, grinning at me, waiting for me to ask what it was.

"What?" I said curtly.

"You're not taking a risk, I am! You're gonna keep yourself right where I decide to leave you and not set a foot near that base," he said with his eyes widened looking at me, then took another bite of the rabbit.

"Well… I mean… I don't guess that's a problem, but where do you intend to leave me?" I asked, letting my eyes wander around before blinking them back in his direction.

He pooched his lips a little and looked up to think while bringing his hand to wipe both sides of his mouth in one downward slow motion with his fingers. "Ok, I'll be honest with ya," he relented, "I hadn't fully decided what I was gonna do with you yet."

"I'm a good hider," I said, trying to conjure up my convincing face. "I can just get close with you and then like, hide in the woods until you come to get me."

Now looking down, his face turned rigid and tense, he brought his eyes up with a slow blink to look at me. He didn't say anything.

Apparently, he just assumed I would gather from his silent look that he didn't like that idea.

"Ok, well what would happen if I got too close and got captured?" I asked, then gave my theory to answer the question for him. "If I'm just a Gypsyin and they don't know anything about the letter, it's probably less likely they'll kill me, right?" I said, trying to minimize my perception of the consequences. "I mean, I realize I don't know everything about them and all but—"

"They'll erase your memory," he interrupted with a harsh tone like he wasn't about to allow it to happen. "You're right, if they don't think that you're a threat and send you to level 4 interrogation first, they probably won't kill ya." His irritation with my theory started to display itself with sarcasm. "Nah, they'll just send you to the Catch and Release brigade. It's no big deal you know, just have your brain freakin' wiped."

"Okay, okay… sorry. Bad idea!" I said, trying to retract my side, seeing he was getting upset. But I was still intrigued by what he was telling me and everything he knew, and wanted him to continue. "What do you mean they'll erase my memory?"

"What it sounds like," he said, his agitation keeping him vague.

I stopped probing him, seeing it wasn't doing any good. I had never really seen him get so agitated so quickly even with everything Seth threw at him. He told me enough that I got the idea, so I didn't want to force him to continue, knowing it might accelerate him to anger. It was easy to see it was a sore subject for him, and he wasn't happy with the thought that it could happen to me. Obviously, without details, I didn't understand the extent of what he meant by 'erase your memory.' I started to let myself ponder the idea and all the roads it led down until he apparently caught on and interjected.

"Stop thinking about it," he said. Now that he was done eating, he started to go through his bags to rearrange them, preparing to leave again.

"Ok, well where are we going next then? What's the plan?" I asked as I helped him gather things to pack.

"Charlotte, I have a couple of friends there. I'm not taking you that far, though. I'll find a place to hide you just outside the city first. They won't patrol the outer edge. It's basically a no-man's zone. There's nothing there to live on and all the houses have been looted past all hope of ever finding anything useful," he said, trying to soften his tone, then stopped to look up at me. "Look, I don't want you scared of me. But the way you feel about the rest of them is probably a pretty healthy fear. It'll keep you safe if you listen to me and do exactly what I tell you." He zipped up the second of the two duffles, stood up, and threw it over his shoulder. "It's gonna take another couple of weeks to get there. Hopefully, the weather doesn't get worse."

He stood there for a second, looking at me in silence, watching as I strapped my bag on and carefully tucked in my coat around the straps. He reached out his hand toward me, palm up. I hesitated, remembering the same gesture in the field during the storm and what it meant. *Was he reaching for my bag again?*

"Are you with me?" He asked, looking at me, then down at his hand.

I tried not to hesitate. "Yes," I said, taking a step forward and grabbing it. "I'm with you."

He smiled, then pulled me in to rest his chin on my head as I wrapped my arms around his waist. "Good. You're my girl now, Kaleah. I'm going to take care of you, keep you safe." He paused to bring his hand to cup my cheek, and lean back to look me in the eye. "You trust me?"

I nodded, trying to hold back emotions that wanted to bubble up. I'd never been important to someone before. "I trust you, Jake." I said softly, blinking up at him.

A mixture of relief and joy spread across his face when he smiled. "Good." He said, leaning in again to kiss me on the top of the head, then he relaxed as he pulled me in tighter. "Good."

II

CRIMSON DREAMS

We walked for so many days that I lost count. Of most of those, the sky blurred the sunlight with such a heavy haze, the day easily blended into the night as one became shorter and the other longer. It was obvious Jake was no longer tense with the fear of Seth's return. Now it appeared all his anxiety was focused on getting through this new mission he set for himself. His movements were all still the same, calm and calculated. Nothing he did showed he was anxious. It was just easy for me to tell by the things he chose to talk about during our conversations.

He didn't speak to me like I was a prisoner of his anymore or just a subject he was temporarily keeping custody of. I was more than that to him now. When he spoke to me, it was almost like I belonged to him, in a good way, like I was a precious stone that he had found and treasured. His mission changed from walking me to my death and turning me in to keeping me safe with him instead. This new resolve within him now laced itself through every conversation. His strength of will and character were honorable and I'm sure even if he tried he wouldn't have been able to hide that.

Seeing how proficient he was in withholding his emotions, I was curious what it was about me that was able to un-bridle them. I was still uncomfortable giving in to my feelings and reciprocating anything back to him. I knew my past, though considerably unclear, was riddled with pain and trauma and because of that I hardly loved myself let alone knew why anyone else would.

How could he see things in me I couldn't even see? If he was true to his word, I didn't want to push him away. I knew I needed him, but more than that, I wanted to show him that I wanted to be with him, like he did me. I just couldn't yet. We walked for days with a tenseness between us. It was like I was an adolescent with a crush, but couldn't straighten out my emotions long enough to share them with him. This made the relationship status complicated, and we both knew it.

I didn't know if he wondered whether I still didn't trust him fully or if maybe I just needed time. I guess to a certain extent both things were true but the real reason was I didn't feel like I deserved it... I didn't deserve him or his affection, and no matter how hard I tried I couldn't reconcile that thought within myself. I tried for days. Anytime there were periods of walking in silence I would think and ponder all the many emotions flowing through my mind. I felt broken, lonely, afraid and ultimately like I didn't even really know myself.

I spent years alone, isolated from everyone, everything. If I didn't fully know or love me, how could I allow someone else to try to? The idea of whether I could communicate this to him wasn't a problem in my mind. I figured he might understand. My problem was I didn't want him to understand, and I wasn't sure why. I didn't want to even give him a chance to.

The silence in the walking never lasted very long before he would break into it with something to say. He was kind. Even in his references to other Coldiers, he rarely spoke ill of other people. He was well trained, too. If it hadn't been apparent enough, it certainly was now. Most of the time, he broke the silence by showing me something else, or trying to teach me more about how to successfully survive out in the wild. I could have been proud and not pretended all of it was new to me, but much of it was new. I was on my own for years, but picking up skills out of necessity still left much to be learned and he seemed to thoroughly enjoy teaching me. I never wanted to stifle that in him. I loved seeing him light up when he thought he was teaching me something new. In those moments, I was able to see past the Coldier agent and see the man himself, unguarded and sincere. It was endearing and helped me in my quest to understand that Jake could wear the Coldier name without letting it define him as a man.

The day quickly turned into night and we found ourselves again, looking for the best place to stop and make camp. I didn't quite know where we were or how close we had gotten to Charlotte, but he mentioned it wouldn't be too much longer, so I assumed it was relatively close. Where we stopped, didn't seem any different from the previous nights. There were no large trees, ponds, fields, or anything to use as a landmark. Most of the day, we walked in a short brush with a few small trees scattered here and there. It was cold, but any snowfall was irregular. Some days we would walk and it would start to come down heavy only to just melt as it landed. Most days, however, it just looked like the air was icy and frigid, but it never actually produced anything to any measurable degree.

As with every night, we went through the same routine. After we picked a place, he would start on the fire as I went around looking for dry wood to bring back. If I couldn't find enough to last us through the night, then he would go out and find an old dead tree or log to cut up. We would eat any rations we had left from the previous day or we'd set some snares and wait to catch more. Then, after supper, we would talk briefly before nestling up against each other beside the fire and falling asleep. This night was no exception, though we both knew it wouldn't be long before we would need to find another way to sleep. Just sharing our body heat wouldn't be enough to keep us both warm in the weeks to come.

The cold wasn't my only concern, however; I was also afraid of how we might get past the byway lines. These were a series of smaller secondary bridges the Coldiers hadn't collapsed and rarely used for anything other than supplies and troop movements. It was common knowledge that anyone caught using them for non-military use would be shot on sight, so they were typically deserted and may or may not be guarded. I wasn't sure why I was afraid of the byway lines, but somehow I just knew they were dangerous. I didn't know if Jake, being a Coldier, would make it easier for us to cross, but either way, I was fearful of us getting caught.

Crimson, the ground turned crimson. A little girl was standing over me just staring intently, waiting on me, but waiting for what I wasn't sure. "Memento schola," a voice from behind broke her from her stare and she looked toward it. "Memento schola," the voice was a man's voice, repeating itself.

The girl turned to leave, then without taking a step, seemed to disappear, vanish into thin air right before my eyes. I looked over at the voice. His stare was penetrating, but his eyes were filled with agony. His face seemed seized with suffering.

"Killmeeahh," he said it so fast I couldn't distinguish between the words. I didn't know who he was, but the way he looked at me was so intense; there was a connection with him like I had with no one else before.

I tried to tell him I didn't understand what language he was speaking, but the words wouldn't leave my mouth. I could barely get my mouth to utter anything.

"Killmeeahh," his voice seethed loudly, filling my senses with his agony.

I didn't understand. I tried again to yell back to him to no avail. I looked away from him toward the direction the girl went, but saw no one. Where was everybody?

He started to groan loudly. Now I noticed his chest. His jacket was black, yet it was raining red all over his feet. I looked back up toward his eyes, still staring intensely at me. "Run," he said as clear as I could have ever heard.

I stopped to try to understand, "Why?" I asked, but I couldn't tell if my mouth actually said it or I just imagined hearing it.

He drew his brows together, wrinkling his face in anguish. I was hurting him, but I didn't know how. I was confused. I didn't know what I had done, why he was hurt, where I was, or what I was even doing there. "Kill meeaah" he screamed it out toward me, his eyes now brimming with misery.

"No" I screamed back, my mouth now starting to function. "No, I can't!" I screamed again.

"Then run," he said softly, lowering his gaze.

"No, no, I won't leave you."

"Run!"

"NO!... NO!... I won't leave you!"

"Kaleah," a loud voice woke me with a strong jolt.

I opened my eyes. Jake was sitting, staring down at me, with both hands gripping my upper arms tightly. He quickly released them when his eyes connected with mine.

"You're dreaming. Wake up," he said. His voice was still a bit firm.

I didn't say anything. I just relaxed against the ground and tried to process everything I just saw and what I was now seeing.

"Are you all right? You woke me up yelling no, and something else. I couldn't understand, you were saying your words too fast." He asked, then let himself relax again as well.

"I don't know." I stared up at him. "I don't know what I—" I paused, trying to think for a second.

"Was it Seth?" He asked, lowering himself back into position behind me.

"No, it wasn't him... I'm fine," I said, "it was just a bad dream, that's all." I turned to gaze at the fire while trying to rewind everything I saw and put it back together with some sort of meaning.

"Okay," he said softly, relaxing against me. He raised his hand to the side of my face then ran his fingers through the loose hair laying against my temple, pulling it back to position it with the other strands. "You don't have to talk about it but I'm here if you want to."

I thought about it for a split second. "I'm all right now," I sighed softly. "It was nothing," I lied. It was something, it was very much something, but I wasn't ready to talk about it. Partly because I really only half understood it myself, but mostly because I was afraid of what I might have done. The dream wasn't new to me. It had recurred many times over the years. Even though I could never fully comprehend it, there was a piece of me that felt like it was real, like I had been there and done something terrible.

"What do you see in me?" I asked, knowing Jake was still listening. I wanted to change the subject for my own peace of mind. "You don't really know me. I mean I could be a killer or I could be crazy. I feel crazy. I mean, you know about Fred… You don't want to be with someone that's crazy."

"So, is that your problem?" He continued to run his fingers through my hair.

"What do you mean?" I asked, thinking I didn't say I actually was. I just said I *feel* like I am.

"Is that why you hold yourself back from me? Are you afraid I'll think you're crazy?" His voice was soft and delicate, close to my ear.

"Maybe," I figured if I was honest with him it might help me resolve some of my feelings. "I just don't feel lovable. I don't know how to reciprocate it if I don't feel it. You know?"

"I thought that might be your problem," he said now resting his hand on my cheek.

"You can't love me, you don't even—"

"Don't tell me who I can love," he interrupted still with a gentle voice. "If you can't love yourself, that's one thing, but that doesn't mean I can't love you… Now if you don't love me back… I'd understand, that's different, but I'd understand."

"That's not what I was saying," I stopped him. "I never said I didn't… I mean I'm just waiting to say I do, I think I do… I'm just scared to say it."

"You're not crazy," he started combing my hair again with his fingers. "You want to know what I see in you?"

"Yes," I said, waiting for his answer.

"When I look at you, it's like looking at an abstract painting. Yeah, most of them are weird and a little crazy. But all of your crazy somehow makes sense, and it mesmerizes me. Everything you think you are that you hate, I see and think it's beautiful."

I was lost in his words, trying to soak them in so I might repeat them back to myself later. "Thank you," I said, "that was sweet."

He leaned forward and placed a gentle kiss to my temple. I stared at the fire as I thought until the trance dissipated and I slowly drifted back off to sleep.

We walked another several days. Jake didn't ask anything else about my dream and I didn't mention anything, trying to forget it myself. I knew we were getting close to the city. Even as hard as he tried to find a route that was far from roads, we kept running into more houses. Every one we saw he would stop for a minute to look at the map then around to see if he could pinpoint exactly where we were. I asked how he was going to decide which house was the best one to leave me at. He said he would know when he saw it.

I couldn't argue with his logic. It seemed reasonable enough. I could tell we were both getting more nervous with the idea of what exactly we were coming into and what we were both going to have to do. He didn't talk much, but kept quiet and observant. He started to use more hand signals to show me when he wanted me to move, to where, and at which pace. Naturally, I didn't know what any of the signals meant, but somehow was able to distinguish what he intended by them.

After a few more hours of walking and randomly stopping to quickly eyeball half a dozen random houses for their worthiness, we finally found one. It was the first one that Jake was able to pinpoint the approximate location on his map. He needed this so he could find it when he came back to look for me.

The house was larger than most of the others. It had two stories with a large attached garage. It was nestled nicely back on a large lot, dense with trees. He was right. Most of the ones we were encountering looked like they had been looted past the point of benefit. We slowly walked around it, looking for the rear entrance. It didn't have as much trash littered all over the place as a lot of the ones we had seen, but the landscaping was definitely out of control. We walked over a wooden fence that had fallen down and past a large pool filled with stagnant green water and leaves. The area was quite desolate, but that was actually comforting to me, considering the circumstances.

Once inside, we looked around for a minute until Jake seemed satisfied. "This will do," he said, nodding his head with approval.

"What exactly were you looking for?" I asked, kicking a few small things on the floor while pondering the idea of how long I was going to have to stay there waiting for him.

"The bigger the house, the more places to hide," he said as he started to open a closet door and peer in. "Seclusion—it's not as visible to the road. But the main reason I picked this one is 'cause I'll know how to get back to you," he said, then looked up at me and smiled.

"I'm glad you know what you're doing," I figured I'd compliment him. I wanted him to see I appreciated his thoroughness.

"Don't hide upstairs. You might think it makes sense, but it's not the best. We need to find somewhere down here for you to hide that's close to a secondary exit. That way if you hear anyone come in, you can run out and not get caught." He said as he started to walk over to open up other doors that were adjacent to the living room.

"That's a good idea," I said, following him.

"Here, this looks like the best place," he opened the door to the closet under the stairs. "It's dark, but it's next to the front door. Most Coldiers would be trained to come in the back door, so if you hear them you should be able to run before they even know you're here."

"All right…" I said, trying to sound as optimistic as I reasonably could, though I hadn't really liked the look of the space. It was tiny and very dark, but I knew he only had my safety in mind, so I was going to do as he said and not complain.

He started pulling out everything that was crammed into the tiny space and threw it into random places in the middle of the living room floor. "I know you're scared, but you'll be fine. Do you want me to stay here with you tonight and leave in the morning or are you okay if I leave you this afternoon? It'll take me a few days before I can be back. I'll leave you all the food rations though, so you shouldn't get too hungry," he said, then paused to look at me, waiting for an answer to his first question.

"You can leave today if you think it would be best. I can manage," I said, trying to sound brave but not really wanting him to leave me just yet.

He smiled and pointed down toward his bag at my feet, gesturing for me to hand it to him, "If you insist," he said, probably hoping I would have begged him to stay. *Maybe I should have*, I thought.

He took the bag and gently tossed it into the back of the long narrow closet. "I'll leave you with the large one and yours. They should have everything you need. If you need to run, don't try to take the bags. They will just slow you down and likely get you caught. You can come back for them later if you have to, but if you do, you need to look around well first and make sure there isn't anyone still here," he said as he took my bag and crawled into the space to set it atop the large one.

"It won't be so bad. I'll just try to sleep the whole time," I said, looking in and down at where he was now sitting next to the bags. "Besides, I can't think of anything else I could do in here with zero light."

"Do you think this will be enough room for you to sleep?" He asked, looking around, probably trying to generate an idea of the size of the space we were working with.

"Yeah." I took a step in and looked around. "I'm just not sure if I can handle it being pitch black when I shut the door. I mean I'm not scared of the dark, but when you add it to such a tiny space, I start to feel a little closet-phobic."

"Shut it then, let's see," he said with a playful smile.

"Okay," I took a deep breath, looking at the door, then reached out to grab the knob and shut it, preparing myself to see how bad it could actually be.

It was dark, just as I suspected. Maybe not pitch black, but dark enough that I could barely catch my hand with my eyes as I tried to wave it in front of my face.

"Come here." Jake's voice said softly from below.

12

MILES IN THE DARK

I was nervous like a child in the middle of a hide and seek game. There was the anxious expectation of getting found mixed with excitement on top of being slightly panicky. I slowly pushed my hands out in front of me to feel for the sloping ceiling, then used it to start to lower myself to the floor. With Jake sitting below me, I let go and let myself fall onto him.

"Ummph," he let out a large breath as I landed. "I didn't know you were going to sit on me." He sounded like he was smiling and accepting of my playful mood.

"Sorry," I laughed a little, "I couldn't help myself." I reached over, feeling his broad shoulders to my side. I turned and positioned myself to face him, letting each of my knees fall to the sides of his waist.

He didn't say anything to respond. Then his hand moved up towards my face, likely also trying to see exactly how I landed.

As it found my hair, he sunk his fingers into it and rested his palm against my ear. He slowly moved his other hand around and behind my waist. "Do you know what else Coddy's do?" He asked softly. It sounded like he was looking straight at me.

"No, what?" I asked with slight hesitation.

"They finish what they start." As the words came out of his mouth, he leaned in toward me, pulling my head closer to his with his hand, and sunk his lips into mine. I relaxed against him.

The kiss was long and slow like he had been saving it up and was waiting for the right time to bring it out and use it. His lips were soft and moist like he didn't just travel through all the same frigid coldness that I had. He held me against him in a way that was gentle yet assertive, rubbing his hands up and down my back soothingly.

I was captivated. How could someone so strong and confident in their movements still be so gentle and tender with every touch? He removed his lips from mine and softly started kissing my cheek, trailing from my mouth down and stopping on my neck just below my ear.

"You have no idea just how beautiful you are, do you?" he whispered softly into my ear.

"No," I shook my head gently. "No one has ever treated me like this… *lovingly*. All men usually ever want it just to use me."

"Never again, baby. You're mine now, I'm going to take care of you… love you… treasure you…" He whispered, bringing his face back to mine before kissing me again. "Are you ready for this… us… like this?"

"I… I don't… I've never…" I let my words trail off as I thought about it. I didn't remember ever intentionally being with a man before.

He stopped and pulled away, waiting for me to finish. "You haven't?"

"No," I whispered.

"Okay, I'll be gentle then." He said softly, then went back to kissing my neck.

I may not have remembered ever letting go and giving myself to anyone before but that didn't seem to affect me. My body acted like it knew exactly what to do. I reached my hands up to run my fingers through his hair. "I know you will."

I lay there resting beside him, cuddled up close to his side with his arm around me, relaxed. If I ever doubted his love, I no longer did now. This man… This amazing man…

Even though it was dark and I couldn't see anything, I closed my eyes and began to regret telling him he could leave so soon. I didn't want that anymore, now all I wanted was to enjoy his presence, his warmth, his love…

Halted from the middle of my daydream, he quickly jolted up, pulling his arm away from me and turning around. He lowered himself and put his hand over my mouth. I couldn't see him, but I felt the heat from his head suddenly against my ear.

"Shhh… there's someone outside." He whispered directly into it. "Button back up as quietly as you can." His whisper was firm and tense. Then he pulled away from me quickly, taking his warmth and everything else I was enjoying with him. I still couldn't see anything and now I couldn't hear him anymore, either. It was as if he had completely disappeared in the black silence that now lay between us.

I reached down to pull myself together as quickly as I could, trying to keep myself from making any sounds. He gently brought his hand down to rest it on my knee. Then slowly he moved it up toward my side. He moved it in a way like he was trying to let me know where he was without surprising me. Probably so I wouldn't make any accidental sounds. With a little help from his support, I slowly sat up without my arms, only using my stomach muscles, trying to avoid leaning on or even touching any of the walls.

"You're a Gypsyin," he whispered softly, now closer to me. I was slightly surprised that he'd call me that but ignored it, trying to listen for instructions on how to proceed. "If we get caught, you're just a Gypsyin to me. All right?" He paused for a second, his voice heavy with brokenness. "I'm sorry," he paused again. "If we get caught, you can't run, they will shoot you. Please don't try. Okay? You're just a Gypsyin, all right? I was… tell them I was in here taking advantage of you before I brought you in." I could hear so many emotions in his voice that I seldom saw on his face. He sounded sorry, and angry and hurt, and maybe even scared. I wanted to hug him and tell him it was okay. I knew it wasn't his fault. I couldn't tell him, though. I knew I had to hold still and be as quiet as possible.

No sooner had he said it, I heard the same sounds he must have initially. There were multiple men's voices. They weren't loud, but they weren't soft either. I couldn't tell exactly where they were coming from. They almost sounded like they were in every direction except above or below us.

Before long, the sounds became louder like somone was coming closer. Every couple of seconds I heard more sounds, someone was stepping on the items that Jake—I thought randomly scattered—but now I realized, strategically positioned in place. He moved one hand up towards my shoulder, then he slowly moved his other hand to gently cover my mouth. At first I was confused. I thought I was being quiet enough, but soon realized what he was doing.

"When I squeeze your shoulder, scream," he said gently, under his breath. "I might do or say things that you won't understand and it's okay if you act afraid of me… just remember I love you," his voice started to break, "and I'm gonna do whatever I can to get you free again, okay?"

Before I could nod to tell him I heard, the sound from outside the room was now at the door along with a shadow, blocking a foot sized spot of what little light had been creeping in from under the door. He squeezed my shoulder and gently push me backward slightly. I didn't want to, but I did what he said. I screamed as loud as I could muster. Most of the sound was still muffled by his hand, but enough must have managed to escape when suddenly a large shaft of light broke into the room. I squinted and pulled away while taking another deep breath to let out another scream, but Jake pushed me to the floor faster than I could think of what to do next.

"Found 'em!" a man's voice yelled out to the others that must have been close by. I turned my head to try to see, but the light was too bright. All I could catch was a large black silhouette standing there.

"Who do you think you're looking for and under whose orders?" Jake asked, with a superior's authority in his voice as he started to stand up almost directly over my head, the only place where the closet didn't make him have to hunch over. I could start to see better now, looking up from under Jake's legs. The guy had his gun drawn and was pointing it straight at Jake. I could barely tell, but it looked like a couple more men were now walking into the living room as well.

"You better show me your tag if you think you're gonna talk to me like that and not get shot." The guy responded with an almost equally authoritative voice.

Jake slowly lifted his arms and pushed down his sleeve. "There! Now tell me what orders you have and why you've come after me."

"Calm down, Miles. We're just here to assist you with your prisoner transport." Another man's voice pipped up from behind the first man. He was talking to Jake. *Wait... was that Jake's real name... Miles? Did he lie to me about his name, too?*

Jake relaxed his arms and started to act as if he wasn't still being held at gunpoint, even though he was. "Well, thank you, but that won't be necessary. The intel we had was false. The prisoner never showed at the arranged pickup location."

"Then who is this?" The first man asked as he pointed to me with his gun.

"Just a Gypsyin I found a couple days ago. I thought I'd have a little fun with her before I returned to base. You know, that's about all they're good for." He twisted around to look down at me. His face was smug with a touch of angst like he was secretly provoking me to play along.

I didn't say anything. I just crawled backward slowly until my back was touching the wall. He might have thought I was an amazing actor, but all the fear that was now covering my face wasn't fake. I might not have been afraid of him, but I most certainly was afraid of all of them and what they could do;

knowing no matter how hard he tried to stop them, he was still only one man.

"If there was no prisoner, then why didn't you drive back to DC? Jones told me your tracker made it look like you went rogue." The man in the middle spoke up again, acting like he was the real one in charge.

"I hit a man and wrecked the car. I had no choice but to proceed on foot. He was a Coldier deserter. I was bringing him in until I lost him a few weeks back. The fool got himself sopping wet trying to fish. I couldn't get him warmed back up enough and he didn't make it to morning… If you don't believe me, track his tag. His name was Victus, Seth Victus."

"You can tell that to Miller when you see him." The men all lowered their guns at this point, seeing that Jake wasn't acting like a threat. "He's not going to be happy when he sees you don't have his prisoner."

While they talked, I looked over and noticed one of the men in the back of the group had squatted down and was staring at me through Jake's legs. His face was expressionless just like I had seen from Jake's so many times.

"Miller's in Charlotte?" Jake asked, surprised.

"O'Neal, we should just take her and say she's the prisoner," said the man from the back who had been staring at me. He stood up and looked over toward the man in charge, who was still partially blocked from my sight by the first man's torso.

I looked up toward Jake, expecting him to flinch, move, look tense, something, but nothing. He acted as calm as I've ever seen him. Then he turned around to look down at me again. "Get my bags out here and hand them to me," he barked the order like I was a peasant.

I hesitated, not clear on what his motives were in this current role play. Though, his face quickly grew stern, and he started to raise his hand like he was going to hit me. I flinched, then began to move deeper down into the closet to get them for him. I didn't know or understand what he wanted from me, then remembered what he said about how he would act, and relaxed, hoping that was all this was, just him acting. I grabbed the bags and started to move them toward his feet. I could hear the men still talking, but I couldn't gather everything they were saying, so I quickly moved back to my previous position after I gave him both his bags.

"Dude, you really think it'd be fair to take her in as the prisoner? I mean, sure she's just a Gypsyin but I've abused her enough, I don't think she should die for nothing on top of it." Jake spoke nonchalantly.

"Fine, but it'd sure be a waste to not use her up before we take her in. I can go first if you all wanna wait your turn." The man in the back spoke up again.

"Shut up, Finnigan!" the man in charge shouted. "You know what the charges are for messin' with a Gypsyin. Hell, Miles here I'm sure will just get a slap on the wrist, but you won't, ya stupid idiot. And I'm sure not gonna allow it when I'm in charge, neither. I don't give a shit if you wanna be foolish when you're runnin' your own team but right now you can keep it to yourself!"

Jake looked down at the bags now at his feet and bent down to pick up the largest and toss it out of the closet to sit beside his other duffle. Then he picked up mine and did the same. I looked up at him but he didn't look down or try to even make eye contact with me.

"Look guys, I appreciate you coming to help with my prisoner transport, but now that you know it's unnecessary, I'm gonna pull rank. You all go ahead without me. I know the protocol. I'll bring her into C and R when I'm done with her," Jake said, changing his stance to look more firm and commanding. At that point, the first man stepped back a couple of feet and I was finally able to see the second man that I assumed was in charge. He wasn't tall like Jake, but not short either. He was stocky with a clean-shaven face and looked to be middle-aged, but older than Jake.

"Miles, I'm sure you'd like that but until I talk to Miller, you can't pull rank. He told me until he sees you again, I'm to treat you like you went rogue. Now it's obvious that you didn't do that so I'll

be nice and not bind your hands but as for letting you finish with…
ah yeah, that won't be happening."

I looked up at Jake, waiting to hear his response. I could tell he was finally a little tense now. He was holding his hand in a loose fist that started to clinch ever so slightly. He wasn't saying anything. I could see he was thinking about his next move. Then finally he looked back down at me. I was surprised to see he looked upset. I figured he would be able to keep better control of the emotions on his face.

"Don't run, Gypsyin!" He said in a strong tone that didn't match his face, "They'll shoot you." I took it as another warning. I knew he was serious if he felt like he needed to tell me twice.

"All right men, round 'em up, let's go." The man in charge yelled out as he looked around and made a hand gesture similar to the ones I saw Jake make.

I pulled myself up to my feet, where the first guy stepped forward toward me and started to pull out cordage similar to how Jake did the first time we met.

"You don't need that, man. She's not dangerous. She's just a Gypsyin," Jake said, looking over toward us, acting like he didn't really care but I could see he was doing everything in his power to hold himself back.

"You heard O'Neal. You're not in charge. I'll do what I want. I'll give you this though," he took a step back and looked down at my feet then back up to my hair, "you sure know how to find good ones. I haven't seen a Gypsyin this nice in ages. I'd like to be the agent who gets to send her back out of Release."

Instantly I realized what C and R meant. Both men witnessed as the epiphany hit me, manifesting itself as panic all over my face. *Release…* Jake warned me about the Catch and Release brigade. I froze. I couldn't move. They were going to wipe my brain, not kill me—take my memory. *Erase me…*

I looked over at Jake, "Wait, no… please don't take me in." Then I looked back toward the man that had now started to tie my hands. "Please, you can't do this, you can't do this to me." He didn't look up, he didn't even act like I was talking to him. I looked back at Jake who was now picking up his bags very slowly.

"Miles…" I said, calling him what they did. "Miles… please, you can't let them take me. Miles…" He looked over at me briefly, his face obviously sorry and upset, then without saying anything looked back away. I couldn't control myself even though I wanted to. I wanted to do everything Jake told me not to. I wanted to run even though I knew I shouldn't. I started to pull on the cordage, making it difficult for the man to wrap it up as he wanted. Then I pulled myself backward and toward the wall all while still begging someone to help me.

"Stop this crap, I'm not fighting with a Gypsyin today!" The man in charge shouted as he swiftly started to walk over to me. I glanced back over at Jake. He lifted his arm toward the guy and started to say something but before I heard it, I felt an intense thump above my ear. I turned to look back at the man but before I could, everything stopped and I lost all control as darkness slowly filtered into my vision.

13

SERUM AND SOUP

"Open your eyes, Kaleah," a soft yet stern masculine voice whispered. "Kaleah, come on… please open your eyes. Tell me you're still in there somewhere… You gotta be… I need you to remember me…" He spoke again hesitantly like he knew what he was asking wasn't realistic.

All I could see was a dull hue of black, with bits of brownish-gray shadows floating around. I tried to open my eyes, but I couldn't. I tried to move my body, but I couldn't.

"Kaleah… please open your eyes…" With every plea, he breathed closer and closer against my cheek, filling my senses with his warm, heavy breath. "Kaleah?" He continued, his voice growing more frantic the longer I unintentionally denied his request. "Dammit, woman… please, Kaleah… please open your eyes." His voice started strong, then morphed into begging.

I couldn't feel my legs or my arms, nothing except warmth against my face. Frustration started to overwhelm me when suddenly I was hit by an onslaught of thoughts.

Why can't I remember anything?

I have no movement, no feeling, no nothing… Where am I?

Wait… Who is this man and what does he want with me…?

120

I wanted to talk but couldn't. So many questions were sprinting through my mind that I wanted to ask whoever this was that was speaking to me.

"Dammit… Where's the vial? How much of that shit did they give you? You should be awake by now." The man spoke again but softer, now sounding a little farther away than before. "I'm gonna get you out of here, okay? You're gonna be all right… I'm sorry… I'm so sorry… You're gonna be all right." He sounded distraught, close to crying but was holding himself back for whatever reason.

Suddenly, something interrupted him, and he stopped talking. It was faint but started as a small click then a heavy thud followed by footsteps. I remembered that sound from somewhere; it was distinct.

Clicking. Click, click, click… It was a woman in heels walking toward us.

"You must be the Release Agent?" A high-pitched voice spoke from my right a few feet away.

"Yes," the man's voice spoke, registering lower than it had when we were alone. "Peterson sent me. I'm new to this, actually. Do you mind?" He ended with an inflection that seemed to match a gesture I could not see thus not comprehend the intent behind.

"Ah, of course," the woman's voice changed from casual to flirtatious. "What do you want to know? I mean most of the time it's pretty simple, your side of it anyway. From what the other agents have said, the release is the easiest part."

"Oh… no, no," the man interrupted casually with a slight chuckle. "Really, I mean your side. It's fascinating to me how it works, ya know. How exactly you do what you do. I'm just so intrigued by the science behind it."

"Ha! Oh, right, that's what you meant. Yes, it is quite intriguing for sure," the woman giggled before going on. "Well, you see the injection itself is simple; that part's quite easy. Getting the subjects here and under control is probably the hardest part. You would think they would be happy to see it's just a little shot, right?" She giggled again. "But no, they act like we're killing them."

She let out a small sigh. "I guess that's what you guys are for.

You're always so helpful getting… people like her under control." She paused for a second. "This one was a mess. I've never seen one of them fight as much as she did. My gosh, you'd have thought she was rabid… But, you know, if I would have had an agent in here about your size with your musculature, I doubt she'd have been as much of an issue."

"Did they hurt her?" The man interrupted. "I mean did anybody get hurt? If she fought that hard, I hope you had an agent that knew how to handle things without people getting hurt. You really do need an agent that knows what they're doing."

"Ha, exactly!" The woman responded now with her voice moving slowly around me. "I don't know if they hurt her but I wouldn't worry about it if I were you. She's just a Gypsyin. I already checked her arm. She has no tag. She can't hear us right now, either. Honestly, with as much serum as I gave her, she'll probably be late to wake up. She was quite feisty, and well to be frank it was a bit irritating to me so I gave her a little extra, but shh that can be our little secret." She chuckled softly, thinking herself cute, I'm guessing. "She will have a few side effects. That can happen but they wear off."

"Oh really, okay," the male's voice responded, not sounding all that much like he cared. "Can you tell me how the serum works, like how does it remove their memory? That's what I think I'm the most curious about. What will it do to her since you gave her more?"

"Yes, well, the science behind it is pretty neat, really. It doesn't actually erase anything in the memories if I'm being honest with you. I mean that would be cool and all but that's not technically how it works. It essentially is an antigen that binds itself to certain cells in the brain where the mind stores memories. It can slowly erode those cells over time, but mostly it just creates a barrier, or umm… a barricade. It keeps their mind from getting to those memories to recall and use them. With most memories, that's how it works, anyway. Then there are some memories the serum just makes blurry, so they might think they remember something but they can't really bring it up very well." She paused for a second.

"I know this all makes me sound like a bad person but I really like to think about it like I'm liberating them, you know?" Her voice changed, sounding more defensive.

"You're just doing your job," the man's voice interjected, I assume, trying to make her feel better.

I didn't know who this man was but from what he said to me before she came in I got the idea he cared for me. I didn't know if he was asking all these questions so I would understand what had happened to me or if he genuinely was curious, but I appreciated the knowledge. I knew I couldn't move, but she was wrong about what I could hear. I wanted to soak up every ounce of what she was telling him. It was obvious at this point what she had done to me. Deep down, I hoped maybe he could persuade her to tell him if there was a way to reverse it.

"Wow, you know your stuff, doctor." The man's voice continued. "Is there a time frame in which the memories disappear?"

"Oh… uh, what do you mean?" She asked.

"Like how much do they lose?" He went on. "Months? Years? Do they forget how to walk and eat? That sort of thing."

"Yes, well… that is a rather complicated question to answer. See, we have different types of memories, but there are seven main ones. You have short-term ones, which mostly are less than a minute. Those then get filed by your brain into your long term to be stored. Under your long term… well… there it branches off into your conscious and your unconscious memories. And each of those branches off again, you get the idea… Under the conscious category, the antigen binds perfectly to your Episodic memories but not too well to the Semantic memories. The Episodic are the ones that are like life events and experiences. Unfortunately, even though it does a great job binding to those, for some reason it doesn't block events all that well that are more recent and relatively traumatic… Oh, I'm sorry I'm using a ton of doctor-y language." She stopped.

"No, it's fine. I think I'm following you pretty well. Please, go on."

"Okay, well… Like I was saying, it doesn't bind very well to the

Semantic type. Those memories are of general knowledge of the world around us, mainly facts or concepts we know to be true. Like the grass is green, babies are cute, you'll die if you inhale water, and so on, you get it."

"Right," he affirmed, then waited for her to proceed.

"Now the other two types are under the unconscious category. They're both similar to what you'd think of like muscle memory. One of them, the procedural memory, the serum doesn't affect at all. So when you release her, she should still know how to ah... I was going to say brush her hair but looking at her I'm not sure she knew how to do that to start with." She stopped to giggle at herself again.

"Implicit memory, however, the antigen seems to work relatively well with. These are memories where we store learned skills or tasks. So if she knew how to kick-box or speak French, yeah... she won't now... Obviously, there are more than the main seven memories, you also have sensory, collective, priming, cultural... Oh my gosh, I'm sorry... this has to be boring you. Sometimes I just can't help myself when I get on a roll." She softly giggled again.

"No, of course not, please. I'm learning so much, I really appreciate your time. This is interesting. That's exactly what I wanted to know. So is there a way to reverse it?"

"Oh... uh... Well, why would you want to do that? I mean—" she paused.

"Oh no, I don't want to. I was just curious if you could. I figured how amazing all this was that you figured it all out. I just thought you probably also had an antidote of sorts, maybe." He was starting to fumble over himself, but I could only tell so much from being forced to listen to them. I had half a mind to fall back asleep trying to save myself from becoming sickened by their endless flattery of one another.

"Oh well, I wasn't actually the first to formulate the serum so I can't take all the credit, but thank you, that was kind. I mean, I do know quite a bit about it and there is one way that it could be countered but I... well I... it's not really something I can share."

"Right, well I've been here long enough. I should get her and go release her before she wakes up." The man's voice was more stern sounding now than it had been previously.

"I wouldn't worry about her if I were you. She will be asleep for quite a while. You're welcome to stay longer if you have any more questions. I would be more than happy to oblige." She sounded beside herself at the thought that he wanted to leave. Like, why in the world would he not want to stay and fraternize with her more? I was irritated with their conversation and happy that I would soon be 'released.'

"Well, if you don't mind could I come back later? I would love to keep talking with you." The man's voice sounded overly pleasant. Even I knew he had to be lying when he said he would love it.

"Of course!" The woman cooed, giddy.

I realized I was going to have a range of emotions that I would have to deal with soon, knowing I just lost everything that I was, and it might never return to me, but at the moment the only thing I felt was ill. Completely and utterly ill, not only from their sickening conversation, but just in general as well. My body was more than worn out, way past the point of being tired. Wherever he planned on taking me, I hoped it was a place I could rest.

Soft thuds, most likely his boots, moved closer to me, followed by the sound of light breathing close to my ear as he picked me up, but I still felt nothing but a subtle warmth across my face. He didn't say anything else to me as he walked. I heard the random noise of what sounded like a door every so often and a few casual salutations from different passersby and that was it. I didn't know where he planned on taking me and with feeling like I did; I didn't really care. Slowly, I let myself drift back to sleep, shutting down the only sense I still had left that wanted to work.

"You eat soup. Yook me, yook me... open you eyes." I was awakened by a small oriental woman. My eyes opened this time when I tried to make them, and I could actually see. Part of me was thrilled and part of me was confused and irritated that I was confused. I was laying in a bed in a small room. It was dark and chilly though I was covered with multiple blankets.

"You feva high," she said, staring at me as I looked down, observing the blankets. "Mies get mec... ahh mecin. I fix you. I fix you, now eat soup." I could barely understand her, but I gathered enough that I got the idea someone was going to fix me, whether it was her or Mies but I was hopefully getting fixed and it must start with the idea that I had to eat her soup. She handed the bowl to me. I picked up the spoon and started to eat.

Well, I guess I didn't lose the memory having to do with how to eat. That was nice. It was delicious. I would have thought maybe the best I had ever eaten, but then again I didn't know if it was. I caught myself starting to feel angry. The idea of finding that doctor after I was healed and injecting her with her own serum floated through my mind a time or two until I suppressed it. I finished the soup and lay back down to rest. I was still extremely exhausted and didn't want to explore yet what other things my body was able to do again.

I was awakened by a man's voice this time, the same man's voice that was the Release Agent. I assumed he must be Mies. It felt like I had been asleep for days since I ate the soup but I knew that wasn't realistic. I heard him talking to the woman outside of my room. They spoke like they thought I was still asleep and not listening.

"See eat soup but feva high, too high. I no fix heh. Give me mecin, I put in soup, I fix heh."

"I don't know if it will work like that. You have to be careful with it so you don't give her too much." The man's voice was low, trying to talk softly, probably so he wouldn't wake me.

"See eat soup. I fix soup. See betta wi mecin in soup. Mies, give me mecin." She sounded agitated with him.

"Okay, please, you have to understand. I'll give it to you but it's not labeled. If you give her too much, it will make her worse." He paused to sigh softly. "Okay, let me help you. I will show you how much she can have, all right?"

"See Mies, you smat, you yisten me, you smat. I fix heh, you see." She now sounded content, like a lady who won an argument. "See wake, you go see heh."

"No, not yet," he said with hesitance, "she looks like she's resting well, I don't want to bother her."

"See wake, I sow you," she said, sounding eager.

"No," he stopped her, "please… I'm not ready," he said softly.

"Fine, you be back when see fixt wi soup?" She lowered her voice now to match his.

"Yes, let me show you how much medicine to use. It will fix her. She should start to remember everything again," He said, sounding hopeful. "I can't come to see her very often. They might be watching me. I have to be careful when I visit, understand?"

"You see heh when I fix heh wi soup?"

"Yes, I'll be back soon. She will probably sleep most of the time but if she gets sicker, send for me. And whatever you do, Ming, please don't let her leave. You understand me, right? She can't leave, it's too dangerous."

"Yes, Mies, you yuv heh. I not yet heh yeave. I fix heh wi soup. You see heh when see fixt."

"Right, thank you, Ming," he said. His voice was now beginning to fade as the conversation slowly moved away, where it was too far for me to hear them.

I assumed he was showing her how much medicine to give me. I didn't know how to feel about all of it. I wanted the medicine; I wanted to remember everything again, but I had no idea what exactly was going to come back up with all those memories and that made me apprehensive.

Who was this man that Ming thought loved me? If he loved me how did I wind up in a position to even have my memory erased to start with? I wasn't even sure what my name was yet. I know he called me by it when I first woke up, but I couldn't remember now what it was he said. I knew Ming's name. I knew Mies name, though I was suspicious if that was even his name, since Ming didn't pronounce most things correctly. It didn't take long before the frustration wore me out again and I couldn't help but fall back to sleep.

I was frustrated that the only thing I could do all day was sleep. In between the times that Ming woke me up to eat more of her soup or help me go to the bathroom, I slept. My fever must have slowly gone away as well because it wasn't long before I was able to take a layer at a time of blankets off of myself and not feel like I was going to shiver to death. The taste of her soup changed from the first few times she forced it upon me. Now it had a taste that was closer to what I thought it might be like to eat grass. Obviously, I didn't really remember what grass tasted like, or if I had even eaten grass before, but somewhere inside of me I had a feeling it would taste like what she was now putting in her soup.

I didn't know if the medicine was helping me yet or not but I started to notice different things about myself that I hadn't initially. I remembered I was right-handed, or well I thought I was remembering it. I might have just observed myself favoring my right hand, but it felt like a memory. I also think I started to remember that I liked fish too. Granted, the only thing I had been eating was a soup that was made entirely of vegetables. So this could have spurred me to overthink and assume that liking fish was now a memory as well. But I was willing to take it as a positive sign that maybe, just maybe something in the soup I was being forced to endure daily was helping. It wasn't long after I finished another bowl that I lay down again and let myself drift back off to sleep.

14
NO BYE FO MING

There was blood everywhere. I looked around but I couldn't tell where it was coming from. It was on me as well, soaking my hands and dripping off my fingers. I tried to wipe them clean, but it didn't do any good. It was still all over my hands and now smeared on my clothes. There was a man in front of me on his knees, bent over, leaning on one arm with his other pressed against his chest. I thought maybe the blood was coming from him but I couldn't tell.

"Are you okay?" I tried to ask him but it was like he couldn't hear me. I bent down to look at him as he caught my eye and turned his face up to meet mine. His expression was grim as he looked back down at the hand against his chest. I could now see that was where the blood was coming from.

"Can I help you?" I asked, but he kept looking at his hand.

"Memento schola," he said still looking down.

"I don't understand," I said, trying to help him stand up.

"Memento schola," he said again this time looking straight at me like I should have known what language he was speaking.

"I don't know what you're saying."

"You must kill me," he replied. His eyes were full of pain, indicating he was serious.

"I… I can't, no!" I said not knowing why he wanted me to kill him but I didn't want to.

"Kill me, Eva, you must!" He said again, reaching his other hand out toward me.

"I can't!" I shouted back, "I'm sorry, I can't!"

He turned away and let himself fall to the ground that was now covered in his blood. "Kill me, Eva, then run," he said, looking down.

"Please don't ask me to do that," I begged him. I felt his pain. It was an ache so deep, like if your heart was being ripped from your chest.

"Eva… memento schola, you must kill me, then you must run," he said again slowly emphasizing every word.

I didn't want to do it, but I was compelled. I looked around. I didn't know where but I knew I had a knife. I just needed to find it. Without realizing it, I looked down again and saw it was already in my hand, clueless how I didn't see it before.

"Eva… Please!" He continued, helpless in his agony.

"Okay…" I screamed, then reached forward with my right hand and plunged the knife into his back. "I'm sorry… I'm so sorry… Please forgive me. I didn't want to do it, I didn't want to… Please," I cried out.

He fell flat against the ground. The blood started to pool up around him. "I'm sorry… I'm so sorry," I kept screaming it out, hoping it would help me release the pain of what I had just done.

"Wake up, Kaleah," I suddenly opened my eyes to a man sitting in front of me, holding my hand. I pulled it away, then pulled myself back to sit up as much as I could. "Stop, it's just me. You're fine…" He reached out to lay a hand on my shoulder but I pulled away again. "Please… you're fine. Kaleah… It's me."

"I don't know who you are, and my name isn't Kaleah either, so you can stop calling me that," I said, trying not to be snappy, but I couldn't totally help how it came out.

"Oh my gosh, of course. I'm sorry. Just relax. I will explain it to you, okay?" He stopped trying to touch me. "It's just me, Jake… Miles. That's my name, Jacob Miles. You can call me whichever one you want, maybe you will remember one of them. Your name is Kaleah. They took your memory but I'm having Ming give you medicine to fix it and get your memory back. You were just having a bad dream. Ming sent for me. She said she couldn't wake you up, and you kept screaming."

"My name isn't Kaleah," I figured I'd try to tell him again and see if he'd listen this time.

"Um, okay… Do you remember what your name is then?" He asked, sounding confused about how I might know it when he didn't.

"Eva," I said, thinking back to the dream. It had to be.

"Okay, did you remember that or… umm… How do you know?" His brow was furrowed, clearly confused.

"It was in my dream. I…" I started to tell him what else was in my dream then stopped myself. I had no idea who Miles was yet, not really. He could tell me whatever he wanted, but I wasn't going to believe him just yet. I still couldn't understand how he could let me get my memory erased if he really cared for me like he was trying to act like he did.

"Okay, that's great! That's great that you remembered your name. That means it's working!" He smiled and tried to sound excited but there was still a look of confusion on his face. I could tell he was conflicted. He knew me as someone else, someone named Kaleah. So now we both had to be asking ourselves the same question. If he knew me as Kaleah but that wasn't who I thought I was, then why did I previously tell him that's who I was? I couldn't remember if I liked to solve puzzles before but in this instance, I didn't feel fond of the idea that there was now this big mystery placed before me. My brain didn't feel like it could function at such a high level yet. I was already starting to feel worn out, and it had only been a short conversation.

"Maybe so," I said, looking away from him.

"Don't be discouraged, Kal... sorry, Eva." He said, looking uncomfortable calling me by another name. "The medicine is going to work. You'll get your memories back, and then we can leave, just like we originally planned."

"I can't be who you think I am. I don't even know who that actually is! I don't even know who you are either! And I definitely don't know what we planned or why I am here." I quickly grew more and more agitated.

"Calm down please, K... Eva," he said as he started to reach toward me then pulled away, probably remembering I wasn't receptive to his touch. "I know... I know you can't remember and it's confusing. This whole thing is confusing to you. It's easy to feel agitated, that's a side effect, but you have to trust me. We're going to get you back, you're going to get all your memories back, all right?"

I started to calm down. I didn't trust him but I knew he was right. One of two things was going to happen. Either he would be right and I would soon relearn everything about myself, or he wouldn't be right and I would be stuck like this. I knew one way or another, I needed him. Either I would learn to trust him again or I would go back to using him again. Whichever one was my original purpose, soon I would know.

"Who are you? How do I know you and how do you know me?" I didn't want to wait to ask him his side of what I was supposed to be remembering.

"It's complicated," he said, tensing up slightly, trying not to look away from me.

"It's not complicated! How did we meet? You met me somehow!" My brain felt fired-up like it could keep going another few rounds but I couldn't ignore the feeling of fatigue quickly trying to overtake my body.

He hesitated, then swallowed hard finally allowing himself to look away from me. This wasn't encouraging to the idea that we had a positive, productive relationship before he somehow let me get my memory erased. I wasn't sure how I could trust him if this behavior continued, either.

"Look, I don't mind telling you. I just don't know if it would be the best thing to do right now or if I should wait until you can remember it yourself," he finally answered. "It might not be safe for you to know that yet."

I couldn't help but think he was full of shit. That sounded like a lame excuse if I had ever heard one. I sat there staring at him, debating if I had enough energy to argue or not. I wanted to make him tell me, force it out of him. I couldn't though, because I could barely keep my eyes open and was half expecting myself to pass out before long.

"Look, not having my memory doesn't make me stupid!" I was becoming irritated again. "I'm not a child, you can tell me the truth." My mind decided to argue against my body's better judgment.

"Eva, that's not what I'm doing. I know you're not stupid, please... You really don't understand, it's complicated. If I tell you right now, it might confuse you more. I don't want it to... Eva?... Eva!" his voice slowly diminished until all I heard was silence.

"Eva!" I woke up now laying on the floor beside the bed with him on his knees bent over me. "Oh my gosh! Are you all right? What happened?" He gently pushed my hair out of my face and slowly let his eyes search my head and scan downward, looking to see if I was hurt. When his eyes came back and locked on mine, I saw something I hadn't seen before: warmth. Their silent intensity radiated an emotion I wasn't ready for... affection. I quickly blinked away.

As he reached toward me to help me up, I didn't stop him. He brought his arms under mine and around my back and hoisted me back up onto the bed. I didn't answer him. I was still a bit dazed by what happened. He took his left hand and gently pushed it against my shoulder, guiding me to lie backward. At the same time, he used his other arm to help swing both of my legs back onto the bed.

"Eva..." he said, sitting down next to me, looking down at my face. "You have to trust me. I promise, I'm going to take care of you… Now, you need to rest. I have to leave again but I'll be back in a couple days to check on you."

"All right," I mumbled back to him. I had lost every ounce of fight my brain still wanted to conjure up. My eyes no longer wanting to function, started to perform their own system shutdown, fighting against me every time I tried to look at him.

"Rest now," I heard him speak softly close to my face, then felt his lips gently kiss my forehead.

"Wake, wake. I got moe soup fo you… open you eyes, wake, wake." Ming woke me up almost the same way every time. She was cheerful, no matter what mood I was in, nothing seemed to phase her. She was a petite little woman. Looking at the lines on her face, she was older, but it was hard to tell because she didn't have many gray hairs in her straight, black bob. Speaking wise, her English was broken at best. But when spoken back to her, she acted like she could understand every bit of what she heard. It didn't take long before I could tell she was growing on me. I very much enjoyed her company each of the days I had been there. She was warm and friendly as long as I never fought her on anything. But anytime I didn't want soup and tried to refuse, she was feisty as all get out. I was never able to win any of those disagreements, even if I tried she would revert to acting like she didn't understand me and just kept repeating, "You eat soup!" over and over.

If I was counting right, which was hard to do with sleeping so much, it had been about six days since I had seen Miles last. When I wasn't sleeping or eating, all I was able to do was lay there and think. I had thought of more questions I wanted to ask Miles when he returned. Things weren't adding up in my head. I guess that was probably expected, but he could have at least given me enough information to help me believe him a little better. I didn't know if before the injection I was the type of person who easily trusted people but that wasn't who I was now. The person I felt like I was now was one who was highly suspicious. Except with Ming, I trusted her, but she was the only one.

There were things I was starting to remember that I thought probably weren't new to me but might have been, I wasn't sure. I knew what a Coldier was, and I knew what a Sicari was. How I knew those things and not other things were beyond me but apparently that information my brain decided to hold on to. What I still didn't know yet was which one Miles was. I didn't know anything about him. Even if he didn't want to tell me how we met, he could have at least told me more about himself. He could have told me more about myself as well, since he acted like he knew me so well. I gathered the idea he was an agent from his first conversation with the doctor. I also knew from what she led him to believe, he didn't know I was able to hear their whole conversation.

I asked Ming to bring me a pen and paper. Her face lit up with excitement. I think she expected that I had new memories that I wanted to jot down. She quickly returned with both, plus another large bowl of soup. She left them with me before retreating back into the kitchen, I'm sure to make more soup. Immediately, before I forgot them, I wrote down all the questions that I had thought of that I intended to ask Miles when he returned.

First, I wanted to know who I was to him. Were we a couple? Then, if so, I wanted to know how he got the doctor to tell him how to get the medicine. Did he sleep with her? Did he threaten her? What kind of agent was he if he wasn't originally a Release Agent? What I wanted to know more than all of that though, was why did he let me get my memory erased. After I wrote everything down, I took the paper, folded it up, and slid it under my pillow.

Three days later...

I woke up to Ming talking loudly to someone. She sounded upset but I couldn't distinguish her words just the inflections in her speech. The voices became a bit louder as they got closer to my room, but not quite to my door. Before long, I could tell it was a man's voice she was speaking with. His voice was low and slow. He sounded like he was trying to calm her down so he could understand her. Once he was able to help her relax, I could start to distinguish her words better. I tried to listen as best as I could without moving. In case they looked in on me, I wanted them to think I was still asleep. Maybe that would help them feel like they could talk more freely.

"See Sicaee, Mies! See no stay no moe. See Sicaee, Mies, Sicaee!" I could tell now she was speaking to Miles. She was trying to talk slowly so he would understand her better but it wasn't working all that well because she was still pretty upset.

"Ok, Ming, try to calm down. I… I think I know what you're trying to tell me but—" he was quickly interrupted.

"Mies," her voice was louder now, "Sicaee, Mies."

"Shh, ok, ok… Don't wake her up. Why do you think that? Did she tell you? Is she remembering it? She doesn't have a tag. She's just a Gypsyin."

"No!" She started to get upset again probably feeling like he wasn't listening to her, "See Sicaee!"

"Ok," his voice was now lower and firm. "Ming… Why do you think that?"

"See toc in heh seep. Mies, see say tings ownee Sicaee know. See no stay no moe. I saahee, Mies, I saahee."

"Ok Ming, I believe you, all right? You can calm down now," he said, talking slowly, probably still confused. "I just don't understand if… She has no tag! Why wouldn't she have a tag?" He said it softly, asking himself, trying to make sense of it.

I knew what she was saying. I understood her. I didn't quite understand what it meant going forward but I could see it was a problem. If she was so concerned about me being a Sicari, then that must have meant she and Miles were both Coldiers. I lay there as still as possible, trying to resolve in myself what it all meant, asking myself the same question Miles was asking. *If so, where was my tag?*

"Eva," His voice spoke behind me now at a normal volume. He must have been standing in the doorway. "Eva, wake up. We have to go."

I rolled over and opened my eyes, pretending to be happy to see him and surprised at the same time, trying to act like I hadn't heard why he would rush me to get ready to leave. "Okay… Why? Did I do something wrong?" I asked, knowing what she had told him but my question was genuine. I wasn't sure why exactly her thinking I was a Sicari was a reason to impulsively kick me out.

"No… you… ah, you're fine. It's just time to go. It's not safe for us to stay here any longer, that's all." He picked up a little black bag that had been sitting in the corner of my room. He opened it and started to rummage around, inspecting its contents. "Ming, will you put the medicine in here, please?" He asked, handing it out past the door to where she was standing in the hall, where I couldn't see her.

"Okay, Eva," Miles looked back toward me, making full eye contact, "I have to take you out looking like we did coming in, all right? I'm going to be your Release Agent and you're just a Gypsyin that hasn't woken up yet. Do you understand?"

I nodded my head in agreement and started to sit up.

"No, just relax. I got you," he said as he walked over to the bed. "Before we walk out, close your eyes and keep them closed. If anyone sees you awake, they might find out what I've done." He bent over and put both his arms underneath me, one under the small of my back and the other under my thighs. He adjusted them briefly then swiftly stood straight, picking me up. He acted like I didn't weigh anything. The motion was slow and fluid without him groaning or making any noise at all, other than his usual breathing.

He walked with me down the hall. I looked around, trying to find Ming. I wanted to thank her before we left for taking care of me. I spotted the black bag sitting on the counter all closed up, propped nicely against the wall.

"Where's Ming?" I asked him, feeling pretty upset at the thought I might never see her again.

He stopped beside the bag and removed his arm from under my legs as he let my weight rest on the counter. "She can't say goodbye, Eva. I'm sorry," he said, picking up the bag with his free hand. He slung it over his shoulder, then placed his arm back under my legs and pulled me back up tight against him again.

"Oh, okay," I said, trying to stop myself from feeling upset. "I understand."

Miles looked down at me and smiled slightly with the corner of his mouth. "Close your eyes now. Go to sleep if you need to, just don't open them until I tell you that you can."

"Okay," I closed my eyes and relaxed into his arms as best as I could. He kissed me again on the forehead, then shifted his weight to open the door using the hand that was carrying my legs.

15
MEMENTO SCHOLA

I must have fallen asleep. I woke up with a force, pulling me to one side. I was laying in the backseat of a car. The gentle vibration was soothing but we must have been going around a corner because I was about to fall out of the seat. I opened my eyes to look around briefly before shutting them again. I didn't know if I was allowed to open them yet.

It was dark outside but there was enough light that I could see snowflakes hit and settle gently against the window seal. The car was nice and warm. I couldn't hear anything except the sound of the vents blowing and the wipers as they chattered every couple of seconds against the windshield.

I opened my eyes again quickly, trying to see if it was just Miles in the front or if there was someone sitting up there with him. I could see him in the driver's seat but my head was behind the other seat so I couldn't tell if he was alone or not. Just in case he wasn't, I didn't want to say anything. I decided to just reach my hand up and gently push on his side so he knew I was awake. Then, if we weren't alone, he could give me a signal to go back to sleep.

Slowly, I raised my arm and reached out toward him. I touched his jacket first. It felt course, but had a slickness to it at the same time. I reached a little further until I hit something hard, I presumed was flesh.

"Whoooah," he yelled as he jumped to the opposite side a little. The car braked and my entire body rolled hard against the back of the seats and then onto the floor.

"Oh my gosh, Kaleah!" The car skidded a little, then came to a stop. "Kaleah!... Uh, Eva, I mean... What are you trying to do? Where did you... are you okay?" His voice was clearer now as if he'd turned around to look into the backseat.

"Yeah," I moaned, facing the floor. I grappled to get my arms underneath me to push myself back up to the seat.

"Ha," he chuckled. "Come here." I felt him grab a hand full of fabric at my back, catching the waist of my pants, then he pulled upward, trying to help me. "Oh my gosh, woman... You love the floorboard of cars don't you?" He asked. Now I was sure I heard him laughing.

"No!" I said, pulling myself back onto the seat. "Why would you say that?"

"Ha," He continued to laugh, "I will tell you some other time unless you remember it first," he said as he began to calm himself back down. "Actually, it's my fault. You'd think I would remember to put a seat belt on you. Ha... Next time I guess."

"Where are you taking me?" I asked, looking around out the windows.

He suddenly got quiet and serious again, like he remembered his mission. He let out a low cough to quickly clear his throat then proceeded to talk again. "How much can you remember?" He asked, turning back around to look at me through the rear-view mirror.

"What do you mean?" His new demeanor was starting to concern me. I wondered if this had anything to do with what Ming told him before we left.

I quickly rehearsed in my mind how it might go if I just told him I knew what Ming thought I was. But I didn't know why she would say that because I didn't remember being a Sicari and wasn't sure what she was talking about. The longer I thought about it I realized he might think I was lying if I told him what I knew. So, I figured it'd be best if I kept pretending like I didn't know.

"I mean, who are you?" He asked, his tone was cold.

"Why would you ask me that? You know I don't remember!" I said, sticking with the route I just concluded was best.

The interrogation didn't last long when he quickly gave in. "You're right, I'm sorry." His tone lightened again as a heaviness lifted off of him. "It's going to take a few days, but I'm taking you to a little house that we found… umm… I still have a lot I have to tell you. I was hoping you would have remembered it all by now. Do you want to sit up here with me? We can talk as I drive."

"Okay," I said as I started to crawl forward onto the armrest then over until I fell into the empty seat next to him. I straightened myself up and looked back over my shoulder to grab the seat-belt and buckle it in.

"Good idea," he said as he started to drive again very slowly. "I deactivated my tracker," he said nonchalantly as he looked over at me briefly and smiled.

"What?" I asked, confused.

He looked at me again this time analyzing my face seeing if I knew what he meant by it or not. "Sorry, I was just checking to see if you remembered," he said then looked back at the road.

"Look, if you don't trust me enough to tell you when I start remembering things, how am I supposed to feel like I can trust *you*? How am I supposed to believe *you* are who you say you are? It goes both ways you know!" I said it as sternly as I could.

He was silent for a minute.

"What are you afraid I am?" I asked, hoping I could make him come out with it first.

"You don't understand. I thought I lost you—" He paused, now sounding upset. "No, I lost you, I did… I lost you… I'm just doing everything I can to get you back, all right?"

"You didn't answer my question." I said. I needed him to answer it. I needed it out so it could be resolved.

"No one… I'm just afraid I won't get back the girl I had," he looked defeated, almost broken by the idea. But I couldn't help but think he was lying. I knew what he was afraid of and I knew he wasn't going to tell me.

"Who was I to you?" I asked, trying to remember the questions I wrote down. I forgot the paper under my pillow at Ming's so I would have to bring them up from memory.

"Kaleah," he said at first. "Who *are* you to me, you mean. Now I'll call you Eva like you asked, but you are still my Kaleah." He paused, a mixture of sadness and pain now visible on his face.

"How did you get the antidote from the doctor? She said she wouldn't tell you?" I continued with my questions, breaking the silence.

"How did you know about that?" He asked, quickly looking over at me, then back toward the road.

"Did you sleep with her?" I wanted the truth but at the same time, I was hoping he would lie if the answer was yes.

"What? No! Kaleah... I would never—" He stopped for a second. "How did you know about that?" He asked again this time more sternly.

"I could hear you, okay? I heard everything. I heard her say she double dosed me. I heard her tell you how amazing you are. The whole time you just... you just acted like you didn't care. Like I was just a Gypsyin, it didn't matter." I said, feeling myself becoming more agitated and slightly fatigued.

"Kal... Eva, I mean." His voice was now lower and calm. "No, I didn't sleep with her. I did care, that's why I went back to her to get the medicine for you. It was all an act. I had to act like you didn't mean anything to me."

"How do I know you aren't acting now?" The argument was starting to wear me out, but I continued, "How do I know when you're acting and when you aren't? How do I know when you're telling me the truth and when you're lying?"

"Come on, Eva, you know I'm not lying to you." He looked over at me when he said it. "I love you... I wouldn't ever do anything to hurt you."

"You're lying right now!" Unable to lower my voice or contain my emotions, I continued. "If you loved me so much, then why the hell did you not stop me from having my memory erased?" I asked, feeling deflated like just used almost every ounce of energy I had left.

He didn't turn to look at me, just kept his eyes on the road as he softly stepped on the brakes, bringing the car slowly to a complete stop then putting it in park. He lowered his hands to let them rest in his lap as he tilted his head back to lean against the headrest.

"You're right, I screwed up." He turned his head to look over at me. "I screwed up, and every day I have to deal with the consequences. Never in my life have I had anything as good as you that I could call mine. Someone with a heart as pure as yours just waltz in and tear me up like you did. I was nothing but a shell of empty emotions and you broke me... You broke me and held me together all at the same time. I haven't been the same since I lost you... So you can think that I'm lying but I don't care; I don't care anymore. No one can punish me more than I punish myself every time I think about what you had to go through, what I wasn't able to protect you from... It kills me inside... Do you have any idea what I wanted to do to that doctor when she told me what she did to you? It sure as hell wasn't wanting to sleep with her." He stopped and looked away again, bringing his hand briefly to his face.

"Okay... I have another question. Do you promise to tell me the truth and not lie to me when I ask it?" I asked, trying everything I could to keep myself awake.

"Of course!" He said, looking back at me. Then he reached down and took hold of my hand.

"Why are you afraid that I'm a Sicari?" I asked, hoping we could be open with each other.

His eyes widened as he looked at me. He didn't say anything, he just stared with his mouth slightly open, as if thinking. I don't know if he was thinking about how to answer or what to do but he wasn't responding.

"I'm tired," I said, trying to keep my eyes focused on him, "please, just answer me."

His face changed. He started to look at me differently. I couldn't keep my eyes focused on him enough to determine what the look was. My eyes kept wanting to roll around, half focusing on everything and nothing all at the same time. I was doing everything I could to stop my eyelids from shutting.

I don't know how long I was asleep but when I woke up; it was daylight, and I was in the backseat of the car again. Something was strange. I looked down and saw my hands were tied together. There was a dark green cord intertwined and wrapped around them. I didn't know what was going on, or why it was there. *Why would Miles have tied me up?*

"Miles?" I yelled out to him.

"It's for your own good," he said calmly, without even letting me ask a question.

"Miles, no... no, it isn't. I don't understand. Why would you do this?" I asked, growing more and more angry.

"You talk in your sleep, Eva. Ming was right. This means your memory has to be coming back soon." He paused for a second. "The doc said that was a side effect," he mumbled softly, talking to himself.

"Whatever. Why does that mean you think I need to be tied up?" I asked, agitated and confused.

"Look, I know you're an agent now. You said enough last night... Well, it's pretty obvious." He didn't act afraid of me or even upset. I couldn't gauge what he was doing.

"I'm not an agent. I don't remember being one. Besides, you even said yourself, I don't have a tag. Please, just untie me. I won't hurt you. Do you think I'm going to hurt you? I won't." I said, trying to reason with him.

"You might not remember it yet, but when you do, I don't know what you're capable of. I'm not afraid of you. I just don't want you to run from me. I don't know what you're about to remember," he said, then paused for a second before continuing.

"As for the tag, I've been thinking about that. There's a special agency within the Sicari, where most of their espionage agents come from. I've heard rumors that at the beginning of the war there were a couple of units that they didn't tag. They just sent them out to look like Gypsyins. It was risky obviously, because they had all these spies out there now that couldn't be tracked. Soon they realized it was a bad idea. There were too many of them that could go rogue or even turn into a double agent and there wasn't anything they could do to stop it. So, what I heard was, over the years if the Coldiers didn't catch and kill them first, whenever they would go back to their station, the Sicari would decommission them themselves. They couldn't risk having a double agent out there so after they interrogated them, they would wipe their memory or kill them. I'm not sure which, it's not my side." He stopped again to take a breath.

"Essentially, that's where the Coldier Catch and Release program started in the first place. They couldn't determine which Gypsyins were really Sicari spies and which weren't so in the beginning they interrogated all of them before sending them to C and R. But after so many years passed without uncovering any more spies, the protocol changed. Now whenever an agent catches a Gypsyin, unless they're deemed a threat, they skip the interrogation and just go straight to C and R."

I didn't know what to say. I was trying to think of some way that I could prove him wrong, but I knew it wasn't realistic with very few memories to work with. "That sounds great and all but I'm not a spy!" I said it fully believing it was the truth, but deep down wondered if he was right. "Please, just untie me. You can't keep me tied up back here forever."

"I don't intend to," he said as he started to pull the car over toward the side of the road. "I'll untie you as soon as your memory of me comes back. When you remember who I was to you, I'll know you won't try to run from me." He stopped and put the car in park.

"What are you doing?" I asked.

"Relax, I'm just getting your medicine out of my bag. It's in the trunk. It's time for you to take it again," he finished, then opened the car door and got out.

"This is bullshit," I shouted. I couldn't believe he wouldn't untie me. I heard everything he said, but still thought it was ridiculous. No way was I going to let him win. If he wasn't going to untie me, then I wasn't going to take his medicine. I rolled over until I was laying with the front of my body against my seat. I curled up as tight as I could, putting my face down into the crack. Before long, I heard one of the car doors open. I assumed it was mine, considering the large gush of cold air that hit me suddenly.

"What are you doing?" He asked, standing outside looking in at me.

"I won't take your medicine, not until you untie me!" I said as loudly as I could, but was muffled by the cushion in the seat.

"Oh my gosh, you're impossible." He paused, probably to think about what he was going to do with me. "Yes, you will take it," he continued with a rather upbeat but firm voice. I think he thought I was playing. He acted almost like it was a game and I had invited him to play along with me.

"You can't make me take it, not unless you untie me!" I yelled out. "I'll only take it if you untie me!"

"Bet me," he said, apparently accepting my challenge.

Suddenly, he took both his hands and hooked them under my arms as he started to pull me out of the car. "I know you're feisty, but I'm bigger than you are, and if I have to manhandle you, I will. You're gonna take your freakin' medicine whether you want to or not. It's good for you… Dammit, woman, why do I always have to save you from yourself?" His voice was more playful than firm, but I wasn't playing even if he was.

As my head passed through the door's opening, the only thing I could see all around his feet was snow. Seeing it and not knowing whether he intended to drop me after he got me pulled out, I quickly worked with him and pulled my feet under myself while using his leverage to stand.

"Wow, I thought you would put up more of a fight." He said now making eye contact with me as I turned around.

I stood there and glared at him, trying to make my face as mean looking as I could muster.

He didn't say anything else. Still looking at me, he started to grin. He turned back toward the car and reached out with his left hand as if to shut my door. Before I even realized what he was doing, he spun his body back around and swung his arm quickly toward me as though to hit me.

I didn't have to think; on impulse, my body moved swiftly into action faster than I knew what its moves were going to be. Almost like it was in slow motion, I caught myself bringing both hands, still tied, up to block him. I looked down. My wrists were now braced against his left forearm. Within the next split second, my body, accepting its instincts, took over once again. Quickly, with one smooth motion, I moved my right leg forward, erasing the space between us. Then I took my left leg and hooked it behind his right leg, where he was now bearing most of his weight. Putting my hands squarely on his chest, I pushed him with all my force, making him fall backward, landing in the snow behind him.

He sat up, bracing himself just staring at me, jaw wide open. "What the hell was that?" He shouted, looking aghast.

I think my face was probably matching his with its own disbelief. "I could ask you the same question. Why did you try to hit me?" I shouted back.

"I wasn't really going to hit you. I was just acting like I was to see if you remembered how to fight," he said as he began to stand back up.

"Well, I don't! I already told you I don't remember anything like that yet. Why do you feel like you have to keep testing me?" I retorted, noticing all the excessive movement was starting to make me feel weak.

"Uh... Yes you do! Whether you realize it or not! Don't you think it's a bit obvious now? I knew it... I knew you had to be getting some of those memories back. That's why I keep testing you. It's obvious they're coming back 'cause Kaleah never moved like that." He said as he began to thoroughly dust off all the snow.

"I'm not Kaleah!" I stepped back to rest against the car. "I'm sorry, all right? I'm sorry I can't be her. You want a ghost... You just want me to take the medicine so I can remember you, so you can have her back... But what about all the stuff I don't want to remember, huh? Did you ever think you might get more than you bargained for trying to resurrect her?"

He didn't say anything he just stood there listening.

"I think I killed people... I could have been a bad person... I don't want to know how to fight. I don't want to be a spy... What do you plan on doing if, after it all comes back, I decide I don't want to be with you anymore? What if—" I started to feel light-headed.

"Eva, stop, you're wearing yourself out." He took a couple of steps toward me.

"I don't care! I remember enough, okay?... I don't want any more medicine. I don't want any more memories. There are reasons I haven't told you what I've already started to remember... Whoever you think Kaleah was, I'm not her and I—" I stopped. Suddenly, I started to feel clammy and nauseous. I looked up to try to remake eye contact with him, but I couldn't focus on his face. There was now more than one.

"Eva?..." his voice quickly grew distant.

The heavy rain was over and now the sky was a beautiful deep red hue. I followed tightly behind Marcus. The byway lines were surprisingly quiet for that time of day, which made me suspicious but I ignored it. We both knew the risk but didn't see we had much choice; we had to cross through them if we were going to meet our contact at Nashville at the arranged time.

The rain had slowed us down enough we didn't have time to go around now. The old metal bridge we were crossing was clear from what I could tell, but Marcus was a better spotter than me so he decided to go first. I felt like I should have been in the lead but I wasn't about to question his orders. I hoped, since the river below was now gorged, there would be fewer, if any, Coldier patrols we would need to slip past.

"Stop!" He spoke firmly under his breath. We had only made it a quarter of the way. I wasn't sure what he saw that made him think it was safer to stop than try to finish the distance, though.

"What?" I whispered loudly toward him, trying to position myself behind one of the large metal trusses.

"Riflemen!" He said as he started to look around for where he could move quickly to be safe from fire.

I didn't say anything. I just stood there waiting for orders. He started to come back towards me. I assumed to get behind the same truss I was using for cover.

He only took two steps before I heard it. A deafening crack tore through the silence. I couldn't tell which direction it came from but it shook me. I quickly looked down to evaluate myself and make sure I hadn't been hit. I didn't feel anything, so I assumed it just missed and we were fine. I looked up, expecting him to keep walking toward me but he didn't take another step. He fell to his knees.

"Marcus?" I yelled, not being able to control my volume. I wanted to go to him to check how bad it was, but was afraid I'd be spotted as well.

"Eva... don't move, baby." He was so calm. For a moment, I thought he must be fine. How else could he be so calm?

"Okay. Are you all right?" I asked, hoping the same shock that hit me was what took him to his knees.

"Eva… Memento Schola?" He spoke to me in Latin.

"Yes, I remember my training. Why?" I was confused. We only used that language to communicate in situations where it was vital to our intel.

He pushed his hand up under his coat to his chest. "Eva… Memento Schola. I'm hit."

"What?" No sooner than I asked, he pulled his hand back down and away to look at it, now slick with blood.

"You can't be hit." I didn't know why I was arguing with him. It was obvious he was but I couldn't help but feel compelled to deny it.

"Eva… they're going to catch you, you have to run." He insisted, looking up at me, his eyes growing weary.

"No, I can't leave you. Here, let me help you—"

"Stop!" He cut me off. "You can't save me. You need to run!" He said it as firmly as he could.

"Marcus," I started to argue again, but knew I shouldn't. Catching movement in my peripheral, I looked away to see men now on the river banks coming towards us. "I can't leave you, they're coming."

He turned to see where they were, then looked back down at his hand to gauge his condition.

"Eva… I love you, baby, but you need to follow my orders now, all right?" He said it slowly so I would understand him, "You need to kill me, then run. You can't let them capture you."

"I can't kill you." I didn't care to argue with him this time. I couldn't do what he was asking.

"You have to kill me, Eva, memento schola. We can't let them have the intel." His voice was coarse. I knew I needed to follow his orders even though I didn't want to. I knew he was right. I couldn't save him, and I wouldn't be able to outrun them now, either. If we were both caught alive, they would torture me in front of him to find out what we knew. If I killed him, they might let me go, thinking I was just his Gypsyin captive, now taking this opportunity to free myself.

I pulled my knife from a sheath at my ankle and got down to crawl over toward him.

"Marcus…" I said softly. He was now laying on his side facing me with the blood flowing a little more easily from the hole in his chest. "I love you… I'm sorry, Marcus… I'm so sorry."

He looked up at me. All I could see was torment in his eyes. I knew he would do it for me if he could. "Killmeeva…" The words slurred together as they flowed from his mouth.

"I'm sorry," I said one last time as I took my knife and thrust it deep into his back where I knew I would hit something vital enough to help him pass quickly. I glanced up to see the Coldiers were getting closer. I waited until I could tell his breathing had stopped, then I pulled it out and struck him with it again, then again, and again. I started to scream with every strike, knowing I needed to make it look like I wanted him dead.

Before I knew it, there were Coldiers all around me. They were screaming something at me but I was too distraught to comprehend it. I dropped the knife and lay myself flat on the ground. My hands were now covered with his blood.

16

EXPOSED

This time I woke up on my own, no one calling out my name, no one shaking me. I was laying there, again in the back seat with my hands still both tied. As I opened my eyes, all I could see looking straight up was Miles. My head was in his lap. He was looking back at me, apparently watching me sleep.

"Who's Marcus?" He asked softly, seeing I was now awake.

I relaxed and looked straight up at the ceiling. I remembered now. It wasn't everything, but I definitely was remembering more. I lay there for a second, trying to think about how I wanted to respond. *Do I want to tell him everything? Do I want to be totally honest and not hold anything back?* I needed to formulate a plan in my head on how to proceed. *Do I trust him?* I asked myself…

"What is worse, never remembering the love of your life, or remembering and realizing you were the one who killed them?" I asked, finally deciding to answer him with a question.

He brought his hand to my face, then using his thumb, he wiped the tears away from under my eyes. "If you could bring him back, knowing he might never remember you or love you again, would you?" He asked quietly, with a gentle demeanor.

I was conflicted between genuinely thinking about how I would answer that question and knowing why he asked it. I remembered my childhood now. I remembered Marcus. I remembered our mission, what we were to each other. I remembered the Coldiers taking me that day, interrogating me. I remembered so much about who I was as Eva, but I still hadn't remembered yet where or why I turned and morphed into Kaleah. I didn't remember Miles yet, how we met, or anything about our relationship.

I knew the answer, but I didn't want to tell him.

I would... If I had a chance to see Marcus again, for him to be alive, I would do anything to save him. Even if he never loved me again, just knowing he was alive would be enough. I knew that was what Miles was trying to show me, the reason he did what he did to bring my memory back, but I didn't want to admit he was right. With the pain I was now feeling inside, it didn't seem fair that I would have to suffer just so that he could have *her* back.

"I can't answer that," I said, in honesty not really knowing how to answer him.

"What happened to Kaleah was my fault, but if I had to erase the memory of her, trying to erase the pain of my failure, I wouldn't." He finally answered my original question.

I didn't respond. I kept my eyes straight, trying to not look at him, my tears now welling up enough to cloud my vision.

"Tell me about him..." He said, inviting me to open up. Probably knowing it'd only get worse if I suppressed the feelings. I saw the kindness in his suggestion, the sacrifice he was willing to make to listen to me talk about another man.

"He was an agent like me, but he wasn't a Gypsyin, he was a Sicari. We met at the Praetorium. I was being assigned to the field for the first time and he was my superior. We were only supposed to be in the field together for a year. But one year turned into two, then three. We worked together so well, he was able to convince them not to reassign either of us. It didn't take long before our relationship grew from being strictly professional to something more. Something that wasn't allowed. It was against the rules. We both knew it... We knew we couldn't let them see we loved each other. It wasn't the disciplinary action we were afraid of though, we didn't want them to pull us apart and put us on different assignments. He was a lot like you," I said, finally allowing myself to look at Miles.

"He was strong, stubborn, handsome… loyal… Loyal to me, yes, but more loyal to the cause… That's what killed him. He wouldn't let me try to save him. Memento Schola—remember your training, he kept telling me. The security of our intel was more important than our lives. But he knew I loved him more than the cause. I would have told them everything if it would have saved him." I stopped there, knowing I was getting too emotional and didn't want to go on.

"Kaleah never told me about him. She told me the Coldiers shot a guy she was with at Nashville but…" He said softly, looking away, speaking almost to himself as much as he was to me. "She didn't remember…" He said it like it was a new profound revelation. "Holy shit, I think I know what happened to you… Eva, were you captured after they shot him?" He asked with a quizzical look on his face, as if trying to solve a puzzle.

"Yes," I said, not wanting to divulge any more information than I needed to.

"That's where Kaleah came from." He said it like he just figured it all out. "You must have already had an injection before I met you. It makes so much sense now. When they released you the first time, you wouldn't have known your name. You wouldn't have known you were an agent… She wasn't pretending… Kaleah wasn't pretending she wasn't a spy, she didn't remember." His face flooded with relief the more he unraveled the mystery.

"Did you think she lied to you?" I asked, trying to figure it all out myself.

He relaxed as the tension from his moment of enlightenment dissipated. "I didn't know. It just didn't make sense. That wasn't her…" He paused. "That's why she called me Jake when you call me Miles. Agents refer to each other with their last names. That's why she didn't fight me. She never fought me. She just ran, anytime she was scared, she just ran."

I was confused. *Why would Kaleah have needed to fight him?*

"You never told me how you met," I said, figuring this was a good time for him to finally tell me since those memories still hadn't come back.

"I guess it wouldn't hurt you to know now," he said. "Wait, if you can remember Marcus, can you not remember me?"

"Not yet." I didn't want to disappoint him but I hoped he could see I was telling the truth. "Just my earlier memories have come back. I don't remember anything after Marcus yet."

"Oh, okay," he sounded disheartened. "If you want, I'll tell you all about us."

"Please," I said softly.

"I got a letter from my commanding officer. I had only been back at base for a few days. I had just returned from a mission. I was tired and irritable but he said it was important and that I was the only man he had available to send. He also told me he couldn't trust anyone else. I'm still not sure why. He gave me the letter and the coordinates and told me it was important that I get the prisoner back to him unharmed. That was my job. I was the one who transported valuable assets, high-profile prisoners. They sent me all over the place."

"Who was the prisoner?" I interrupted him to ask.

"You," He paused to look back down at me.

"What? You just agreed that I didn't know who I was. I wasn't a spy anymore. Why would you come after *me*?" I asked, now turning myself to sit up so I could face him.

"I didn't have to chase you. You came willingly. You said you were tired of being alone and knew the consequences, so you sent for us… Ah well, you sent for the Sicari actually to come pick you up."

"Well, if I sent for the Sicari, what did I do when I found out you were a Coldier?" I asked.

"Yeah uh… that's a really long story. You weren't happy, I will say that, but you learned to trust me." He reached his hand down to rest it on top of mine, both still tied together. I started to pull away, but didn't. I needed him to feel like I was trusting him again.

"Did I love you?" I asked, trying to get all the information I could out of him in case I needed to use it against him later.

"Kaleah was complicated but yes, I believe you did. I can see now for obvious reasons why you had a hard time letting go though, and accepting how you felt for me."

"What made you love her?" I asked.

"How could I not?" He relaxed, "I still remember the first time I saw you." He looked at me, his eyes lost in the memory. "I knew the letter said you were dangerous but I could tell early on it wasn't true. When I slipped up on you that day, you were just sitting there, not a care in the world. You didn't turn to see who was coming. You didn't even act like you knew I was there. Of course, memory or not, you were still the same stubborn, smart mouth that you are now. You didn't make it too hard for me, though. After I had to tackle you, you seemed to comply quite easily." He smirked and looked away for a second.

"It's weird though, you know… the way things happen? I never expected to feel for someone the way I did, so quickly or easily. It wasn't love at first sight. To be honest, you were a little rough looking at first and I was still pretty irritable from my workload and all. But it didn't take long before I knew. A couple of days in, we were walking through a field and you got soaking wet. Granted, with my training, it was pretty instinctual what I should do; you would have gotten hypothermia if—"

"Are you serious? You didn't!" I interrupted, remembering what the Sicari trained us to do if that happened.

"No…" He said with a loud chuckle. "Believe me, I wanted to, but no. I just warmed you back up inside my jacket." He looked back down into my eyes. "The way your hair, all soaking wet, laid against your face. I hadn't even touched you yet when I knew I was falling in love with you. I think it shocked me more than anything else. I fought against it for days, weeks even. I told myself you can't feel like that for someone so quickly. It's not possible… On top of that, I knew you were a Gypsyin. I told myself I couldn't love a Gypsyin. I knew what they were going to do to you when I got you back to base. It messed up my whole mission. I was compromised, and I knew it."

I regretted asking the question. He answered it so well; I felt compelled to like him. I needed to ask him harder questions. I wanted to trip him up. I didn't know what, but he had to be hiding something from me. "If you knew they would erase her memory, and you loved her like you say you did then why did you still take her to your base like you were ordered?"

"I didn't take you like I was ordered," he said defensively. "That's not what we were doing there. I was taking you just outside the city to hide you so I could go and deactivate my tracker. They were never supposed to find us together."

"Well, you said you screwed up. What did you do?"

"I loved you too much… If I would have left you sooner, they would have never found you." He paused briefly, tensing up a little as he pulled his hand back. "Are you happy? Is that what you wanted to know? I know you're trying to manipulate me. You're using the classic interrogation techniques. But I can see right through it. I'm an agent too, remember? Your spy shit isn't gonna work on me, but nice try." He was obviously upset. He quickly turned, opened his door, and got out of the car.

"Miles… I'm sorry," I said, but the door shut too quickly for him to hear it.

I sat back and watched him as he walked around to the front passenger's side. He opened the door, bent down, and started rummaging around, looking for something in the seat directly in front of me.

He was a Coldier and I, Eva, a Sicari was his enemy. An enemy he thought was intentionally holding hostage the apparent love of his life, Kaleah—also me. *This is insane…*

"Jake," I said, trying to get his attention.

"Don't call me that," he snapped back at me. "Kaleah can call me that when she comes back. I'm Miles to you."

"Fine then, Miles, I have to pee," I said, trying to look at him through the gap under the headrest.

"Sure, I'll let you out to pee when you take your medicine." He replied still rummaging around.

"Oh my gosh, are you freakin' serious?" I asked, knowing he probably was. I didn't want to take the medicine but knew if I refused I wouldn't like the alternative. "What's next? You won't feed me unless I comply?"

"Hey, don't give me good ideas if you don't want me to use them," he said, standing up with the medicine now in his hand. He took a few steps back to my door and opened it.

"I have to pee too bad! Let me go first and then I'll take it," I said, looking up at him.

"Nope, I wasn't born yesterday. Sorry," he reached in and took hold of my arm to help me out of the car.

I got out and stood there looking at him. He held up a small brown glass bottle and started to unscrew the cap.

"Eva," he looked at me dead in the eyes, "I know what you're capable of now. Please don't try anything. I don't want to accidentally hurt you, all right?"

"Just give it to me," I said, figuring I might as well get it over with.

He held up the bottle and poured the liquid into the cap until it was almost full. He slowly moved it toward my face and set it against the top of my lower lip. I sipped it and swallowed.

"Thank you," He said as he replaced the cap and put the bottle in his pocket.

He let me pee even though I wasn't allowed to go farther than the other side of the car. I asked him one more time if he would remove my ties but he refused. It didn't take long until I was completely drained of energy again as well. I crawled back into the back seat of the car and lay down before I realized he intended for me to eat. He reached out to hand me some food from the front seat. I was too exhausted to ingest anything, so I declined, then turned over to snuggle myself back up to the seat-back. Without much effort, I swiftly drifted back off to sleep.

We drove for what had to be another few hours; half of which I was still asleep and the other half awake but pretending to still be asleep. It was the perfect time to lie there and think to myself about everything. I had more memories that were starting to come back. It was strange how I could tell there were new ones while still trying to separate them from the old ones. It was as if they had been there the whole time but they were just in a shadow and for whatever reason; the shadow dissipated, and they were revealed to me again. Some would reappear if I thought about them hard enough, like Marcus, for example.

I wanted to remember more about him, so I lay there thinking, almost daydreaming. Then, as clear as the memories from the last day, I could see them. I could see him again standing in front of me. I could feel him again the way he touched me. The way his words sounded coming from his mouth, he had an accent. It was southern. I could remember his smile. He had the most handsome smile. It didn't take long before I could feel the pain of his absence boiling up inside me.

I didn't want to fall in love with Miles the same way Kaleah did. I was still in love with Marcus. I could feel the hatred for the Coldiers slowly building within me as more and more memories revealed themselves as well. Miles didn't seem like a bad guy, but to be with him felt like I would be stabbing Marcus in the back all over again. *What would he think to see me with the very side that made me kill him before they tortured me, erased my mind, then left me to die?* Even if Miles had the best intentions, I couldn't let myself love him again. I wasn't Kaleah anymore, and I didn't have her memories yet either, so until then I wasn't about to allow myself to see in him whatever she thought she did.

I was afraid to keep sleeping so much even though my body was giving me no choice. I realized every time I did I was potentially giving Miles insight into every memory that was returning without even knowing it. The longer I lay there the more I thought about what I wanted, and how I was to go about getting it. I didn't want to love him. I couldn't let myself be with him. I still belonged to Marcus, not anyone else. I wanted to go back to the Praetorium. I had to return to give them the intel that I now remembered from before Marcus was shot. I didn't know where Miles intended to take me, but I decided my mission was to now get free from him and return to the Praetorium, the Sicari's Central station.

I realized since he knew I was an agent now he would most likely keep a closer eye on me than he had Kaleah. Just like he knew I was using interrogation tactics earlier, he would now be watching for more of my training to come out.

I was too weak to go anywhere on my own yet. I could barely stay awake long enough to have a decent conversation. I knew I had to stay with him until I could fully recover and potentially long enough to make him trust me again. He would be able to tell if I was acting like I was Kaleah, and without her memories that wouldn't be easy to do, anyway. I had to pretend I, Eva, was now falling in love with him just as she did. I just needed to buy myself enough time for the plan I devised in my head to work.

I was shaken from my thoughts by a sudden rattling of the car as we turned onto a gravel road. I rolled over to face the front, used my hands for leverage against the seat, and set myself up to look out the window to see where we were. It was nearing dusk. The sky was a pretty golden color. Wherever we were, it had to be far from the city. I could see as we passed, the trees were very dense and full.

"Where are you taking me?" I asked, acting afraid.

"I'm hoping you will remember it when we get there. It's the little cabin we stayed in together. It had almost everything left intact, beds and all. I think it's too far out for looters to bother with it. You loved it there." He said, his voice was now upbeat and optimistic.

I didn't know how to respond. I just kept staring out the window as we went further down the gravel rabbit hole. I wanted to try to be more kind and gentle with him. I assumed the way Kaleah had been, what he probably fell in love with. But I also didn't want to do it so abruptly that it was obvious that I was trying to manipulate him, either. It was going to be tricky. I was going to have to feather the effect of turning myself slowly into her, all while hoping I didn't lose who I actually was now in the process.

"Don't be scared. You really did love it there before we had to move on. That's why I wanted to bring you back. I think it will be a nice little home for us," he said it so gently I was starting to feel bad for him, almost guilty, knowing my intentions.

We pulled up and parked the car just in front of a large old two-story pole barn that set just to the left of what, I'm sure, was the little cabin he had been referring to. From what I could see through the window, it looked small but quaint. It also looked like it wouldn't be hard to keep it warm inside; I could already imagine a billowing pillar of smoke emanating from the small brick chimney set atop the tiny shingle roof.

"Wait here while I go and inspect it, make sure it's safe for us still." He said getting out and making sure the child safety locks were flipped on on both back doors before he walked away.

I wasn't sure what he did to prevent me from escaping through the front doors but I didn't attempt it. I didn't have enough energy; maybe he knew that. Before long, he returned and got all his bags out of the trunk and took them in, still leaving me to wait in the car. Then finally, after a few minutes of who knows what he was up to inside, he came back out to retrieve me.

To no surprise, it was just as quaint on the inside as I had expected it might be from what I saw on the outside. Everything was nice and tidy and in its place; nothing like I would think an abandoned house might look. He had already started a fire in the little wood stove that sat next to one of the side walls in the living room. It wasn't quite warm inside yet but I could tell it probably wouldn't be long until it got that way and I would need to remove a few layers.

"What do you think?" He asked with a smile, seeking my approval. "I'm hoping it can help bring back some memories for you.

You enjoyed sitting in that chair and looking out the window." He said as he pointed over to a large gray recliner perfectly positioned beside the fire facing the window.

"I bet I did," I smiled back, trying to create pleasant small talk. I wanted him to feel comfortable enough around me that he might finally release my hands. "It's nice here. What is the bedroom like?" I asked as I sat down in the recliner and started to stare out the window. Even though I just had ample sleep in the car, I already wanted to lie down and pass out.

"Are you tired again?" He asked, looking down at me. "The doctor said the medicine would do that. You should feel better once all your memories come back and you don't need to take it any longer."

"Yes, I'm exhausted. It's getting annoying, I would like to feel productive again." I responded. I caught a bit of information however that he might not have intended for me to and shoved it into a safe place in my mind to bring up later. I wouldn't be tired if I stopped taking the medicine. That was excellent knowledge I needed for my future plans.

"The bedroom is as nice as it is out here. There are two of them, actually. Only one of them has a mattress on the bed though," he said, answering my original question.

"Are you going to make me sleep all tied up?" I was hoping I had been nice enough that he wouldn't still feel the need to restrain me.

"I was thinking about that, seeing as you're dangerous now and all." He took a chair from beside the kitchen table and pulled it up to sit in front of me, so he could see me as we talked. "If you were trained, like I think you were, those restraints aren't going to stop you from escaping. They wouldn't even stop you from trying to attack me, but you haven't. Why?... Could it be because you're making plans up in that little spy head of yours?"

Dammit, he's smart! He was already a step ahead of me. This made me rethink the previous intel I thought he let slip. It could be a lie to trap me or he could be using reverse psychology so I would keep taking it. I wasn't sure anymore. It was as if my life was one big constant chess game and until now I was always the winner. I had yet to find an opponent as skilled and bright as myself. But there he was now, sitting in front of me, almost like he could read my thoughts.

"Well, if you know they aren't doing you any good, I would like if you removed them now." I was intrigued by him and interested in seeing what would come from our verbal volleying.

He leaned back in the chair to observe me. "If you don't want them on anymore, that's fine. Go ahead and take them off. I know you can do it yourself. I won't stop you, go ahead."

I stared at him for a minute. I didn't want to show him he was right and boost his ego, but at the same time; I was thoroughly over having my hands bound. Without looking down, still staring at him, I worked my hands around themselves and maneuvered them until the cordage was loose. Before too long, I was able to pull them away from each other and was free, with the cord now sitting in a loose bundle in my lap.

"Happy?" I asked, now irritated that he gave me no choice but to expose both my plan and my skills.

"Very!" He smiled, seeing he had won this round. "So here's your choice… You can sleep on the bed with me so I can wake up if you attempt to escape or you can sleep in the cellar."

I was now more irritated with him than before and I was sure he could see it all over my face. "That's not a choice! Besides, how do you know I won't try to kill you in your sleep?"

He chuckled. "Okay, let's say you could kill me…" a large smile overtook his face, "Let's just say it was possible, 'cause I mean… I don't know, maybe you are more bad-ass than me. How likely do you think it would be that you could do that if you don't even have enough energy to stay awake for ten minutes without collapsing; let alone fighting a fully trained Track and Capture Agent that's probably twice your weight?"

Dammit, he has a point. I wanted to sit there and devise an alternative plan since he just crapped all over my original one but he was right about that too. I didn't even have enough energy to sit there and argue with him, so I sure wasn't about to attack him while he slept.

"Ugh, fine! Just let me go to bed now then." I said, looking toward the hall where I assumed the room was.

"No problem, but you're gonna eat first. You haven't eaten all day. How are you going to be able to kill me if you won't eat? I'm gonna have to help get you all built back up. If you're plannin' anything, you're gonna need your strength, don't ya think?" He said it sarcastically, half-serious but obviously joking.

I complied. I sat there, trying to hold myself up long enough to get something down until he was satisfied. Before long, he gave me the all-clear and said he would show me the bedroom. I don't know if I really had eaten enough or if I just looked so close to passing out again that he felt bad and agreed so he wouldn't have to carry me to bed.

I followed him back to a small room off of the end of the hall. It was so dark I could barely make out the silhouette of a large bed frame.

"The window won't do you any good if you're still thinking about escaping. I already tied it shut from the outside. I'll come lie down next to you when I'm ready to go to sleep," he said, holding my arm as he gently helped guide me over to the bed.

"Did you make Kaleah sleep with you, too? Is that why you think she loved you? 'Cause she didn't fight you every time you forced her to—"

"Stop it!" Now irritated, he quickly interrupted me with a slight jerk of his hand against my arm. He slowly lowered himself to look me directly in the eye. "I never forced you to do anything with me you didn't want to do." He said, earnestly.

I didn't say anything else. I just turned away from him to lie down and curl up on my side, facing the darkness of the rest of the room. It wasn't long before I drifted off to sleep.

17

APPLES AND ARROWS

I don't know how long I had been asleep but when I woke up, it was still dark outside and very dark in the room. I didn't hear Miles laying next to me but reached out my arm to feel with my hand just in case he was there and it was too dark to see him. He wasn't; I was alone. Part of me didn't mind and thought maybe I should just go back to sleep but part of me was curious to see where he was.

I rolled over to find the edge of the bed. I must have been too tired to notice when I got into it but the springs were quite loud. If I had wanted to use this opportunity to be sneaky, the mattress sure hadn't done me any favors. Wherever he was, I'm sure Miles already heard me coming.

Realizing I lost the element of surprise I gave up on any clever ideas I had and just let myself act normal. After standing up from the edge of the bed, I made my way slowly through the dark to find the door. I expected more light to come in after opening it, but when I did, it was almost just as dark in the hall as it had been in the room. I ran my hands along the hall walls as I walked closer toward the living room, now really curious to see where Miles was and why he had not come to lie down like he said he would.

Running my fingertips along both walls as I walked forward, I could feel where they ended and the hall stopped. The living room was barely brighter than the hall or the bedroom. I could make out shadows, but not well. The light from the fire that was there from when I arrived had now dissipated into nothing and the room was quite a bit colder, verging on chilly. Miles must have let the fire go out. I stood there and looked around, trying to make out what shadows were what and where I should walk next.

"Why do you hate me?" A deep voice murmured from the general direction I had expected the recliner to be in.

"Miles?" I asked, not sure what mind games he was attempting to play.

"Answer my question, Eva!" His tone was low and stern, not sounding like the same man I had been accustomed to since I woke up in C and R.

"I… I don't hate you. What are you doing in here? Why didn't you come to bed like you said you would?" I asked, still trying to make out the room so I could move closer without falling over something.

"You don't have to run. When you're well enough to leave, I'll let you go if you want. I won't keep you here," he said, his voice now sounded a bit distraught.

"Okay, but by *well,* do you mean I have all of my memory back or I have my energy back?" I asked, wanting to get a good idea of what kind of deal we were making.

"Either… If Kaleah never comes back, then I'll just have to deal with the loss then. I'm not going to hold you against your will trying to make you love me." his voice was still low and somber.

I used my hands to try to feel for anything large that I might run into as I slowly walked toward him.

"I know you have a bad history with men but I didn't force you to do anything with me."

"Jake, I'm sorry I said that to you. I didn't mean to hurt you," I replied, still taking sweeping steps in his direction.

"Stop…"

Stop? Instantly I realized I called him Jake without being aware of it, honestly not trying to manipulate him again.

"Stop!" He said again louder.

Before I got a chance to tell him I said his first name accidentally, suddenly a sharp stabbing pain pierced my thigh. I must have run into something.

"Ow, what the hell?" I didn't know what I hit, but it hurt badly.

"I told you to stop! Stand still. I'll get some light." The clang of the recliner springs crunched as he stood followed by the thud of boots walking over to the table. A quick hiss of a zipper indicated he'd found his bags.

"How can you see where you're going?" I asked, taking my hand and trying to inspect my leg as well as I could in the dark.

"Maybe I have night vision goggles, maybe I don't. Maybe I just ate a crap ton of carrots as a kid, wouldn't you love to know?" he said sarcastically as he continued to rummage through his bags.

"Shit, I think I'm bleeding," I said out loud, but more for myself than for him.

"You might be. You ran into the wood rack next to the stove." His voice now sounded closer to me.

My eyes picked up the light of the flame before my ears recognized the sound of the match that he struck suddenly against something close to me. He reached over and lit an oil-burning lamp that he must have found somewhere, considering I hadn't seen it when we first came in. His face, set aglow by the lamp, appeared before me now more ominous than friendly with the flickering of shadows and light bouncing off of it.

I looked back down at my leg. I had started to bleed through my pants. I had been in much worse pain but that didn't mean it didn't still hurt really bad. I pulled my hand up to look. My fingers were now saturated with it. I rubbed them against themselves as I held my hand up close to my face to examine them. It didn't take long before I noticed the sight of the blood was starting to bother me. *This is new.* I never had issues seeing blood before.

"Come, sit down. Let me take a look and see what you did," Miles said, pointing toward a chair at the dining table.

I walked over and pulled the chair out, then sat on the edge of the seat, extending my leg out toward him.

"You're bleeding a lot!" He sounded surprised. "I won't be able to get to it by pulling your pant leg up, you'll have to take them off." He looked up at me with a face full of professionalism.

I didn't say anything. I was trying to stop myself from feeling sick, still thinking about the blood on my fingers. I didn't think he had bad intentions, but wasn't feeling much like caring. I stood up, pulled them down, gently kicked them off then sat back down on the edge of the seat again.

"It's cold in here." I couldn't help but state the obvious.

"Yeah, I didn't have enough time earlier to gather firewood. Sorry, I'll do it later when you're asleep," he said, now bending over to examine the wound. "It's deep. I'm going to have to run some stitches through it," he said, looking up at me.

"Dammit, okay… that's fine. What did I even run into?" I looked back over toward the stove. Really, I was just trying to avoid looking down at my leg since I didn't want to see the blood again.

"There's a thin piece of metal on the top edge of the wood-rack that's sharp. I almost cut myself on it earlier when I was making the fire. I didn't think to tell you about it, sorry." He was now back up, sifting through his bags again, most likely looking for his sewing kit.

"Miles, I think I'm going to pass out. I'm getting light-headed." I couldn't stop myself from thinking about the blood.

"Okay, are you feeling tired again? Do you want to lie down on the floor?" He grabbed a few things out of his bag and sat them down on the table.

"No, that's not my problem, it's the blood," I said, glancing back down at it, "I've never had this problem before but I—"

"Don't worry about it. Here, let me help you." He came around to my side and cradled me like he was going to lift me. Then, holding my weight, he slid me off the chair and slowly lowered me to the floor. "I'm not sure it's the best idea but there is some alcohol down in the cellar. If you want, I can get it for you. It might help with the pain while I stitch it up and probably help with whatever issues you're having thinking about the blood."

"Okay!" I didn't hesitate. The idea sounded pretty attractive to me at that moment.

"All right," he said, standing up. "You can't drink much, though. I'm not sure of the proof. It looks homemade." Then he turned and opened the door to go outside.

I lay myself back against the floor. It was freezing, but now with all the blood centralizing at my core in preparation for me passing out, the floor's chill against my back was soothing. I lay there for what felt like an eternity, trying not to think about the blood, without much luck. It didn't help that I could feel it now trickling down my leg, since my pants were no longer there to collect it.

"I got it," a voice spoke as the door opened then shut all while letting in a large gust of frigid air. "You still with me, or have you already blacked out?"

"No, but I'm close. You need to stop it from bleeding. Just give me a shot of that stuff so you can sew it up," I said it quickly, so he knew I was in a hurry to get it done and over with.

"Ok, here." He took off the cap and handed me the full bottle.

I sat up, took the bottle from him, and started to take a few large gulps until suddenly he jerked it back away from me.

"You can't have that much. Stop it! Did you not hear me when I told you I didn't know how concentrated it was." He scolded, then replaced the cap and looked down at me with a face full of disapproval.

"Sorry," I said it but I didn't mean it. I wasn't sorry at all. I wanted it to disappear. I didn't want to see the blood anymore. I lay back down against the floor and relaxed. "That stuff's strong. I should be fine now, sew it up."

"You're ridiculous!" He said, still sounding critical, "You know... maybe Kaleah *is* coming back 'cause that's the shit she would do."

I didn't respond. I just lay there waiting for him to get the needle and thread ready while he cleaned up the wound in preparation for the stitches. After a while, still expecting to feel the pain, I was surprised when I didn't notice it any longer. I thought I was still awake but wasn't sure of that anymore, either. It was easy to relax with the thought of the blood no longer bothering me. For a moment I thought I must have been asleep because I couldn't hear anything anymore but then I heard Miles speak again.

"Am I hurting you?" He asked. "I can't tell whether that stuff did the trick or you can really handle your pain."

"I wanna say I can handle my pain," I chuckled, not able to control it, "but… that stuff is pretty potent. I feel really nice and kinda float-y, ya know?"

He might have responded, but I didn't hear him. I was starting to feel extremely calm and peaceful, a nice change from the mental anguish I had been used to since my memories of Marcus had returned.

"Ok, I'm almost done. Give me a minute and I'll get something to cover you up. You have goosebumps all over your legs. I knew it was cold in here but I…" He kept talking but I could only understand pieces of it until I drifted back off into my own little world.

I wasn't sure how I got there but the next thing I remembered was lying in the bed, now with a heavy cover draped over me. There was a dim glow barely emanating from a little lamp over in the corner sitting on a small table. It was just enough to see figures without much detail. He was laying there next to me, fully clothed outside the covers.

"Why do you have your clothes on?" I was confused about why he didn't want to snuggle up next to me. We always snuggled at night before going to sleep.

"What?" He looked over at me, confused.

"I'm cold, I need you to warm me up." I smiled sweetly.

"Uh, I… but you uh…" He still sounded confused for whatever reason.

"Do you not want to?" I asked, curious why he was hesitating but also trying to hurry him up.

"Ah, yea that's fine. Hang on, if you're cold… Yeah, I guess that's fine." He sat up and pulled his shirt off. I couldn't help but stare at him, letting my eyes trail down his muscular frame. Then stood up and unbuttoned his pants and slid them off as well before getting back into bed with me.

I lay there facing him, waiting for him to come over and curl up next to me. He got close but not quite up against me like he was waiting for something.

"Uh, it might be easier for me to warm you up if you turned around. Your back can take all the heat from my chest." He acted clueless to what I really wanted.

I looked up at his face. His head was above mine so I couldn't see his eyes. I pushed with my feet against the bed slowly inching myself to where our faces lined up.

"Why are you acting so coy? We both want the same thing," I said now looking him straight in the eyes.

"Eva, I don't think—" he started to respond before I got impatient and leaned in to kiss him.

His kiss was different from what I remembered. Even though I surprised him, he didn't pull back. He leaned into me and kissed me back like he meant it. He was assertive, at the same time gentle. He wrapped one hand behind my head and used the other one to push himself up off the bed just enough to get closer to me.

His lips were soft and warm, as was his body. I had been kind of cold but I mostly made it up for an excuse to make him get closer. He kissed me like he hadn't kissed me in forever, like I died and was just resurrected. It didn't make sense to me but I didn't mind. He was passionate, and I liked it.

"Make love to me," I whispered.

Suddenly, he stopped kissing me and hesitated slightly before returning to it. I wasn't sure if what I said bothered him somehow but was too worked up to care.

"Now, Marcus… please…" I begged.

His body tensed up as soon as the words came out of my mouth. He paused and lowered himself away from me slightly.

"What's wrong?" I asked, not understanding why he would stop.

He didn't answer. He just lay there, looking down at the blankets, thinking to himself.

"I'm… I'm sorry, did I do something wrong? Why did you stop?" I thought he might answer if I asked him again.

"Ka… Eva, it's… ask me in the morning. I'll tell you why if you ask me when we wake up," he said, sounding disappointed.

I tried again. "I don't understand. I'm sorry if I did something to—"

"Stop, you're fine. You didn't do anything. I really… I…" He paused. "It was nice. I missed you. I wish I could have… uh… Ask me in the morning, I'll tell you if you ask me, okay?"

"All right," I said, trying not to feel rejected. I rolled over slowly and pulled the cover back up over me. I lay there for a minute trying to think about why he would stop but nothing was making any sense. My thoughts were haphazard at best. Before long, I slowly relaxed and fell back to sleep.

The next morning, I wasn't sure where Miles went. He wasn't next to me when I woke up. I couldn't really remember anything after he stitched me up but I still would have expected him to be in the bed with me like he originally said he would. Unless he was still mad about what I had said that he made Kaleah do… *Did he decide to sleep in the recliner after all?*

I worked my way into the living room. There was now a sharp pain in my leg that made it difficult but I managed. I didn't see Miles there, either. If he was comfortable enough now to leave me without guard, he must have been serious the night before when he said he wasn't going to stop me from leaving if I wanted.

There was food on the table and a fire now in the stove. The room was warm and cozy again. It also looked like he attempted to clean up all the blood. I sat down at the table to eat and looked over toward the wood-stove to see what I had run into that would have cut me so badly. There was nothing there anymore. He must have removed the wood-rack while I slept as well.

After I finished eating, I worked my way over to the recliner to sit down and watch for him out the window. I didn't have anything else to do but sit there and think. I wasn't sure what I wanted to do anymore, and that bothered me. He was disrupting the plans I made in my head.

It was like what I had seen in movies as a child. I had a devil on one shoulder and an angel on the other. I guess to Miles the devil would be Eva and the angel was Kaleah. Kaleah wasn't even back yet but I couldn't help but think about her and what she would want. Even though I still didn't have her memories, I realized there was a side of me that was her. I didn't want her memories to dominate mine when they returned, though. That concerned me.

I wanted to sit there and think about Marcus. This was probably the first chance I had to mourn for him. However, at the same time, I couldn't stop thinking about Miles and what Kaleah saw in him. I was torn between the two. Miles wanted me to love him, but he didn't really love me, *Eva*. He loved Kaleah and wanted her back. Plus, even if I wanted to, I couldn't love him. My heart was always going to belong to Marcus.

The angel shoulder wanted me to see there was no choice, and I just needed to move on and let go. After all, it had probably been years since I lost Marcus. However, the devil shoulder wanted me to live in the past and stew over what I had done and what the Coldiers had done to me. It also wanted me to think of Miles as the enemy. After all, he was a Coldier, and the Coldiers were no longer good in my mind, not after everything they had done and all the pain they caused me.

I was stuck between my past and my present, waiting for myself to decide which to choose so that I could formulate a plan for my future. I had to ask myself again what I wanted. How could I stay with Miles and live in this cabin with him alone just the two of us, for the rest of our lives? If I chose that path, I wouldn't really be choosing. I would just be letting him and Kaleah choose for me. But would my other option be any better of a life? If I left him, I would go back with the Sicari but I knew that was risky. Did I want to be a spy and be forced back out in the field again? I wasn't sure anymore. I sat there, beginning to daydream, trying to decide what I wanted to do.

I hadn't felt tired again. Maybe it was because I hadn't been awake for long or maybe it was because I hadn't taken any more of the medicine yet. Either way, it made me want to get up and do something.

Looking out the window, there were a few small outbuildings in the distance next to a small grove of trees, what I assumed was an orchard. I felt like I probably had enough energy to walk to the orchard and back without help. I thought it would be nice to see the trees. Depending on how long I would be here, potentially into spring, I wanted to know what different types of trees there were.

I got up and went over to the table. I didn't want to wear the pants that I had taken off that had blood all over them so I went through the bags to find another pair. It didn't take long until I got myself all suited up and ready to brave the cold, nippy air. I wanted to leave a note for Miles, but couldn't find a pen or paper. I thought for a second then walked back over to the window and drew an arrow on it in the condensation that had built up from the heat of the stove against the chilly air outside. Then next to the arrow I did my best to draw a little apple.

Upon opening the door, I was taken aback by the bite in the air. I hadn't quite expected it to be so cold. Thankfully, though, I had put on one of Miles' coats so I was confident that it would keep me relatively warm on my small trip across the yard. I stepped off the porch and walked toward the East where the sun had already risen but was hazy from all the cloud cover. I didn't take more than a few steps when suddenly I heard my name.

"Eva! Stop!" Miles yelled out to me. I looked over to see he had been collecting firewood quite a ways behind the house in an area I wasn't able to see out the window. "Don't take another step!"

I wanted to explain to him I wasn't trying to escape. I was just trying to walk over to the orchard but the cold dryness in the air made it hard for my throat to get enough moisture worked up to yell loud enough for him to hear me.

"I…" I tried to cough then swallow hard, "I'm…" I tried to cough again, "I'm just going over to the orchard." I pointed toward the trees that were in the direction I wanted to go.

"Don't move!" He yelled again as he dropped the pile of firewood that he had been carrying and started to run toward me.

"Fine! I won't. I wasn't trying to escape, you have to believe me." My throat was now cleared enough to yell it back over to him.

"Why would you even be out here? It's too cold? And you don't need to be walking on that leg, you might rip a stitch!" He said, slowing down as he got closer.

"I have enough energy now. I just wanted to get out and see the orchard," I said as I took another step in that direction.

"Eva, I swear if you take one more step when I told you not to, I'm gonna drag your ass back in to that house and tie it to a chair," he said it with a stern look like he probably meant it.

"You're not my boss. I can do whatever I want and go wherever I want," I argued back, not liking his threat.

"I am today! And right now you're gonna do what I tell you. What if I wasn't out here and you passed out again? How would I know how to find you?" He raised his voice a little, getting more upset.

I didn't respond. I just turned toward the orchard and took another step before I felt him pull against my arm.

"Eva, Stop! Dammit!" He tightened his grip to keep me from walking away. "I don't want to hurt you."

I spun around to pull my arm back and push him away from me with my free hand but he didn't let go. He gripped it tighter, then reached up and took a hold of my other arm now, too.

"Let go of me! Now!" I pulled again, trying to break my arms loose from his grip but he wouldn't release them.

Since he wouldn't let go when I asked, I moved in closer and twisted my arms around, bringing both my hands up and out forcefully breaking his grip.

His reflexes were faster than I anticipated. After I broke his grip from my arms, he didn't try to stop what I was about to do with my hands. *Throat punch him.* Instead, he shoved his whole body into me and wrapped his arms around the outside of both of mine at my waist. Then threw his weight against me, taking me to the ground to pin me below him. *Dammit!*

"Eva, stop it! I don't want to hurt you. Stop trying to fight me!" He said, breathing harder, still keeping all his weight on top of me.

"I don't want to hurt *you!* So get off me and let me go. You know what I'm capable of now, don't say I didn't warn you." I yelled back.

"Why won't you just listen to me? I'm trying to protect you!"

"Protect me from what? You're the only thing that's making it hard for me to breathe right now." My voice was softer but only from not being able to get more air to strengthen it.

"From killing yourself! There's a ten-foot hole in the ground somewhere over here." He started to relax after saying it, releasing just a little of his pressure off of me.

"Let me go," I said again, but more like a request than a demand, hoping he saw I had relaxed and wasn't still trying to fight him.

He looked down into my eyes, "If I let you up will you listen to me?"

I was about to respond until something reflective caught the corner of my eye. I turned my head to see what it was. It looked like a pen but I could tell it must have been something else. It was silver at one end and blue at the other. I stared at it for a second, forgetting to respond to his question, forgetting that he was even on top of me.

He looked over to see what I was looking at. "Eva! No… Don't!" He said, probably thinking I wanted to use it to stab him.

The longer I stared at it, the more I started to recognize it, then finally I realized what it was. The hairpin Jake gave me the day we left the cabin. Suddenly, so many new memories flooded into my mind. One after another, I could visualize them. I was alone… then Jake… then Seth… Seth's death… Jake and I together in the closet… We were captured. I remembered. It was all back. I remembered everything!

I looked back at him, now looking at me. His eyes were full of worry, probably wondering what I was about to do. Then his face changed along with his eyes. He could see something in mine, something that wasn't there before. "Kaleah?" He said softly.

"Jake…" No sooner had I said it, he released all his weight and sat up off of me.

"Kaleah!" He said as if releasing every ounce of agony he had built up thinking he would never see me again. He reached down to wrap his arms around me, then pulled me up to sit with him, holding the embrace. "Kaleah…" He tightened his hug, "I didn't know if you would ever come back."

I didn't say anything. I wanted to sit there and ruminate on all the memories and soak up his presence. I missed him so much.

"I'm sorry, Kaleah… I'm so sorry." His voice started to break up. "I never meant for you to get caught. I love you so much, baby. I'm so sorry."

Baby… The word instantly brought memories back up of Marcus. I wanted to sit there and feel immersed in the moment just as Jake was, but I couldn't. My memories of being Eva were now stopping me. Instantly my mind was like a battlefield, and my thoughts were now the weapons between two enemies.

"Take me inside. I'm cold, Jake. Will you take me inside?" I wanted him to enjoy this moment. He needed to be free of his guilt. But I needed to move. I had to distract myself. I could feel Eva inside me, her thoughts grappling for control. She didn't want him to win, she didn't want to love him.

"Sure," he said as he picked me up and carried me toward the house. My leg had bled into my pants again, but it didn't bother me like it had the night before.

I could tell he knew this changed things, and he wanted to talk

178

about it. I did too, but I wasn't sure how to explain to him that Eva was going to be a problem. However, if *I* was Eva, was *she* the problem, or was it Kaleah that was the problem? I didn't know who to be anymore, and I didn't know how to tell Jake about it. Also, if he knew, what would he even be able to do?

18

COLDIERS CREST

"Jake, we're not safe here. Eva didn't tell you everything," I told him as he lowered me to sit in the recliner.

"What?" I'm sure that's not what he thought he would be discussing with me the moment my memories returned.

"We're in danger. I have to tell you before she stops me." I could feel my mind trying to shift. I wanted to maintain control but my memories of being Eva were too strong. If I didn't hurry, my training would kick in and I wouldn't be able to tell him anything at all. "There's a lot I... *she* didn't tell you. She was trained not to. My memories... Eva's memories, they're fighting for dominance and she's stronger than me—Kaleah. If she takes over, I won't be able to tell you anymore, so you have to listen closely." I paused to take a breath. He sat down in front of me and nodded for me to continue.

"Do you remember when you told me about the Gypsyin units the Sicari sent out at the beginning of the war? You were right when you said they didn't have trackers on them since Gypsyins don't have tags. But you were wrong when you said they would decommission them when they went back. When I... Eva went back, they knew it was a problem, and they gave her a tracker."

"What?" His face was confused but I could tell he was still listening.

"I have a tracker, Jake. They put it in my head somewhere. Eva didn't tell you because she was hoping they would send Sicari to come find her. They could already be on their way, I don't know but we're not safe here."

"No, that doesn't make sense. If they were going to track you, they could have done it this whole time. Why would they come to get you now? It's been years since you had your memory erased in Nashville." He looked confused.

"It's complicated. I… she never told you who she really was… Who I really am… Jake, there are things I have to tell you, but I can't right now. I was never supposed to get caught at Nashville." I wanted to tell him everything all at once but I could feel resistance within myself.

"Ok, I believe you but I don't understand how we're in danger. Why would they track you now and not after your… once you turned into Kaleah? Why didn't they track Kaleah?" He was clearly trying to organize his thoughts, and he needed more information before he could make a game plan.

"The serum they use to erase people's memories has heavy metals in it. My tracker is like a radio beacon. Before you gave me the antidote, when the toxin was heavy in my blood, it interfered with the signal, so it couldn't broadcast. When your medicine flushed the toxins, it cleared my memory, but it cleared the metals that were disrupting the signal too." I finished, hoping it was more clear to him now.

"Oh my gosh, that makes sense." He looked down for a second to allow himself to process it. "Who are you that they want to track you down and bring you in so bad?" He asked, looking back up at me.

"The intel that I… Eva had, the Coldiers would kill to get it. That's probably why you were sent to pick me up, Miller… he's… Oh my gosh, she won't let me tell you… I, ugh… Jake, I'm sorry I want to but… She won't let me tell you her secrets…" I was beginning to feel quite frustrated with my dueling minds. "I started taking the medicine when I was at a Coldier base. My tracker might have come back online there. If that's what happened, the Sicari will think I'm a double agent. Both sides will try to come after me now."

"Okay… Don't worry, we're going to think about what to do. I'll keep you safe, baby, okay?" He sat back slowly, trying to concentrate.

"Jake, you have to be careful. Eva… She's not on your side. She's still very much a Sicari. Her motivation is to finish her mission. Marcus died for the intel that I'm carrying." I tried to think of the best way to warn him but didn't know how exactly to say it.

"How do I know when it's you or her talking to me, then?" He asked, looking back up at me.

"Use your instincts. You know Kaleah better than anyone else." I felt psychotic, but it was the truth. I didn't trust myself enough now, being a mixture of Eva and Kaleah, to be able to always steer him in the right direction. If I couldn't trust myself, he shouldn't either.

"Okay then, I'd ask you how much time you think we have until they're here but I can't see how that would change anything. If they're tracking you, they'll just follow us if we leave." His said, looking conflicted.

"You're right, you're not safe with me. When they get here hide and let them take me." I said, trying to convince him.

He looked up at my face and gave me a strange look. "Why would you say that? I would never just hide and let you get captured again!"

"Miles, I'm just thinking it might be the only way. I don't think they'll hurt me, and if they try, I can fight them off." No sooner had I said it than his face changed and his eyes began to look suspicious.

"Don't ever suggest something like that to me again, do you hear me?" He spoke the words clearly so I would know he was serious.

"Okay, then what do you think we should do?" I asked.

"I got a plan. But I can't trust… I'm not going to tell you. You will just have to trust me all right, Kaleah? It's best if you don't know right now. I will tell you what to do when the time comes." He started to rub my leg as he said it.

Suddenly I could envision myself, Kaleah, as a pawn stuck in a chess game with Jake and Eva as the opponents. Both trained, intelligent, sharp, and both fighting for and against me.

"Ok, I trust you." I smiled and put my hand on top of his. I was happy to have my memories back. I really did love him. I tried to focus on that and not think about Marcus or any of the memories I had of being Eva. I was in control when I didn't think about anything in that part of my past. It was when I let those memories slip in that I could tell it might turn into a downward spiral and I didn't know where that would lead but ultimately nowhere good for Jake.

He stood up and looked out the window not saying anything else. I wasn't sure what his plan was, but I was happy that he left me out of it. I couldn't trust that I would stay in my right mind and not try to sabotage him if Eva's memories somehow took over and tried to cloud my judgment. I wanted to stay here with him, love him as he loved me, and forget about my past. But I could tell the part of me that remembered everything she was and everything she had done wouldn't let me settle. It wanted to return to the Sicari.

"Did you see Miller after we were captured at Charlotte?" I asked, breaking the silence.

He turned to look at me, furrowing his brow. "Who's asking?"

"Does it matter?"

He turned back toward the window. "You have your past and I have mine… For right now, let's just leave it at that."

I didn't respond. He turned back toward me again. "There's snow coming. I can tell by the air. We need to get ready. I need to go get more wood or I won't have enough to keep the fire going tonight. We have some time to prepare. We drove here and they'll most likely use horses." He paused to look down. "Your leg is bleeding again. Do you need me to help you restitch it or will you be all right if I go get some more wood cut up to bring in?"

I looked down to see how bad my leg looked now. It was bleeding again, but not much. "I'll be fine. I can sew it back up myself if I need to. Go, do what you have to do to get ready."

He smiled, then bent down to kiss me on the forehead. I tilted my head back to show him I wanted more than that. He looked me in the eyes and smiled again. "I missed you." He said, then leaned in to kiss my lips. It was exactly like I remembered. His lips were soft and moist, and the stubble above his mouth tickled mine every time he moved in for more. He stood back up, still looking at me. "My Kaleah," he said with a half-smile. Then turned and walked out the door.

T he rest of the day went on relatively uneventfully. I was able to restitch my leg without having any issues with the blood. As long as I kept it off my fingers, I felt fine. Jake was gone for a while initially cutting and gathering wood. I wasn't nearly as tired as I had been every other day preceding this one so I found myself in an unusual position that I hadn't been before. I was bored.

I couldn't take a nap. With every thought and new memory surging through me, my mind hadn't been able to stop long enough to even begin to rest, let alone sleep. I rummaged around, looking at what things were in the cabin, keeping an inventory in the back of my mind if I needed anything in the future. Then I remembered the hairpin. It was still out in the yard. I knew Jake wouldn't want me to go outside again, especially nowhere close to where the hole might be so I decided to wait and ask him to get the pin for me when he came back in.

I wasn't sure what his plan was, or how he intended for us to sleep that night. It was hard for me to not sit there and make an alternate plan in my head. I trusted him, but everything in me couldn't help but take my training and put it to use as well. As I ran across something while rummaging, if it looked like it could be used as a weapon, I would either position it so I could use it later during a fight, or I would hide it so that no one could use it against me. I found myself doing this several times; each time making sure I had the right motives, Kaleah's motives, in mind.

For the first time, I didn't feel scared as Kaleah. I knew what I was capable of and it didn't bother me to think that I might have to fight Sicari. What scared me was the thought that Eva didn't want to fight them, she wanted them to take her. That was her original plan.

I only hoped when the time came, whenever they got to us, that I could do what Kaleah needed me to do. I also hoped that the Sicari wouldn't be able to say or do anything that would make me change my mind. I didn't want anything to happen to Jake. Ultimately, whether I felt like Kaleah or Eva, that was one thing they agreed on. I would give myself up and sacrifice my mind, not knowing what the Sicari intended to do with me before I would let them hurt him.

Jake came and went multiple times, bringing in wood and setting it next to the stove on the floor. Each time stopping on his way back out for another quick kiss. He didn't say much. I think he took me seriously when I warned him about what the Eva in me might do, what she had been planning.

It had already started to get dark when I sat down to eat. Jake still had a good bit of food he had brought from the base. I knew he would be hungry when he got back in so I took a portion of it out, put it on a plate that I found up in one of the cabinets, then set it aside for him. As I sat there eating, I noticed the crest on the pouch of food. It was a large C with a black circle inside of it and a few words circling the outside, all elaborately embossed onto the bag. I turned my head to read what was around the C:

United as one, against all others. We fight tyranny, not our brothers.

First reading the words, my mind wanted to concentrate on the meaning and let it resonate. But before I could, flashes of different memories and symbols shot through my mind. It was like I had been under a spell that was just broken. I recognized the crest. I had seen it a hundred times at that point. For the first time, though, I recognized it as something else. Memories of the men surrounding me on the bridge flashed into my mind. The crest... It was on their jackets, their bags. One even had it tattooed on his arm.

I could still feel them, the way they grabbed me and dragged me away from Marcus. It didn't matter how many times they saw me stab him; they didn't treat me like I was just an innocent Gypsyin. They were cold and calloused. They didn't care who they just shot. They didn't care about me either. I didn't fight them, I just let them take me, but that wasn't good enough. Before they took me to interrogation, they did things to me... things I wished I couldn't remember, things I wished I could blot out of my mind.

"Don't worry she won't remember anything..." "She's just a Gypsyin, they're fair game..." "You're taking too long, it's my turn..." The memories were as fresh as if it just happened. Campbell, Baker, Robins, Sanchez, and Miller, I remembered them all, every single one. They didn't try to hide their names, their faces, any markings they had on their bodies, and definitely not what they intended to do to me.

Initially, it was so awful I thought it was a part of the interrogation until they were done and then moved me. It was the first time in my life I genuinely wanted to die. I knew they were going to erase my memories, but I didn't want that. All I wanted was for that little glass vial to be poison, one that would kill me, not just erase me.

I remembered now why I wanted the Sicari to come get me. It wasn't as much that they were my people, or that they would save me from the Coldiers. I wanted to be free again, free with my memories to go and take revenge. I wanted to find those men and do worse things to them than they did to me. I wanted to not only avenge myself, but avenge what they made me do to Marcus. I wanted them all to suffer. I hated the Coldiers, and they all had to pay for the things they did and the things they allowed to be done in their name. I knew it had been years but my intel had to still be good. If I was able to get it to a Sicari station, it would hurt the Coldiers in a way they might never recover.

"Kaleah?" Jake spoke, quickly followed by the sound of the door shutting.

I didn't turn to look at him. I knew he would be able to tell I was thinking differently. I didn't know how to control my face yet. It had never been a problem until my memories of Kaleah had returned.

"I made you some supper. Are you hungry?" I tried to ask it in the most pleasant voice I could come up with, something sounding like Kaleah.

"Yes, thank you!" He said as I heard the wood falling to the floor behind me. Then the thud of his boots taking a few large steps to come back over to the table to sit.

I hadn't decided if I was going to keep playing like I was Kaleah or if I was just going to come out with it and tell him I changed my mind and I knew what I wanted. I wanted to leave and go with the Sicari when they came to find me. He would just need to step aside and allow them to take me. As soon as the thoughts hit me, I realized that he wouldn't allow that to happen. *He'll never allow me to take Kaleah from him.* Without me having to fight him, he would never listen to me. I hated Coldiers, but I really didn't want him hurt. Whether it was as his prisoner or not, he kept me safe. I knew I didn't have a choice. I couldn't tell him that I changed my plan and wasn't going to stay with him any longer. I had to pretend to be her. There was no other way. I just hoped in the process I didn't let the same spell that he had over me the first time return.

He started to eat without saying much to me. I think he was afraid of who was ruling my thoughts now, just as I was afraid he might see it was no longer Kaleah.

"Did you get yourself stitched back up?" He asked, looking up at me finally.

Dammit, why's he so smart? I didn't know why I constantly underestimated him but I did it again. He knew I had issues with the blood. That was why he was bringing it back up, to gauge my reaction. I wanted to look away, but I knew that's what he was watching for.

"Yeah, it's fine now," I said, keeping eye contact with him.

"Was it bad?" He asked, not letting the subject go just yet.

"Nope," I wanted to say more. I knew he would be suspicious of a one-word answer, but I couldn't. If I tried to say more than that, I would have to think about it and then that would really give it away.

"Really? 'Cause it looked bad. It had started to bleed through again and looked like you needed to restitch it." He continued prodding to see if it bothered me.

"No... uh, I got it," I said a bit flustered but trying to hold it all together.

He didn't say anything for a minute. He just looked at me and smiled, then down like he was trying to think of how to reply.

"You know you still talk in your sleep, right?" He looked back up, his face now appeared different, like it was hardened and he had caught on.

"Um... I guess I knew it. Why?" I asked, trying to keep up the act and respond to him how he would suspect Kaleah would just in case I was wrong.

He looked down and started picking at his food with his fingers. "I know what you want. I know what they did to you. But you're good. You never talked about your intel. I didn't know the Sicari were coming, and you never said you had a tracker either. How did you hide it?"

The jig was up. He caught on quicker than I suspected he might. He knew I had reverted to thinking like Eva again. "The memories are what I can't control. All you hear are the memories. It's the knowledge, the intel, my plans... You'll never get that out of me unless I want you to." I said, taking his cold demeanor and matching it.

"Right, 'cause you're a spy. I guess if you didn't give it up being interrogated you're not going to for me either, no matter who I am," he said, looking back over at me.

I froze. "Oh my gosh," I gasped. I couldn't stop myself. My face had to be showing him everything. I just figured it out. Maybe he thought I already had, and that's why I wanted to leave but I didn't. How could I not have? The epiphany hit me like a ton of bricks. "He sent you! Miller sent you to get me…" I backed myself away from the table, still keeping him in my sight. *How have I have been so naïve? Kaleah… this is her fault!*

"Yeah, but you knew that this whole time. I told you Miller was my commanding officer. Why are you acting like it bothers you now?" He asked, his face no longer cold but rather genuinely confused. "Is it because of what you said he did to you? I mean, I didn't know that until the night after we left Charlotte, when I heard you talking in your sleep. If I had known before that I would have—"

"Stop!" I backed up a little more. "Stop acting dumb and like you care about me. You know I figured it out. I caught you. Miller sent you for the intel. He knew who I was. That was the plan this whole time, wasn't it? Pretend you fell in love with me so that when you brought my memory back I would feel comfortable enough with you to tell you the intel." I pushed myself back again to where I could get up from the table when I needed to.

"What? No… no, no, no," he said, realizing I was tense and trying to back away. "That's not the truth, please, you have to believe me. I didn't know who you were before I met you. Maybe Miller knew, I don't know, but that's not the way it went. I was never… Oh my gosh." He raised his hand to his forehead to push his hat back off his head. "Please, that's not the truth. I know what you think it looks like but it's not the truth. I really do love you. I'm not pretending just to get the intel. I swear! If that's what you think, don't tell me what it is. I don't want to know. That's not what I want."

He could tell I didn't believe him. As I turned myself to face the door, he pushed himself away from the table slowly and, leaning forward in his chair, angled himself to intercept me in case I ran.

"Don't do this, please don't do this," he said, knowing what I intended to do. "You have to believe me. I would never hurt you intentionally. That was never the plan. I didn't know anything about why Miller wanted me to pick you up. Besides, how do you know it's the same Miller? There are a ton of Millers?" He looked ready to chase me if I tried to move.

"Because he was the one interrogating me. He knew I had intel that I wouldn't tell him. You wouldn't even begin to believe the things he did to me. I begged him to kill me, so he did. He drowned me, then brought me back over and over again. He knew I wasn't afraid to die. My death wasn't going to make me talk. He saw what I did to Marcus, too. He saw my weakness… my only weakness. *Love.* Did you not wonder why he sent you, a good looking single man to pick me up alone, all by yourself? This whole time, even if you say you didn't know about it, that was his plan. He wanted you to fall in love with me, or me fall in love with you. He knew that was the only way he could make me talk." I looked away and released the tension with a deep sigh, feeling physically drained.

"Okay, I believe you. All right? Look at me, Eva, look at me," he said, still sounding on edge. "You have to believe me now, okay? I swear I didn't know any of that. I was just his pawn, all right?"

I looked back at him, trying to stare straight into his eyes. I could see he was telling the truth. I didn't want to believe him. I wanted to hate him just like all the other Coldiers, but I knew he wasn't lying. Whether I liked it or not, he loved me and he was on my side. "Fine," I sighed.

"This means the Coldiers are probably going to be after us as well, but they can't track me anymore so they won't know we're here," he said now relaxing a little.

"When the Sicari get here let me go with them. Once they get the intel, they'll let me go." I turned my body away from the door and back toward him so he knew I didn't still intend to run.

"No!" He brought his fist down hard against the table, making a loud thumping sound. "I'm not losing you again!" He said through clenched teeth, his face now red. He sat back and looked down at his fist, then released it a little as he looked back up at me. "You know they won't let you go. If anything, they'll erase you again. If you went with them, I'd never be able to find you or know where you went. I wouldn't even know if you were still alive... It'd be the last time I saw you. You're not going with them. I'd give my life fighting to keep you before I would let you go."

Dammit, I knew it. I knew he'd say that. "What do you want me to do then, just stay here with you and play house until they come? I need to find the unit that killed Marcus, the men that raped me. I need to find Miller and make him pay for what he did," I said it as I looked down at his fist.

"Revenge will never complete you, Eva," he said, relaxing a little more.

"And loving you will?" Memories of walking with him through the woods and talking to him at night before we slept started flooding into my thoughts as soon as I asked it.

"That's what I want, what I was hoping for... I would be enough for you. Your memories of me, of us falling in love. I hoped they could be enough to drown out the memories of your past—what's been done to you..." he said.

"You can't drown those out, not unless you drown Eva, but then you're killing me in the process. I'm broken, Jake. I'm broken; you don't want this." I said as I brought my knees up to my chest and wrapped my arms around them, burying my face in the crack between my thighs. I started to cry. I couldn't control it, it was all too much for me. I couldn't stop myself from releasing all the pain.

I heard him get up and walk around the table before he wrapped his arms around my back and my legs, hugging me just as I sat. He lingered like that for a moment without saying anything then squeezed tighter as he slid me off the chair and down into his lap. I let go of my legs and wrapped my arms around his back, pulling myself tight against his chest, letting him cradle me.

"I'm scared, Jake," I said still crying into his shoulder. Eva would never admit it, but Kaleah would.

"I know, baby, I know," he said, tenderly running a hand through my hair.

I sat there unable to control the crying, releasing it all. His embrace was warm and relaxing. I never wanted it to end. He slowly started to rock forward then back, gently stroking my head. "Shhh, it'll be okay," he said softly. "Shhh…" he rocked forward. "Shhh…" then rocked back. I let myself relax and close my eyes. I wanted to sleep. That's when the pain stopped, when my mind was quiet.

After awhile he rearranged his body to stand up and carry me. He walked with me down the hall and into the bedroom where he laid me on the bed then turned to walk back out.

"Don't leave me." I rolled over to look up at him, reaching out for his hand.

"I'll be right back. I have to lock up and stoke the fire." He said gently, pulling his hand away as he bent down to kiss me on top of my head then walked out.

I closed my eyes and let myself fall asleep. Before long, I woke up to the sound of him coming back into the room. But he didn't close the door behind him this time like he had when we were here with Seth. He also didn't remove any of his clothes. I wanted to ask him why, but I knew why. It was obvious protecting me was more important to him than continuing what we started in the closet at Charlotte. Knowing Sicari were on their way, he wouldn't be able to relax until they were taken care of and I was no longer in danger. He took the quilt and pulled it up over me, then lay beside me on his back on top of it.

"Aren't you afraid I might run? Shouldn't you put your arm over me like you did our first night?" I asked, knowing I wouldn't be able to get what I really wanted out of him, but maybe at least he could be closer to me than he was.

"Believe me, I want to. But I need to keep an eye on the door. I can't do that if I have my back to it. And I'm not going to put you between me and it either," he said as he looked at me, now curled up facing him.

"Okay," I said with a small smile, then pulled my arm out from under the cover and gently rested it across his torso.

"Go to sleep now, baby. I'll keep you safe," he said as he leaned over to kiss my head again.

19

BLOOD AND SACRIFICE

Jake was gone again when I woke up. It was light outside, so I figured he had already been up and awake for a while. He was the early riser, while I was always the one who enjoyed my morning sleep. The fire must have gotten pretty toasty during the night. Before going to check for Jake, I needed to collect all the clothes that I had removed randomly while I slept and put them back on.

I noticed the room felt chilly when I removed the quilt. *That's odd.* He brought in enough firewood the day before that there shouldn't have been any reason why he would let the fire go out. I walked out into the hall. It was chilly there as well. It was brighter outside than usual, too. The living room had more light flowing in and down the hall than the previous morning when the sky was dreary.

When I entered the living room, I expected to see him but he wasn't there. I looked out the window above the recliner but I couldn't see him outside either, not from that view anyway. There was snow on the ground, just like he said there would be, but only a thick dusting. I walked over to the table to see if he left a note or anything telling me where he might have gone but I saw nothing.

Maybe he went to get more wood. I looked over toward the stove. There was a lot less wood there than the night before but there was still plenty. I walked over and opened the stove to see what the fire was doing and if I needed to stoke it again. It wasn't out but there were only a few embers left. It must have been hours since he stoked it last.

Something didn't feel right. Something was wrong. I quickly tried to settle the panic that wanted to well up inside of me. So many thoughts and feelings began to barge in all at once, both from Kaleah's memories and Eva's alike. They were tussling. Like my mind was a ship that was about to capsize. I made myself stop and breathe deeply a few times, hoping it would help me clear my thoughts. Everything in me that was Kaleah wanted to be afraid. It wanted to go hide and hope that if Jake were in trouble that he would be able to save himself. Everything in me that was Eva wanted to go and find him, but not to save him as much as just so she could find the Sicari and let them take her.

Now more calm, I looked around. I grabbed his coat, the same one I wore outside the day before, and quickly threw it on along with my shoes. As quickly as I could, I went to retrieve a couple of items that I could use as weapons that were small enough to carry with me. I pulled out a kitchen knife from the bottom left drawer of the cupboard in the corner. Using it, I cut a small hole in my sock above my ankle to stick it through, letting the elastic hold the handle against my skin and the blade stick out of the fabric. Then I reached into the large front pocket in Jake's bag and pulled out the spool of cordage that he used to tie me up while in the car, and I stuck it in the pocket of my pants.

I opened the door to walk out and shut it behind me as quietly as I could. Then I walked to the edge of the porch and looked down into the snow, observing any tracks I could find. I could see Jake's boot tracks but they weren't headed in the same direction he went to cut the wood. They were headed in the direction of the orchard.

I walked slowly, following them, putting my foot in each of the prints. After a few steps, something caught my eye again in the same area it had before. It was the hairpin. I reached down to pick it up while still staying observant of my surroundings and listening for Jake. I reached up and wrapped my hair into a small bun and weaved it through to hold it tight. Now, if I were to get in trouble for any reason, I had something at my feet, my waist, and my head that I could use to help me.

I followed the tracks slowly, looking ahead to where I suspected the ten-foot hole might be so that I would miss it. I couldn't hear anything. There was no breeze, no birds, or even any sounds that I could distinguish, really. As I kept going, I looked around, trying to stay aware of what else might be around me when suddenly I heard something. It was faint and I couldn't tell what it was but it was in the same direction the tracks headed.

I followed them until I was almost to the orchard. There were so many trees and outbuildings that I had to move slower to make sure I wasn't missing anything. I wanted to follow the tracks, knowing they should ultimately lead me to him, but all my instincts as Eva wanted me to start to duck and cover behind the trees. Then I saw it. Something was hiding behind one of the buildings. The only thing sticking out that I could see looked like hair flipping up and back. I heard them not long after I saw them. They were horses. The Sicari were here!

I still didn't know where exactly they were, while I keep in mind they most likely weren't with their horses. I didn't know if they had found Jake yet or if they caught his trail like I did and were stalking him as well. I hadn't seen any other boot prints, so I stayed close to his, slipping between trees and buildings as stealthily as I could. I didn't want to go near the horses, knowing they might spook and alert the men to my presence.

Before long, I started to hear something again. It was men's voices. They weren't with the horses. They were ahead in the same direction Jake's tracks led. There was another small barn further that way. They must have been in there. I realized they probably had already captured Jake, but I couldn't let my emotions overtake me. I would get worked up in a frenzy and make stupid decisions so I needed to keep the element of surprise if I was going to be any help to him.

I ducked behind a tree and looked at where I knew I was now headed. I spotted each tree that was between it and myself and charted in my head each move I was about to make before I made it, making sure I would get there without being seen. I moved quickly from that tree quietly to the next one, treading softly against the snow. I could hear more the closer I got. They had him. He screamed. My heart beat faster and faster as more thoughts popped up one after another, cluttering my mind.

I stopped and made myself take another couple of deep breaths while trying not to close my eyes. I knew what I had to do. I couldn't go into this with the same mentality that made Kaleah who she was. I had to let Eva do it. I had to put all of my fear that she wanted to leave Jake aside and let her take over, trusting she'd make the right decision when the time came. That was the only way I knew how to save Jake. I had to trust myself, who I really was, Eva. I closed my eyes and thought about Marcus until all the memories of that day rushed in. Then I opened my eyes again and locked them on my target.

I moved into position behind the shed where I could hear the men with Miles. The wood had started to rot on the bottom of the boards so I knew I couldn't get close or they might see my feet. Looking back, there were only two horses, so it was reasonable to believe they sent no more than two men to capture me. I had to be patient and pick the right time to move in. I couldn't rush it. If I did, I could get myself hurt, get Miles killed, or let one of them escape. If that happened, they would come back with more men. I positioned myself behind a tree close to the building and listened for the right time.

"Why you guys always gotta make it hard on us, you Gypsyins?" One voice asked. He had an accent that sounded like he was most likely northern, possibly Canadian.

I heard the sound of a thud followed by Miles letting out a large breath with a groan.

"Ya know, we'll stop if ya just give us the answers we came here looking for…" the same voice said again.

"I'm not telling you anything!" Miles groaned again, sounding like he was in pain.

"Morin, man, we should check and make sure he doesn't have a tag." another man's voice spoke this time. He sounded younger than the first man, but I couldn't detect any accent.

"You're right. I'm the Gypsyin you're looking for. But you're going to regret treating me like this when we get back to the Sicari station." Miles' voice sounded raspy now.

"See, Perry, I knew he was the one. You can see it all over him. He's pathetic, trying to threaten us. That's probably why his daddy passed him down a girly name, isn't that right, Jordan Eva." Morin, the northern man, said my name like it disgusted him. It was obvious they thought Jake was me.

I stayed close, but slowly walked from one tree to another to get closer to the entrance of the building, setting myself up for when I needed to attack.

"You think we're going to just take you back to the Praetorium right like you are, huh?" The younger man took a turn at taunting Miles.

After he asked the question, I heard another loud punching sound then saw a shadow flicker in the light that was coming from under the barn boards. Miles loudly groaned again, sounding lower like he was on his knees. "Man, they must just let every idiot be a spy these days. Do you really think they would let a double agent waltz right back into the Praetorium and start barking orders, aye? Nah, 'cause we Sicari aren't that dumb like you Gypsyins." Morin hissed.

"You're gonna talk to us or we're gonna erase ya." The voice of the younger man spoke.

The older man laughed. "Good idea, *delere eum*!" He spoke in Latin, taunting Jake further.

Delere eum… Delete him!

I almost gasped in shock, but caught myself. The Sicari hadn't developed a memory-erasing serum when I was with them. *Shit!* I hoped they were bluffing to just get him to talk, but I knew it wasn't likely. The Sicari had multiple serums they were working on before I was erased. With how many years it'd been, no doubt they had ample time to develop their very own.

I heard another large thumping sound, then Miles cried out again. I didn't know what they were doing to him, but I couldn't let them give him the serum.

I walked out from behind the tree and sneaked around the building to peer in through a crack in the wall near the entrance as best as I could without them seeing me. There were two like I suspected and from what I could hear, one was larger than the other and obviously older, making it realistic for me to match their voices to their names. Neither of them had a larger build than Miles but they weren't small men either. It wasn't going to be easy, but I knew I would have to kill them both.

I sat there for a second, watching them. They had both Miles' hands and feet bound so he couldn't fight back. One would taunt him while the other would punch or kick him. Then they would switch. The older man, Morin, was left-handed and had a small limp in his left leg. He must've had a previous injury. I made a mental note seeing I could use that against him.

The smaller of the two and younger one, Perry, was more muscular like Miles but it didn't look like bulky, strong muscle rather a quick, wiry, lean kind of muscle. I would have to take him out first. I had the element of surprise as well as being a woman. I knew they would underestimate me. If I miscalculated them and wound up caught, my backup plan was to play like I was helpless so they would try to use me against Miles to make him talk, which he would most likely play into easily. That would give me the opportunity to get close enough to them for me to kill them even though I wouldn't have the element of surprise anymore.

I watched for another minute or two, trying to detect any weaknesses in Perry, as well as looking to see where they might have put the vial of serum. I didn't want them to use it as a weapon against me or try to use it against Miles, either.

I stood up and backed up so I would come through the entrance at a running pace. I pulled the knife from my sock, positioned it in my dominant hand, and started to run. As I turned the corner, the men were standing almost in the same position I last saw them. I ran as quick as I could toward the younger one, and as I suspected he was quicker, he ducked low and away before I could stab him. My momentum not stopping with stabbing him as I intended, took me to my knees against the ground past him. I straightening my leg and spun myself around to trip him, trying to get another chance to stab him again. It worked. He fell backward, hitting his head hard against the back wall of the barn.

I quickly moved over to position myself above him. I took the knife and brought it down as quickly and as I could with all my force, striking him in his upper right chest. I felt the air in his lung release with the initial blow. I pulled the knife out, then plunged it in again closer to his heart. But before I could pull the knife back out and turn to find Morin, suddenly my body was pulled back and away.

It was Morin. He had a hold of my feet. I rolled to my side to get him to release me, then I tried to crawl away from him as quickly as I could but he kept pulling me back toward him. Memories of Seth instantly flashed into my mind. I looked over and saw Miles just laying there, not moving. I didn't know what Morin did to him but I knew he wouldn't be able to help me.

Morin grabbed my foot again to pull me toward him. He could see I was just a woman, and a small one at that. Feeling like I wasn't as much of a threat as a man would be he started to taunt me, playing with me like he was the cat and I the mouse.

"You think you can save your little boyfriend here, do ya, aye?" He said as he pulled me under him then proceeded to sit on me.

I squirmed to turn over and onto my back. He didn't let me at first, still taunting me.

"Who do you think you are, trying to fight a Sicari?" He released enough tension to let me turn over. Then he reached down and grabbed my left wrist. Holding my arm tight, he pulled my sleeve up to look for my tag.

"Why… you're the…" he started to speak.

With his attention on my arm, I used my right hand to pull the hairpin from my hair.

"I'M EVA!" I screamed as I plunged it into his neck, hitting his artery.

The blood was everywhere. My hands were covered in it. My clothes were soaked in it. I sat there and stared at it, and the ground was now saturated with it.

I looked over at Perry. He wasn't moving, his skin was now pale as well, so I knew he wouldn't be a problem any longer either. I looked over at Miles. He was still breathing, so I figured Morin must have just knocked him out. I hoped that was all, anyway. Then, suddenly, I remembered the serum. I had to find the serum and make sure they didn't give it to him. I crawled over to Miles and looked at him. His face was red, but not beaten that badly. I didn't see the vial anywhere around him. I tried to pull the sleeves of his jacket up to look at his arms, seeing if I could tell anywhere they might have given him the injection.

"Miles, can you hear me? Wake up! They're dead now. I took care of 'em. We're safe for now. Wake up!" I said, patting his face gently, trying to get him to rouse.

I looked around again but couldn't see the vial anywhere near him. I crawled over to where the younger man was laying. His face was now white, like a ghost. I moved his hand so I could feel inside his coat pocket. His skin was cool to the touch now, too. There wasn't anything in either pocket. I rolled him a little to one side to feel for the vial in his pants pocket but nothing, then the other when I finally found it. I reached in and pulled out both the vial and the needle they needed to inject it. Seeing I had it, I sat back and relaxed.

Just knowing they didn't use it on Jake was the biggest relief. I didn't know what I would do if they took his memory away. I pulled the knife out of Perry's chest and crawled back over to cut Jake free, then sat next to him, waiting for him to wake up. I sat there and stared at the vial.

How could something so tiny cause so much trouble and pain? It was no bigger than my thumb. It was a clear glass jar that had a thin metal cap that you could plunge the needle into. The liquid inside looked like gray metallic molasses. It was thick and slow-moving when I tilted it. I took it and put it in the chest pocket of my coat, then turned back toward Jake to try to wake him up again.

"Jake, baby, wake up. I killed them. You'll be so proud of me. I killed them. I didn't think I could do it, but I did. We're safe now," I said, firmly stroking his face.

I lifted his shirt and jacket to look at his abdomen to make sure he wasn't bleeding anywhere. I didn't see any cuts just a lot of bruising. A large section of his right side had already started to turn a dark purple. It must have been where they kicked him. Thankfully, his upper chest didn't look like it took too much damage.

He started to move slightly. His eyes didn't completely open, but began to flutter. I couldn't help but think of Marcus. This was how I was supposed to save Marcus.

"Miles, it's safe now," I said again loudly, trying not to get too close in case he startled upon awakening.

The rush of adrenaline that had been surging through me started to dissipate the longer I sat there. In its absence, I began to feel a sharp pain in my leg where I had the stitches. I looked down to see if it was bleeding again but there was already blood all over me, all over my pants, my shirt, my jacket, and now all over Miles. I brought my hands up to look at them. It was all over my fingers, a glossy cherry red smeared here and there into a lighter reddish-orange hue that faded into a dark rusty brown where it had already started to dry.

No sooner had I looked, I immediately realized I shouldn't have. Almost instantly, I felt chilled and started to shiver. My head began to feel float-y at the same time the edges of my vision started to tunnel in toward the center. I knew what I had done. I tried to blink out of it while laying flat and keeping my knees up, telling myself to think about something else. It wasn't helping. Now I was clammy and nauseous like I needed to puke. Realizing my vision was still narrowing and I could no longer hear anything except a dull ringing sound, I relaxed and let it overtake me.

"Killmeeaahh…" I could hear Marcus but he was quiet and I couldn't see him or respond.

"Kilmeah…" He began to get a bit louder. I tried to look for him but couldn't see him.

"Kalmeah…" He now sounded like he was right next to me.

"Kaleah!" The voice finally broke through. I opened my eyes.

"Oh my gosh, Kaleah!" The voice was low and husky. "Are you all right? Are you hurt?" I looked up to see Jake sitting above my head, looking down at me.

"Jake," I said, trying to get my voice to fully work, happy to see he was now awake.

"Are you hurt?" He asked again, probably wondering whose blood was all over me.

"I'm fine. But I killed them, Miles… I killed them." I said, losing the initial excitement Kaleah felt now realizing I just killed two of my own men. *I'm in so much freaking trouble. Holy shit, what did I just do?*

"I know, baby. We'll figure out what to do next. I just need to make sure you're okay," he said, trying to help me lift my head to sit up.

"Are *you* hurt?" I asked, trying to turn my head to look at him.

He moved around to position himself in front of me. He acted a bit stiff, like the movement hurt. He started to respond then stopped, realizing he hadn't actually assessed himself yet. He looked down briefly, softly patting his chest and stomach with both hands. "I'll be all right. It's only bruising. I'll heal," he said calmly, trying to not take too deep of a breath.

"Did they break anything?" I asked, looking down at his chest, implying maybe he should check for pain around his ribs.

"No, I'm fine," he said quickly, wanting to move on to another subject.

"They brought the serum. They intended to use it on me before they took me in," I said, trying to keep myself together. "Their trackers will stop here and mine won't. The Praetorium will know what happened and send more men." *Holy shit... Breathe!*

"I know," he said, looking away from me over towards their bodies. "Let me help you to the house. We'll talk about what to do next when we get there."

"I can walk, I'm fine," I said, standing up trying not to hyperventilate. "I might need you to stitch me back up, though." I looked up at him as he stood, trying to stop myself from looking down at all the blood everywhere. *Breathe!*

He walked over to inspect the bodies before we left. He stood above the younger one, then bending down he reached over and ran his fingers lightly across his chest. "You stabbed him," he said, surprised.

"Yes, twice. The first one I missed the vitals." I tried to look, but didn't let my eyes linger.

He stood back up and walked over to Morin. He didn't bend down, he only looked at him while still standing. He didn't say anything at first just stood there staring down at the body.

"You never told me your full name," he said finally looking up at me and moving toward the door.

"You never told Kaleah yours," I responded now following him out and around the barn. The air was fresher outside, not nearly as stifling. I could breathe way easier.

"True!" He said, looking back at me with a little half-smile.

We walked together back to the cabin. Once back inside, he loaded the wood stove back up and began to restart the fire. We drank all the spring water he had collected the day before and I didn't want him to leave again to go get more so I got a bowl from the cabinet and quickly went outside and collected as much snow as I could fit into it. Then I brought it back in to set next to the stove to melt. After a minute or two, I was able to use it to saturate a rag to wipe the blood off of myself. I removed all my clothes that were now soiled by it and rummaged around through Jake's bag until I was able to find more.

Before putting more pants on, I stopped and let him restitch my leg. I asked for a little more of the alcohol but he refused. He said even though he didn't want me in pain, now wasn't a good time for me to not have clear thinking. He needed me to help him decide what we were going to do next. I could see his reasoning almost immediately so I didn't fight him. I sat there and thought about what I had just done, and how brave that was.

We sat there in silence while he stitched my leg. He didn't talk, probably trying to concentrate on what he was doing. I sat there and thought more. Ideas from Kaleah and Eva both dropped into my mind, trying to pull me one way then the other. Even though they were like oil and water, I did everything I could to try to come up with a plan that would work the best for both of them as well as for Jake. I knew what I wanted to do. I just needed to see what Jake's ideas were first.

"I hope I'm not hurting you too badly. I'm almost done," he said still trying to focus.

"No… it's… you're fine." I tried to reassure him as best as I could, but it was painful and I started to feel sick again from the thought.

"I can tell you're worried. But just relax. We're going to figure out what to do. I won't let them hurt you again," he said as he pulled his hand up to tighten the thread.

"They're going to keep coming for me. You'll never be safe if we stay together." I could tell it was an Eva thought that slipped out. As soon as I said it, I regretted it and wanted to tell him Kaleah didn't feel that way. I didn't get a chance though, before he responded.

"Eva, stop it. I told you last night it's not gonna happen," he said, looking up at me with a stern look.

"I killed my own men, Miles. It's not like what you did with

Seth. I can't just lie and tell them it wasn't me. They'll know I did it. If they didn't already suspect it before, now I'm guaranteed to be labeled a double agent." I was upset. I realized for the first time my actions compromised my mission.

"It doesn't matter what you are to them. They aren't loyal to you. Did you not hear what those men were going to do to me, thinking I was the spy. They would have done the same to you or probably worse since you're a woman!" He raised his voice a little, but I could tell he was trying to hold back.

"They'll never stop looking for me. And with this thing in my head, now they know exactly where we are too. They'll send more!" I was beginning to get frustrated.

"Just relax. I'm going to think of what to do. I'll make a plan and we'll both be safe. Besides, we have horses now that we can use to go somewhere else. It's perfect since I didn't bring enough gas for the car to make it much farther than here. We can just both be outlaws, wandering the countryside. It'll be an adventure. Look at it like that." He must have been done with the stitching. He took the needle and started to put it back in the sewing kit.

"But we'll always be running, we'll always be in danger," I said, now lowering my voice.

"Is there a way we can deactivate your tracker like I did mine?" He asked.

"No, it's not that simple. I wish there was a way, but it's in my head. I don't even know how, I just know one of the times that I went back to the Praetorium, they put me under and put it in my head. It's somewhere up there in my brain. I don't know exactly where. I don't even remember if I had a scar. So unless you feel like doing brain surgery, I don't think that's a viable option." I was trying not to get worked up but I could feel the frustration building.

"Okay, well, we have some time to think about it, plan what to do, and get prepared. Even if they saw as soon as it happened that you killed those men, and they immediately sent more to come and find you, it would still take days for them to get here," he said, trying to reassure me.

I didn't respond right away. I knew what we should do, but I wasn't sure how to tell him. I figured he wouldn't like it and I might have to fight with him to listen to me.

"What's wrong?" He asked, seeing the look on my face.

"I know what we have to do. It's the only way. I just… I don't think you'll listen to me," I said hoping he could see my thoughts weren't currently being dominated by any one side.

"If it's a good plan, you won't have to worry about me. I'll listen to you. Just tell me, baby." He leaned in toward me, placing his hand on the thigh that he didn't just stitch up.

I hesitated, looked down, readjusted myself in the chair, then looked back up at him. "Do you promise you will at least listen and think about it before you say no or get all mad at the idea?" I asked, trying to make sure we were both ready for me to tell him.

He took a deep breath as he sat up straight in his chair, then let out a silent sigh. "Yes, I promise," he said, letting his eyes connect with mine so I could see he genuinely meant it.

I sat there looking at him for a second, trying to think about the best way to tell him and the best words to use. "You need to give me the injection again. I kept the serum. I found it before you woke up. You can use it to—" He interrupted me before I was able to finish what I was trying to say.

"No!" His face quickly became upset. He let go of my leg and leaned back. "Are you kidding me? Really? You're serious?"

"You promised you would listen and think about it," I said, trying to get him to let me continue.

"I said I would listen if it was a good idea. That isn't a good idea. Why would I let you do that?" He asked, now letting his face relax a little.

"Because… it's the only option!" I unintentionally raised my voice.

"No! No, baby, it's not. We can come up with something else. We don't have to do that," he said, trying to convince me to let the idea go.

"You can't come up with anything else. Stop saying that. You know it's the only way. You're just too scared to let me do it." I was irritated that he wouldn't hear me out.

"Okay, fine, if that's what you want to call it, I don't care. But I lost you once and now I finally got you back. I'm not just going to turn around and let you erase yourself all over again. I won't lose you again!" He said, leaning forward toward me.

"But you don't have to lose me," I said. "If you'll just listen, I will explain it!"

He dropped his head and looked down, now resting his elbows on his knees with his hands clasped. "Fine, I'll listen, but will you at least put yourself in my shoes and think about why I don't like it?" He asked, still looking down at his feet.

"I know why. I know what my memories of being Kaleah mean to you. But you're not losing me, not who I really am. You're only losing memories. We can make more… together. You can reteach me everything that I need to know. You can tell me about how we met, about how much we loved each other." I paused to sit back a little, trying to relax at the same time he looked back up at me and remade eye contact.

"It can be a whole new life for us. Besides, it would fix so many other problems. I wouldn't remember everything that happened to me when I was with Marcus. Everything the Coldiers did to me. Everything I did to Marcus." I stopped, knowing I would get too emotional if I continued.

"So it's more than just hiding your tracker?" He acted like he might have been starting to understand.

"Yes! It'd fix that and so many other things… I loved Marcus, and I know I can't get him back. But the memories of what I did to him haunt me. Every night, I'm haunted by Eva, by my past, by the pain. Not to mention the intel. It would be best for everyone for me not to remember that. I know what it would do to you. I know it would be a lot of work. I'm sorry I don't want you to have to deal with that, but I don't know any other way." I reached out and took a hold of his hand and put it back on my thigh.

"It's not the work I care about. Kaleah loves me back. Eva

doesn't. How do I know the next version of you will?" He tightened his grip on my thigh as he said it.

I smiled. I found his insecurity endearing. "How much do you think I love you right now?" I asked.

He paused and lightly wrinkled his brow, trying to think. "I don't know, I guess you've never really told me."

"Exactly, but you know I do. You can feel it. If I couldn't stop myself from loving you when you had me all tied up as your prisoner, then why would I when you have me safe by your side, caring for me. I love you enough that I trust you and you alone to bring me back to life… Tell me what I need to know. Teach me how to fight like Eva and how to love like Kaleah." I got down on my knees between his legs and looked up at him. "We can make more memories together, Jake. Those are the only ones I want. I only want the good ones, the ones with you… Not the ones of killing people… or being tortured or… having to—"

He leaned down and kissed me. "Okay," he said, resting his forehead against mine. "Okay," he said again, followed by another kiss then leaned his head back a little to look into my eyes. "I love you, I'll do it for you."

20

BROKEN SHADOWS

I smiled, then leaned in to kiss him back. "I love you too, baby." I said, wrapping my hand around the back of his neck.

He broke the kiss with a large smile, then went back to it before breaking it again to lean forward and pick me up. He carried me down the hall and to the bedroom. "We have to be easy with your leg. You might break that stitch again, then the poor thing will never heal right," he said as he gently placed me on the bed.

"Okay." I said softly, laying back, looking up into his waiting eyes.

Keeping his hungry eyes trained on mine, he stood beside the bed for a second, took off his boots, then undressed. He looked down at me with a soft smile, then slowly climbed in and over me and lay down beside me. I needed him, his comfort, his protection, his love… I wanted it all. And I knew if I was going to let myself trust him, really trust him, I needed to be vulnerable with him, and let him be vulnerable with me.

I turned to my side to mirror his position then began to kiss him again. I reached my hand up to his side to find his hand and thread my fingers through his.

"Does lying like this hurt you?" I asked, remembering his bruises.

"No," his voice was soft but husky. "I'll be fine."

"Okay," I pressed my forehead against his to look into his eyes. "I want what you want... this... us..." I whispered.

"Aww, baby," he groaned. "You have no idea how happy that makes me to hear you say that. I missed you so much." Then he continued to kiss me slowly and gently as he traced his hands up and down my back, following my curves.

His kisses were passionate, like if he thought they were the last ones he would ever get to give me. Long and slow, he pushed his mouth into mine, then pulled back before doing it again.

"Kaleah..." He said, pulling away, his breath ragged. "I love you so much, baby." I could hear so many emotions in his voice. So many I never saw on his face.

"I love you too, Jake." I murmured. "More than you'll ever know."

Now relaxed and satiated Jake curled up behind me, nestling his chest tight against my back. He rested his arm against my waist, then tucked his hand under my side and pulled me in tight toward him just as he did the first night after Seth's death.

"I won't go back on what I agreed to, but the thought of not having you... like this... It's hard. I know I'll still have your body and we can make more memories, but... that's not the only thing that makes me love you. Those memories of us together, ugh... it's like when someone dies. Even though I had you as Eva, you losing the memories of Kaleah, not being able to talk to me like you were her, it was like she died. You died." His voice was low and tender.

"I'm sorry, I'm sure I'll never know what that feels like," I said, trying to think about what he was telling me and put myself in his shoes.

"Don't do that," he said still speaking softly.

"Do what?" I didn't understand what he was talking about.

"I'm trying to lie here and think about how awful this is for me and how much it hurts me to think about what you're willing to do for us. How am I supposed to wallow in my self-pity when you actually stop being stubborn for once and agree with me? Now I feel worse thinking about how selfish I sound when you're the one that will lose all your memories, not me. You're the one willing to sacrifice yourself so we won't be in danger. Then I think, dammit, that's why I love you, 'cause that's the stuff you'd do for me. Then the whole process starts all over again with me feeling bad, feeling like I'm about to lose you again."

I realized it wouldn't help if I said sorry again so I lay there trying to think of the best way to reassure him that it would all work out. "I'll still love you, Jake… umm whatever your middle name is Miles."

He let out a soft chuckle behind me. "It's Adrian… Jacob Adrian Miles. I'm sorry I never told you."

"To be fair, I never asked," I said, trying to make him feel better.

"What is yours? Do you remember?" He asked as he brought his hand up from my waist to stroke my hair.

I did remember, but Eva didn't want me to tell him so I hesitated. "Ellice." I whispered finally.

"Ellice, I like that," he said, then leaned forward and kissed me on the back of the head.

Neither of us said anything else. We just lay there in silence, enjoying each other's presence, until we fell asleep.

He was still lying next to me when I woke up in the morning. I tried to think back, realizing I didn't have the best memory, but thought it was probably the first morning that he was still next to me when I awoke. I lay there staring at him, watching him while he slept. He was so peaceful.

I wanted to wake him up with kisses but at the same time; I didn't want to wake him at all. I just wanted to lie there forever, watching him. I wanted to embrace all the little nuances of his body. If I stared at him laying there long enough, maybe I would be able to remember them after the injection. Maybe if I tried to think of him hard enough, I could make a memory that would last.

I was mesmerized watching the rise and fall of his chest and the long, lean lines of his torso. I looked back up at his face again. His beard was starting to come back quickly, since he hadn't been able to shave it for a few days. It was no longer just stubble. The skin on this face was smooth, tempting me to take a finger and trace it, down his nose and across his cheekbones. I also wanted to take my hand and sink it into his hair and stoke it as he had mine. It looked so soft. I was afraid to touch him, though, knowing he would most likely wake up with any little movement.

The longer I lay there the more I realized I didn't want to forget him either. I didn't care about the other memories. I wanted everything else in my past to disappear, but not him. All the moments we shared, the days and months we spent together, just the two of us walking and talking. I wanted to be his forever. I didn't want to be Eva anymore. I didn't want to perpetually mourn for Marcus. I didn't want to be Kaleah anymore, either. I realized she was merely just a broken shadow of who Eva was made to be. I never wanted to feel lonely and powerless ever again. I didn't want to keep running.

I was starting to feel nervous, as if I was mentally preparing myself for a big surgery. My mind would start to wander off on different rabbit trails, thinking about all the bad things that could happen if I went through with it. Then when I tried to recenter and refocus to bring it back to think of all the reasons it had to be done, it didn't last long until it would wander again.

I thought about making a list of things I wanted Jake to make sure to tell me about and a list of things I never wanted him to mention to me ever again as well but I didn't have any way to write it all down, so I didn't. The intel, on the other hand, I decided would now forever be my secret, one that would die right along with all of Eva's other memories.

It wasn't long before Jake woke up. He looked over at me still laying there, staring at him.

"G'mornin' beautiful," he said with a smile, then leaned over to kiss me.

I smiled back as best as I could, trying not to alert him to the mental distress I was just dealing with before he woke up. "I love you," I said, realizing it might be the last morning I would wake up next to him, with all the memories of how we first met and how we first fell in love. Deep down, I was just as scared as he was. What if I woke up as someone who didn't love him the same way I loved him in this moment?

"I love you too, baby. Don't worry it's going to be all right, we're gonna be okay." He must have sensed my trepidation.

We each started the day out like we did the others. We got ourselves ready and went to the living room. He got the fire going again, and I got the food ready for us to sit down and eat. Neither of us initially talked much, both feeling tense about what we knew was about to happen. Before long, he sat me down to talk again, knowing it was important for us to decide how we were going to proceed.

For hours it seemed like we sat there, him asking me questions and me answering. I told him about my life before the war, so then when I woke up after the injection he could tell it all back to me. Even if they weren't memories, that way I would still know who I was and where I came from. I told him the things about my past I wanted him to recant to me and I told him the things about Eva and what she did that I didn't want to know about.

When I wasn't telling him memories of events or details about myself, we would discuss what I wanted us to do in the future. He asked me if I liked where we were, though we both knew we wouldn't be able to stay. We discussed where we would go once I woke up and how we should get there. I told him it'd been too many years since I'd ridden a horse. I couldn't really remember if I still knew how so if I needed to relearn either way, it might as well be after my memory was erased again.

Miles asked me which name I wanted to be called when I woke up, since I now had so many. It didn't take me long before I knew what to tell him—Elliceva. Though I was still fine with Eva for short. I knew it was an odd name, but it had a special meaning to me. When I said it, he looked confused and maybe a little taken aback but he agreed nonetheless and we went on.

I knew we were running out of time and he wouldn't be able to remember everything I was trying to tell him. I could tell he was starting to get mentally weary after so many hours as well. The sky hadn't grown dark yet, but it didn't look too far from it. At that point, I knew any questions he was still asking were just trying to prolong the inevitable.

"I think it's time now," I said, looking over at him from the recliner.

He didn't say anything initially, he just looked down. "Just one more day. I think we need another day. We can do it tomorrow." He looked back up at me. His eyes now glossy.

"We can't… I'm sorry. I wish we could wait too but I don't know when they'll come. You need enough time for me to recover. You will need time to prepare for us to leave and be able to take enough with us. Enough time to explain things to me in case I don't understand, in case I don't want to go with you…" I could have gone on but I could tell I said enough for him to get the idea.

He swallowed hard. Then stood up slowly. "Okay, where's the vial?"

"It's in the chest pocket of your coat... the one I wear," I said. "Here I'll get it." I stood up and walked over to the table to retrieve it. I reached in and pulled it out along with the syringe.

"Should I lie down? We can go back to the bedroom?" I looked back up at him to ask.

"No, I'll carry you back there if I need to. Right now, just sit in the recliner. You'll be able to stay warm if you're next to the fire," he said it as he motioned in that direction.

It was obvious the whole experience was awkward for us both. Neither of us wanted to do it but we both knew it needed to be done and we had no other option.

I sat back down and started to hand the vial over to him then thought about it quickly and pulled it back. "Did you want to do it or did you want me to?" I asked, realizing we never discussed it.

"I'll do it," he said, reaching out for the vial.

He took it from me and held it up to look at it. "There's a problem we didn't think about." Then he looked back down at me.

"What?" I asked, thinking he was just trying to stall again.

"How much do I give you? I don't want to overdose you like the last doctor did. But if I don't give you enough will it stop the tracker signal or just mess your brain up?" Even though this was a dilemma for him there was still a sense of relief in his voice, knowing it delayed what needed to be done.

"I don't know, I guess I just assumed you would give me the whole vial." No sooner than the words came out of my mouth, a terrible look grew across his face.

"That's not happening! We will move on to Plan B before I give you the whole vial and just hope it doesn't kill you," he said with his face as serious as he could make it look and his voice as stern as I'd ever heard it.

"We don't have a Plan B!" I said, looking up at him.

"Well, you might not but I do," he finally broke, and cracked a small smile, thinking he was witty.

"What the hell do you think your Plan B is, then?" I asked slightly disturbed that he hadn't already shared it with me.

"A metal hat," he said without smiling at all. He was serious.

I didn't know how to respond. I just sat there and stared at him. "You're lying. That was never your Plan B. That was your Plan A, this whole freakin' time. That's not even realistic, it won't work, and we're running out of time!" I said, trying not to scold him too harshly.

"Okay fine, I knew it was a hail-Mary, but I thought maybe you'd change your mind," he said, letting his face relax.

"I don't want to do it, it's not that I just want it so badly. I don't know any other way. And we don't have time, we have to do it now!" I said, taking the vial back from him. "Here, give me the needle. I'm gonna draw up half. That shouldn't be too much. If I still have memories tomorrow, you can give me a little more." I looked up at him, hoping he was listening to my instructions.

"Please give me more time. I can think of something else," he begged as he hesitantly handed me the needle.

I stared at him for a moment. I could see so much angst in his eyes. "Okay," I said, instantly seeing a relieved look on his face. "You got as much time as it's gonna take for me to draw up the serum and stick it in my arm," I finished, now seeing his previous look vanish and morph into a panic.

Three days later...

"Elliceva, wake up, baby."

It was hard to open my eyes, the room around me wasn't extremely bright but it was bright enough to make it difficult to stay asleep. "We have to get ready to go," he said, sounding more alert, not like he'd just woken up as I had. I reached up to rub the crust off of my eyelids to help allow them to open easier. Then I looked over and saw him. He was standing next to the bed getting his clothes on, first his shirt then his pants, and last his socks and boots as he sat back down on the bed.

"I finished packing everything last night after you went to sleep.

If you need help getting yourself dressed, I can stay here. It might take a little longer though," he chuckled to himself. "If not, I'll go check on the horses again and make sure they're ready to go." He reached over to grab the jacket that was hanging on the bedpost. Then he paused and looked over at me. "You're awake, right? You're not going to go back to sleep as soon as I leave?" He asked, straightening up his collar.

"No, I'm fine," I said, smiling at him.

"Good." He put a knee on the bed and crawled over to kiss me. "Remember, it'll be an adventure." He smiled again, "I love you, baby, I wouldn't want to do this with anyone else." He leaned in to kiss me again then crawled back off the bed and walked out.

He did it. He thought of another way. I guess the best ideas come to us when the right amount of pressure is applied. We're going to travel to the grotto lands, the only area within the nation that agents on either side won't travel through. It's not exactly a safe-haven for Gypsyins, or really anyone, for that matter. It's a land of ghosts and shadows, known for its many caves and caverns. For agents, it's a place of great danger as the inhabitants are known to be hostile toward both sides of the conflict but who exactly the inhabitants are is more myth than fact.

The area is home to the biggest cave system I'd ever seen as a child. Rumored to now be nothing more than an abandoned network of stairs and handrails, hidden places, and dark chambers inhabited only by the bats and bugs that replaced the tourists. Without even trying, you could get lost, trapped, or both and never find your way back to one of the system's many entrances. To most, it was too dangerous, too mysterious, too unknown… but to us, it was none of those things. It was a perfect refuge and we would make it home.

**Jake and Kaleah's love story continues with book two of the ERASEHER series - Finding Fallen Angels.
CLICK HERE to download now.**

A note from Sara…

"The main thing I want my readers to get from my books is that no matter how broken and flawed you are, you are still worthy of unconditional love and no matter how weak you feel, there is still strength inside you." - Sara Nichol Quincy

About the Author

SARA NICHOL QUINCY is a novelist born and raised in Indiana. She's a mother, wife, and entrepreneur. The ERASEHER Series reflects her passion for writing romances that are tender and twisty yet still edgy. Add in a little dystopian suspense and a touch of crazy and you have yourself an epic love story that only she can tell.

To read more of her personal story and see what other books are in the works, you can visit her website at:

SaraNicholQuincy.com

There you can subscribe to get new release updates and exclusive offers!

Plus… only subscribers get:
- *Launch date perks (1st week sales get 20% off!)*
- *Cover reveals before launch date!*
- *Exclusive Bonus Chapters that aren't available anywhere else!*
- *FREE books! (When available)*
- *ARC Reader offers for new book series and much more…*

Got a question or comment about her work? She'd love to hear from you. Reach her anytime at **SaraNicholQuincy.Com**

Thank you again for taking your time to read Battling Broken Shadows. Please consider leaving an honest review. It would help immensely!

facebook.com/saranicholquincy
twitter.com/SaraNQuincy
instagram.com/saranicholquincy
tiktok.com/@saranicholquincy